I0788600

Sharia Rising

Carolina Danford Wright

Copyright © 2026 Llourettia Gates Books, LLC
All rights reserved. This book or any portion thereof may not be reproduced or used in any manner whatsoever without the express written permission of the publisher.

Llourettia Gates Books, LLC
P.O. Box #411
Fruitland, Maryland 21826

Hardcover ISBN: 978-1-953082-40-4
Paperback ISBN: 978-1-953082-39-8
eBook ISBN: 978-1-953082-41-1
Library of Congress Control Number: 2026901046

Photography by Andrea Lõpez Burns
Cover and interior design by Jamie Tipton, Open Heart Designs

*This book is dedicated to all grandmothers —
those who are avengers and those who wish they were.*

Contents

Author's Note

I wrote this manuscript in 2016 and had decided I would never publish it. However, with the upswing in terrorism, I changed my mind and decided it was timely.

This book is a work of fiction. It is not an attack on the many honest and hard-working Muslims who live in the United States, respect our laws and our culture, and live in accordance with the U.S. Constitution.

This book is an attack on those who choose misogynistic sharia law.

About The Granny Avengers

THE GRANNY AVENGERS is a series written by Carolina Danford Wright. *Sharia Rising* is the third book in the series. Each of the protagonists in this series is old enough to be a grandmother. Each is brave and on the side of truth and justice. Some of these heroes act on the spur of the moment because it is the right thing to do. Some, because of circumstances, seem to stumble into being avengers. Other Granny Avengers take over when the criminal justice system has failed to do its job. You will enjoy getting to know these feisty women as they struggle to right the wrongs of the world.

Map of Oregon

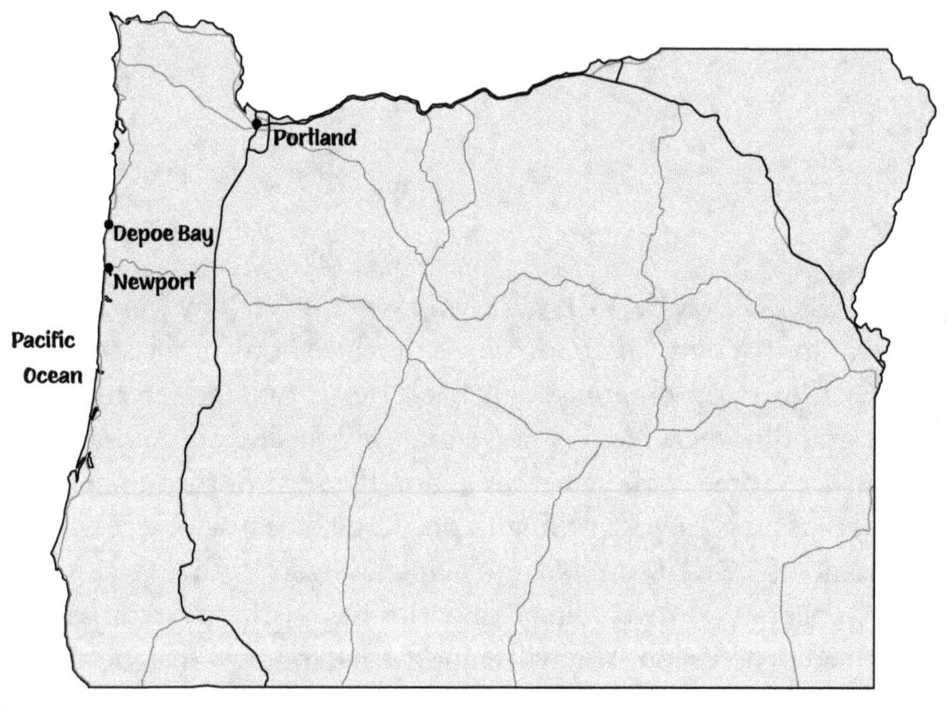

Chapter 1

Looking for a Place to Hide

I was moving to Oregon to get away from it all— away from the past and the present and the future that stretched out in front of me with boredom written all over it. Maybe I was just trying to get away from life or from myself. If the latter were the case, it wasn't going to work out, but I was going to give it a shot. I don't know what I was running from, but I knew I had to get away from it, whatever it was.

I wanted to go someplace where no one knew me. I intended to maintain an almost invisibly low profile. I didn't want anybody to welcome me or even know I had moved to Depoe Bay. I didn't want the neighbors to send over casseroles or brownies. I wasn't going to join a single club or any organization. I wasn't even going to register to vote. It's a waste of time for a Republican to register to vote in Oregon anyway. When I moved to Oregon, I was going to disappear from the human race. I was going to become a recluse, a hermit, an eccentric old woman who never came out of her house. I'd been to Depoe Bay once for a long weekend many years before, but I didn't know a single person who lived in the town. That was the way I wanted it to stay. I'd had many years filled with people, and now I wanted some years with not so many. Or that's what I was telling myself.

I had bought the oceanfront cottage on the Oregon coast sight unseen. Actually, I'd seen the house on the internet and looked at more than seventy-five photographs of the outside and the inside as well as views from the various windows. My real estate agent had measured rooms for me, and lawyers in two states had finalized the paperwork. I'd sold my big house in Connecticut and put a lot of furniture and household goods in storage. I decided to take to Oregon only the furniture and rugs I loved. I was careful to select exactly what would fit into my one-story, one-bedroom cottage. I packed up the clothes and books I wanted to have with me and sent my belongings ahead to Oregon.

All that remained was for me to organize myself, my West Highland Terrier, and my various electronic devices with their chargers. I put my medications, some clothes to wear on the trip, and the fragile personal items I didn't want to send with a mover into my Chevy Suburban. I started out on my journey to cross the country from the Atlantic Ocean to the Pacific Ocean—from sea to shining sea.

I had sent a plan of where I wanted each piece of furniture to go and told the "relocation specialist," hired by my real estate agent, what I wanted in the various drawers in the kitchen. Wi-Fi had been set up and all the utility bills were going to be paid automatically out of a checking account. A housekeeper and a gardener had been hired to help me out with the cottage and the yard. Not many people are interested in buying a one-bedroom house. No one else had been willing to pay the exorbitant price I had paid for my cottage. But this property had prime views of the Pacific Ocean. I'd fallen in love with the place and decided I had to have it at any cost. The house had already been completely redone and was in excellent condition. I wanted the house to be move-in ready when I arrived. I had a bench added to the already large shower and changed the paint colors on the walls of all the rooms.

One thing I wasn't expecting were the absolutely gorgeous gardens that awaited me. There was an English perennial garden in the truest sense of the word, and an herb garden was planted by the back door. The real estate agent had mentioned the herb garden, and I had asked her to have the gardener plant lots of basil, flat leaf Italian parsley, and several varieties of thyme. The mint and chives were already there. Although I had pretty much given up cooking, I loved having fresh herbs in case I was inspired.

I knew there was at least one excellent diner in town, a pretty good Mexican restaurant, and an Italian place with terrible atmosphere but really good food. They would all deliver, for a fee. There was a hotel with a good dining room and a country inn that specialized in comfort food like fried chicken and mashed potatoes and gravy. There was a well-known and reliable seafood place that also made good cheeseburgers. I had cooked and entertained my entire life and had something of a reputation in those areas. I was so terribly tired of all of that, and I wanted other people to cook for me from now on. I wanted to eat well, but my cooking days were over.

Some people would say I was too old to drive across the country by myself, but I took it easy and didn't drive too many miles in one day. It took me almost two weeks, and it had been a delightful trip. I was ready to meet my new home, my cottage by the sea. I was tired from the long days of driving. We arrived in the middle of the afternoon, Gaela and I, and she was glad to be someplace, too. I don't think my West Highland Terrier cared much where that someplace was as long as I was there with her and there was plenty of food.

I'd had my real estate agent stock the pantry and the refrigerator with our specific food requests. I was going to have to purchase some things online, but what I'd already ordered would keep me going for several days. I was hoping I didn't have to leave the house for at least a week.

The fence I'd had installed looked better than I'd hoped. How often does that happen? The fence and a whole-house back-up generator had been the two things the house did not come with that I absolutely had to have. I wanted to be able to let Gaela out the back door and not have to worry that she would run away. Gaela means "a source of happiness," and she was indeed a source of happiness for me.

I'd had a garage door opener sent to me so I could drive right in, and no one would know I had arrived. I pulled into the garage and put the door down behind me. I was too tired to unload the car, so I grabbed my medications, electronics, chargers, and Gaela's bowls and went inside the house. It looked exactly right. It had been smart to trust the real estate agent and the "relocation specialist." They had done a good job getting the house in turnkey order.

Hundreds of hydrangea bushes surrounded the house, and the pinks and blues that filled my yard, even this late in the summer, were breathtaking. Oregon's coast promised lots of water, and my favorite flowers were called hydrangeas for a reason. There were rose bushes and camellia bushes and other beautiful things I wasn't expecting. I knew I would want to look it all over and admire it carefully at some point. My cottage was even more wonderful than I had imagined it would be. I had chosen well.

Right this minute, I didn't want to do a thing except collapse on the bed and look out the windows at the Pacific Ocean. I'd come a long way to enjoy this view, and I wanted to glory in it. I had paid a boatload of money to be able to lie on my bed and watch the Pacific Ocean waves. I knew that sooner or later hunger would motivate Gaela even if it didn't motivate me. I didn't want to think about that. I didn't have to. Gaela and I both fell asleep, and it was dark when we woke up.

I was trying to keep myself away from the news so I didn't turn on the TV set. I'd become too much of a news junky in my old life, and I was trying to learn to keep my blood pressure down without the use of medication. I let Gaela out the back door and decided I would make myself a cup of green tea and skip dinner. Gaela wasn't a fan of green tea or a fan of skipping dinner, so I knew the least I would have to do would be to fix something for her to eat. Gaela ate, and I drank two cups of tea with local honey. I took a long, hot shower and climbed into bed with my electronic books. Neither the housekeeper nor the gardener was coming until next week, so I had an entire week to pretend I wasn't here yet, an entire week to practice being a recluse.

After my drive west, my time zones were confused. I woke up once at seven o'clock the next morning and went back to sleep until eleven. There was no reason for me to make myself get out of bed except that Gaela insisted. I let her into the yard and decided to check out the kitchen. The coffee maker I'd ordered was there. The Dunkin' Donuts coffee was in the freezer and the fat-free vanilla-flavored creamer was in the refrigerator. I filled my cup half with coffee and half with creamer and walked out onto the front porch. It was chilly so I went back inside to find a sweater. There was a blue sweater in a drawer, and it was mine, folded and put there by the ever-efficient "relocation specialist." Gaela and I enjoyed our view of the Pacific on this sunny morning, and I drank a second cup of coffee on the porch. Gaela was always ready for a nap, and eventually we both decided to go back to bed. We slept until three in the afternoon.

I thought maybe I should unpack the car, so I brought in one suitcase and one box. I put the box in the kitchen and the suitcase in the bedroom, and that was as far as I got with the unpacking. It would wait. I could wear the blue sweater I'd found for the rest of the week. Who would know? I began to understand how old people got into their bad habits of not eating, not changing their clothes, losing track of time, and forgetting to pay their bills. I didn't want to fall into that trap quite yet, but it was nice not to have to fit into any structure for the day, even a structure of my own making.

I was hungry and decided to see what was in the refrigerator. I found a nice thick Porterhouse steak and some Bob Evans sour cream and chive mashed potatoes. There were frozen French green beans that I could put in the microwave. Gaela was always happy to share a steak with me even if it was just the chance to chew on the bone. I opened a bottle of Pinot Noir and poured myself a glass. It was too chilly to eat on the porch tonight, so I turned on the gas fireplace in the living room and ate at my dark wood antique card table.

I'd sent the table ahead to Oregon for this specific purpose. It would serve as a dining table for one. It could seat two in a pinch. It was an attractive and substantial inlaid wooden table and had beautifully carved legs that didn't fold. The food tasted great to me, and so far I loved being alone in my new home and hiding from the world that I knew would, sadly, find me sooner or later.

When I was in my fifties, I'd decided I would try my hand at writing. I found that I loved it and had quite a few good stories to tell. I'd always been a voracious reader and knew what kinds of books I loved. I wanted to write books that I would like to read. I had no idea that anybody else would want to read what I'd written. I put an old photograph of myself on the dust cover of my first novel and adopted a pen name. I didn't think it would amount to much, and I self-published my first book, not ever imagining that a publishing company might be interested in it. Much to my surprise, in fact it was downright shocking, my book was a huge best seller.

Several publishing companies wanted to publish my book. I got an agent, and she negotiated a favorable contract for me. Since the book was already a best seller, I suddenly was making more money than I'd ever thought possible. I signed a lucrative contract for a second book which I had already written. Even though I was comfortably fixed financially, after publishing three books, I was downright rich. It was fun to be rich.

I went on some book signing tours, and at first, that was fun, too. People didn't recognize me from the picture on my books. That was also kind of fun. I put on a blonde wig (my hair used to be blonde) in the hairstyle of my former self who appeared on the dust cover of my books. I had a little plastic surgery done to my neck and eyes. I realized I loved the writing part of writing, and I liked the money part. But after a while, I really didn't like the being famous part.

Fortunately, I had used a pen name for all my books, and I'd refused to allow anyone to find out my real name. That was the only thing that saved me when I decided I'd had enough of public life and wanted to become a recluse. I wanted to keep on writing, but I didn't want to do any more book signings or any of the publicity tours. Of course, publishers always want you to do the promotions and all of that; so I quit. I continued to write but didn't publish anything anymore. I eventually realized that the only thing to do was to get completely away from my East Coast life. I made plans to move to Oregon.

Because I suffer from osteoarthritis, the choice of the Oregon Coast was probably not a great one, but I wanted someplace with beautiful views and wild weather. I wanted a place I had been before but a place where I didn't know anybody. I wanted a place that would lose population after the summer season ended and become a kind of ghost town. So here I was beginning my life as a recluse and wondering how many days I could stay indoors without going out. At some point I might have to accept the fact that my real problem was that I was depressed.

The sun had been shining on my first day in Depoe Bay, and I'd ventured outside twice. I'd sat on my front porch for short periods. Gaela had loved sniffing around and investigating her back yard. I knew I would want to turn on the television set one of these days, but for right now, I was happy to just be hanging out, getting to know my new home.

The weather accommodated me on my second day in Depoe Bay when the tail end of a September typhoon from the Pacific

Ocean or Japan … or someplace … hit the Oregon Coast. The rain pounded down and pounded down some more. My weather radio told me that the Coast Guard was staying in port unless an emergency arose. Fishermen were told not to go out because of the rough seas. The wind gusted to seventy-five plus miles per hour. I was thrilled to finally experience the wild weather I'd been seeking. I loved to watch it and see the way it tore up the surf in the Pacific Ocean. If the Coast Guard and the fishermen were not allowed to go out in the weather, how could I be expected to go outside in the rain?

I felt warm and safe inside my house. I slept late, drank coffee for breakfast and lunch, ate a big dinner, and went to bed early. I was not observing healthy eating habits. I had already beaten the odds at seventy-four and wasn't about to take up granola bars and vegan cheese at this late date. Vegan cheese was an abomination and an oxymoron, but I liked granola bars. But not in place of real food.

Finally, the four-day storm subsided, and I decided I was going to have to go for a walk sooner or later. Gaela was ready, and although I was not, we set out on a route that I'd been told would take me on a gently winding path down to my rocky coastal beach. I put on my waterproof windbreaker and set off with Gaela who was delighted to see her leash come out of the closet. After walking for about fifteen minutes, my knees were aching so we turned around and went back to the house. The Oregon Coast was even more beautiful than I had remembered. The scenery was spectacular, and I felt somewhat invigorated after the walk. Gaela was pumped, and I resolved to do this daily. I knew I would have to go farther down the path next time.

Feeling so good about my morning out, I put Gaela in the car, and we drove to the town diner. I was tired of my own cooking and decided I wanted to try the diner I'd heard was one of the best in Oregon. I loved diners anyway and was glad they had not completely disappeared during the years of trendy nouvelle cuisine and burrito bowls. The diner, even in the early off-season, was crowded, so I took a seat at the counter. I ordered a large bowl of homemade chicken noodle soup and a turkey club on whole wheat toast with mayonnaise, plus Russian dressing on the side. The diner roasted its own turkey breasts and didn't use the processed plastic turkey most places put in their turkey club sandwiches. The sandwich was delicious, and I promised myself that I would be back soon to try some of the other diner foods I loved. Gaela enjoyed the leftovers I brought to the car.

I was still feeling energetic, so I decided to run a few errands to buy some things I'd either run out of or had forgotten to bring with me to my new house. I was out of milk and didn't have any Band-Aids. I couldn't find the white thread for my sewing machine, and I needed an additional wastebasket and some thumb drives to back up stuff on my computer.

Although I had already made a large pot of my own homemade spaghetti sauce and frozen most of it, I wanted to try the Italian place for dinner, the place with great food and no atmosphere. It was my kind of place. I'd had an acquaintance once who loved places with lots of atmosphere and didn't care much about how the food tasted. We could never really be friends, with such opposite goals when it came to going out for dinner.

I drove to the local mall and turned my errands into an entire afternoon's worth of activity. The Italian food was even better than advertised, and the décor was even worse. So I had a great time eating minestrone and veal parmesan with a side of pasta. I was pretty tired when I drove myself home, and Gaela, who had spent most of the afternoon in the car, was also glad to be back at the cottage.

My housekeeper was arriving for the first time the next morning, and I decided I wanted to at least be awake, if not dressed, when she arrived at ten. She preferred to come late because she took her grandkids to school and had other things to do before she came to my house. This was fine with me as I didn't want someone running the vacuum cleaner while I was trying to sleep.

Chapter 2

Not Really Looking

That morning I started the coffee pot and made myself a cup which I was drinking in the kitchen when Anne Marie Peterson, my new housekeeper, arrived for her first day of work. She was younger than I was, but not by much. She had curly gray hair and was a tiny little thing. She would work for me four hours a day. We shook hands and she asked me what I wanted her to do first. There was no socializing, no sharing of family or personal information. Anne Marie was all business. I told her I'd love to have some freshly squeezed orange juice. She immediately went to the refrigerator and began to take out oranges. I told her I'd also like some toast and bacon. She got to work on that, too. I asked her how old her grandkids were. She answered my questions as if she were a well-prepared witness on the stand who had been instructed not to give the defense attorney any more information than he asked for—just the facts, ma'am, just the facts. We were going to get along fine.

She knew I had been here a week. She stripped the bed, put on clean sheets, and started on the laundry. She unloaded the dishwasher and put away the dishes. She knew exactly what to do. I decided to take Gaela for a short walk down the winding pathway to the rocky coastline. It was overcast but not raining. We walked farther than we had the day before, but when my knees started to hurt, we turned back. Gaela didn't want to turn around, but she knew the pain in my knees was the boss.

When we got back from our walk, Anne Marie decided Gaela needed a bath. She took her from me and plopped her in the sink. Anne Marie was right. My West Highland Terrier's hair had begun to resemble the wall paint color builders call Swiss coffee which is a cross between off-white and light beige. After the bath, Gaela's hair was bright white, and she looked great. Gaela loved the bath and was drying herself in front of the gas fireplace in no time.

Anne Marie said she would put the roast beef in the oven before she left for the day. She set a timer which would let me know when to turn off the oven. She had cooked the broccoli and said she would make gravy the next day if I didn't want to make it for myself tonight. I gave her a grocery list for the next morning, and she said the store would put the charges on my account. They would send me a bill at the end of each month. How easy was that?

I was now more than somewhat bored with being a recluse and was thinking about starting to write again. But who would I be writing for if I didn't want to publish anything? Maybe I needed a new pen name and a new publisher. Would my fans not recognize my writing style if I didn't try to change it? I could see now that the boredom I had tried so hard to outrun had followed me to Oregon. It was living right here with me in my secluded and remote cottage with its herb garden, hydrangea bushes, and fenced-in back yard. Maybe I would take up painting? Basket weaving and macramé were definitely out. I opted for taking a nap as soon as Anne Marie had left for the day. The house looked great, and all the laundry was done and put away. What would she ever do tomorrow? What would I ever do tomorrow?

My life as a recluse as well as my boredom would come abruptly to an end when Gaela and I took our morning walk the next day. Anne Marie arrived and put away the groceries. She made my orange juice and bacon and toasted two English muffins for my breakfast. I could tell she loved Gaela and was softening her professional and impersonal exterior a little bit. After our breakfast, Gaela and I set out for a walk. It was still overcast and misting. Oregon weather is like that a lot, at least along the coast in the early fall. I wore my rain jacket with two sweaters underneath.

We'd found our way almost all the way down to my beach when I saw something which I had, up until this moment, only written about. I spotted what I thought looked like a dead body lying in a lump on the shore just out of reach of the incoming waves. Gaela was straining at the leash, anxious to get to this intriguing and probably smelly pile of clothing. I held her back, and I kept my distance. I knew from my research as a writer and from watching TV shows that it was essential not to disturb a crime scene.

The last thing I wanted to do was touch this poor soul, this mass of protoplasm that had once been alive. I didn't need to be a medical examiner to be able to tell that it would be a waste of time to try to find a pulse or to try to do anything to save a life which had been lost days before. The body looked like it was male, but who could tell these days? He wore a windbreaker with a hood and black pants. He was small and slim, but maybe all bodies that wash up on the beach seem diminished by their solitude. Keeping Gaela and myself away from the body, I reasoned, was essential to the preservation of the scene. Whether it would turn out to be a crime scene or not would be for someone else to determine. Maybe it would be just an ordinary drowning, if any death can be said to be ordinary.

It looked to me as if the real crime scene, if indeed there was one, was not anywhere within many miles of this dead body. There wasn't any blood and there were no bullet holes or injuries caused by blunt instruments, at least that I could see. I held Gaela tightly in my arms and took my cell phone out of my pocket. Because I am a responsible person, I always carry my phone with me in case I fall and need assistance. I called 911 and gave them all the information they would need to find me and their newest investigation. I kept Gaela in my lap, and I sat down purposefully and carefully among the cold rocks to wait for the police. I called Anne Marie at the house and told her what was going on. She said she would bring my lunch if I wasn't back at the house by 1:00 pm. The woman could read my mind.

Two uniformed patrolmen from the Oregon State Police finally arrived at the scene. They were polite, introduced themselves, and showed me their identification. They asked me to tell them, several times, how I had happened to discover the body. I explained it all to them, and then I explained it all again. I even told them my real name. I was sure this was going to get me into trouble eventually, but what else could I do? I had no reason to lie to the police, especially now that my cover as a reclusive hermit was blown.

The body looked to me as if it had been in the water for several days, but what did I know? It had long, dark hair, but in these times, having long hair meant nothing. It could have been a man or a woman. It was not anyone I knew. How could it be? I didn't know anybody in the state except for my real estate agent and my housekeeper Anne Marie. And now I kind of knew two policemen. The policemen told me I could go back to my house, but of course they wanted my phone number and all of the information they would need to hassle me in the future.

Sitting and waiting for the authorities to arrive had rested my knees even as it had frozen my behind. I struggled to stand up. Once I had resolved the stiffness in my joints, it was not too hard to walk back up to the house. I had a spectacular view, and the ocean was always changing, never the same from one day to the next or even one hour to the next. I loved the ocean. I knew the wind had made my face ruddy, and my hair was damp. I'd had enough of the outdoor life for one day.

When I got to the house, it was such a pleasure to be greeted with a fire in the fireplace and lunch set out on my beautiful wooden dining table. Anne Marie served me a bowl from the pot of homemade tomato soup she had on the stove. Where had that come from? It was buttery and delicious, and Anne Marie had added little ribbons of fresh basil from my herb garden on top. She had made me a hearty sandwich of thinly sliced rare roast beef with cheddar cheese on rye and Anne Marie's homemade potato salad. Where had that come from? The woman was a magician as well as a mind reader.

I was hungry after my walk, the discovery of a dead body, and my interrogation by the police. I ate every bite of food except for what I shared with Gaela. Anne Marie had prepared spiced hot cider to go with my lunch. Amazing! As I ate, I told her all about everything that had happened. She could see I was enjoying all of her food immensely and seemed pleased that I liked the soup and the potato salad so much. She told me she had left a saucepan of roast beef gravy on the stove for my dinner. She'd frozen some of the delicious tomato soup and showed me where she'd put it in the freezer. She had also made some chocolate chip cookies which were still warm. I am not crazy about sweets, but she had managed to hit my one soft spot in that department. Warm bitter-sweet chocolate got to me every time. Anne Marie washed the lunch dishes, and after she left for the day, Gaela and I took a nap.

It was four o'clock when we were awakened by loud knocking at the front door. Who could that possibly be? Nobody came to the front door. Nobody had ever knocked on any door at my new house, but if they had, they would have come to the back door because it was closer to the road. So much for my withdrawal from the world. Sure enough, someone was indeed at my front door. I roused myself and reluctantly opened it to find a tall young man in a raincoat standing there. Was he going to flash me or did he have a camera hidden behind his back? It turns out he was neither a flasher nor a reporter but a detective, an investigator with the Oregon State Police. I should have guessed that he would be here at my house sooner or later. I just hadn't expected him so much sooner.

His name was Detective Nathanial Broderick. He showed me his identification, and he wanted to come inside. He was quite good looking and had nice gray eyes, bushy eyebrows, and light brown hair. I asked him to sit down in my living room and offered him some coffee or some hot cider. He opted for the cider, and we both had a cup. I brought a plate of cookies and some cloth napkins. Here he was, my first guest. And I'd never intended to have any guests at all, ever, in this, my hideaway. So much for that. He didn't want to take off his raincoat, although I'd asked him if I could hang it up. He seemed nice enough and repeated all the same questions I had already answered for the cops on the beach.

Nathanial said I looked familiar to him. I said I had "one of those faces" and that people were always telling me I looked familiar. I didn't feel I had any obligation to tell him that I had once written best-selling novels under a pen name and that he probably recognized me from the picture on the dust covers of my books. That had nothing to do with what I'd discovered on the beach. I asked him some questions, too, figuring he wouldn't tell me anything about anything. That was the way cops in novels treated the person who discovered the body. My fictional detectives won't give out any information right up until the moment when they start suspecting the person who had discovered the body as their number one person of interest. Nathanial was different. He answered my questions, or at least he pretended to answer my questions.

I asked if there was any ID on the body. I wanted to know how long he thought the body had been in the water and if it was possible to identify somebody who had been in the water that long. I asked if foul play had been involved in any way. Could an autopsy show the cause of death if the person had been in the water for a long time? I asked if the person I'd discovered was male or female. I asked if his or her clothing gave any clues about his nationality. I am an unusually inquisitive person.

Detective Broderick squinted his eyes, wrinkled his forehead, and looked at me with curiosity. I guess I'd asked questions a person in law enforcement might ask. Or they might be questions a person who wrote books about murders and solving them might ask. I'd never seen a crime victim except on TV and in my own mind, of course, as I imagined them and wrote my stories about them. I'd never seen one in the flesh until this morning. And maybe that hapless soul I'd discovered on the beach was not even a victim of a crime. Maybe he or she was a victim of a drowning, a fall from a boat, or some other kind of natural or accidental death. I assumed the person I'd discovered had been washed up from the sea, but I didn't even know that for sure.

"Are you a retired law enforcement person, Ms. Linder? You seem to have quite an interest in the person on the beach and a lot of questions regarding what we have found out about him."

"Of course, I am interested in that person. A 'him,' you say? Wouldn't you be interested if a body had washed up out of the ocean onto your beach, and you had found it? Wouldn't you want to know who that person was, how they got to your beach, and how they'd died? Anybody would want to know these things. Maybe I just watch too much CSI and NCIS and all of those shows on TV. I want to know everything you can tell me about the person I found. I want to know that whoever that person is that he or she will be returned to his or her family and will receive a proper burial and will rest in peace. Being washed up dead on the Oregon Coast is certainly not an everyday occurrence for whoever it was that I discovered this morning. Finding a dead body on my property is not an everyday occurrence for me either. I want to know everything there is to know."

"We don't know anything much ourselves, at least not yet. The victim appears to be a male in his early to mid-twenties. He didn't have any identification on his body, but we believe he is of African or Middle Eastern origin. We believe that because of his facial structure and the color of his skin and his hair. We will run some DNA tests to determine his precise genetic origins. There aren't any identifying marks or labels in the clothing that might help us determine where any of it was purchased. The labels on the victim's clothes have been cut out, which is unusual and suspicious. We don't know anything about the cause of death, and I won't have any answers about that until after the autopsy has been performed. We may not have answers even after the autopsy."

"Well, detective, thank you for sharing all of that information with me. I'm surprised you've been so forthcoming, and I am very appreciative."

"I know this was a shock for you, and my philosophy is that if the person who discovers a body wants to know as much information as possible to help them deal with the trauma of making the discovery, I want to give them that information. Now you know almost everything I know. I appreciate your time and cooperation. I also thank you for the delicious hot cider and the cookies. They more than hit the spot with me after the past two hours walking with the forensics team and the medical examiner on the beach. You have been very hospitable. I am going to leave my card with you, and if you think of anything else you forgot to tell me or if you have any more questions, please feel free to call me on my cell phone."

"You are welcome. I am happy to do whatever I can to help bring this young man home to his family, wherever that home might be. I hope you will let me know if and when you find out anything more about him. You are correct that the more I know the better I can recover from the trauma of the discovery. The unknown is always the most difficult thing to deal with—for me anyway. Again, I appreciate your telling me as much as you have. I look forward to hearing from you when you have more information."

Detective Broderick left the house, and I have to admit I enjoyed having him here. Maybe I was not as reclusive as I'd thought I was. He was my first guest, and I'd never planned on having any guests here at all. It had not been that painful, and I'd almost been sorry to see him leave. Gaela wanted my attention, a short trip to the back yard, and her dinner. In spite of the enormous lunch I had eaten, I was hungry again. Finding bodies on the beach works up an appetite. I'd never realized that until today, and I would have to remember to put that in my next book. Except, I reminded myself, I wasn't going to write any more books.

I reheated the roast beef from the night before and warmed up the gravy Anne Marie had made and left on the stove. I had the rest of the Bob Evans mashed potatoes, and there was plenty of leftover broccoli. Some microwaved frozen cheese sauce on top of the broccoli completed the hearty meal, and I ate a lot of the rare roast beef. Maybe finding bodies on the beach depletes the body's protein. I might have convinced myself of that fact except that I had also helped myself to large amounts of Anne Marie's delicious gravy. What excuse could I find for that?

After a hot bath, I snuggled down with Gaela and read from my Kindle. I was already imagining a story about the body on the beach. It was one thing to make up a story about an imaginary body, but I did not have poetic license to make up stories about this real victim. I fell asleep wondering about my adventures of the morning and my interactions with Broderick. He was much nicer than the detectives in my own fictional stories. Maybe I had made my detectives too harsh and taciturn. Maybe I could learn something from Broderick's friendly, open-handed style of dealing with the public.

I was a member of the public now and certainly not in control of this story. It felt strange not to be able to push the action forward using my own imagination. Waiting for real facts, especially for facts which might never be known, was frustrating. I needed to find something to do. Being a recluse with nothing to do had become old in just a little over a week.

Chapter 3

Looking For Something

The next morning after breakfast, Gaela and I went down to the beach again. I was determined to search for clues, clues that, of course, a professional forensics team had failed to find. Maybe that only happened in my novels, but you never knew what could happen until you looked. And wouldn't you know it; the morning tide had washed up a backpack! There it was lying on the beach just begging to be noticed. It might belong to the body of the previous morning, or it might be entirely unrelated.

I didn't have any plastic gloves to put on (like a professional investigator would have) so I used some seaweed from the beach to keep my fingerprints off the fasteners of the backpack. When I opened the largest compartment and looked inside, I shut it immediately and backed away. There was something in the backpack that looked to me like explosives with wires and things coming out of it in all directions.

It looked disturbingly like a bomb. It was now completely soaked with sea water, and hopefully in its current state, it was not in danger of exploding.

I wished I'd done the right thing at first and called Detective Broderick before opening the backpack, but I hadn't. How could I have known it was trouble until I'd opened it, looked inside, and seen what appeared to be a bomb? I had tried to investigate on my own, but I didn't think I'd compromised any evidence by opening the one compartment of the backpack. I realized now that this was way out of my league and that professional attention was required. I called the detective, and he picked up his phone right away.

"This is Abigail Linder, Detective Broderick, and I have just found a backpack that washed up on my beach this morning. The backpack has what I think are explosives inside it, and you probably need to see it right away. I don't know if it has anything to do with the body that washed up yesterday, but it washed up in exactly the same spot on the beach as yesterday's body. I opened the backpack to look inside, but other than that I didn't move it or disturb anything. I won't touch it again. I will stay here with it until you or someone else arrives to take it away. The backpack is soaked. I don't think the bomb is in danger of going off."

"Stay right where you are and don't touch anything. I will be right there myself. It will take me about fifteen minutes. Thanks." Detective Nathanial Broderick was so polite. I liked that.

I was almost afraid to call my housekeeper Anne Marie to tell her that I'd found something else on the beach that might cause trouble. She'd arrived at my house earlier that morning. I'd already become irrevocably attached to her cooking and her way of taking care of the house for me. I didn't want to lose her because of the weird things that were happening on my property or because there were always policemen wandering around. I did call her, and she asked if I needed anything. I told her I just wanted her to make me the same exact lunch she'd made for me yesterday. That would make me feel much better. Gaela and I sat on the beach and waited for Detective Broderick.

When he arrived, he had two technicians in tow. They took lots of photographs of the backpack and asked if I had moved it. I hadn't. Nathanial insisted that I call him by his first name since it looked like we were going to have a long-term relationship. I explained that when I'd found the backpack and opened the large compartment, I'd tried not to leave any fingerprints. I told him about the seaweed. He didn't laugh at me or scold me about that; he just said he was glad I hadn't moved the backpack.

Finally, after asking me to repeat several times how I had happened to find the backpack, he told me I could return to my house. In fact, I hadn't "found" the backpack. It was just sitting right there in front of me on the beach. I looked at it, and then I opened it. Then I'd called Nathanial. As Gaela and I walked back to the cottage, I thought seriously about whether or not I wanted to take any more walks on the beach, the next day or on any other day in the future. Maybe I could just admire the Pacific Ocean from my porch from now on.

I went back to the house and enjoyed my wonderful lunch again in front of a warm fire. Anne Marie asked if there was anything new in "the case." I guess she also watched CSI or some of the other crime shows on TV. I was old enough to remember Perry Mason, Della Street, and Paul Drake and how they'd solved crimes mostly by just figuring them out.

They didn't have DNA or sophisticated fingerprint databases or voice recognition or facial recognition software. But every week, they got their man, or their woman. And then there were Nancy Drew and Hercule Poirot. They were so brilliant and so low tech. I knew I was an anachronism longing for the good old days. That afternoon Gaela and I watched an old World War II spy movie on TV. We woke up late after taking a nap, and I decided I needed a change of scenery. We opted for the famous fish restaurant in Depoe Bay, The Sea Dog.

We were late enough that getting a good parking place was not a problem. I ordered a large shrimp cocktail and the large fried seafood platter. It was called the Neptune Platter or something like that. I rationalized ordering the large because I would take some of the leftovers home for lunch the next day. The platter was huge with a mountain of fried everything on it, fish, shrimp, scallops, clams, oysters, and a crab cake. There was also a big pile of fries and a side of delicious coleslaw, so there were plenty of leftovers to take home. Stuffed and happy to have discovered a new place to eat, Gaela and I were anxious to be back at the cottage and went immediately to bed.

The next morning after breakfast, Gaela and I started to get ready for our walk. Anne Marie, who hardly ever initiated a conversation, asked me if I really wanted to take a walk on the beach this morning. I told her I thought it was probably safe to go today. What were the chances I would find something else the third day in a row? It looked like it was going to rain at any minute, so we needed to hurry if we wanted to finish the walk before we got wet.

We didn't even make it all the way to the beach when I saw it. As we went around the last bend in the path, I looked down and to my left, and there were what looked like the remnants of a rubber raft. The battered rubber boat was on the beach in my cove, a cove that half belonged to me. The other half of the cove belonged to the empty property next to mine. I didn't know exactly where the lot line was that divided the cove, but it looked like the raft was on my half. It was difficult to get down to the cove. There was no gently winding path to take me there. It was a steep climb down to the cove's beach, an impossible hike for somebody who uses a cane … like I do.

I called Detective Broderick right away. He needed to know there was something suspicious in the cove even if the raft wasn't completely on my property. He was surprised to hear from me again today. I told him I'd seen what looked like the remains of a rubber raft in my cove. I told him I hadn't approached it and had only seen it from a distance. I took a photo of it with my phone and sent it to him. Of course, neither of us knew whether or not the raft had anything to do with the discoveries of the two previous mornings. Detective Broderick said he would meet me in fifteen minutes. I told him where he could find the raft in the cove. I told him he could find me inside my house.

By now, the rain was coming down in earnest, and both Gaela and I were drenched. I don't run anywhere these days, but I did try to hobble as fast as I could back to my dry house. As soon as we dripped in through the door, Anne Marie gathered up Gaela and toweled her off and put her in front of the gas fireplace to get warm. I peeled off my soaking clothes in the bathroom and decided I would take a shower – not because I needed to be cleaner but because I needed to be warmer. I decided that if I was going to continue to take walks on the beach, I would have to invest in more protective foul weather gear. My thigh-length "waterproof" anorak was not able to handle the Oregon rain. I needed serious fisherman's oilskins to make my daily journeys of discovery. I dressed in dry jeans, a turtleneck, and a heavy cable knit sweater. My bedroom slippers felt great on my feet. I decided I was staying in the house for the rest of the day.

Anne Marie had made beef barley soup with mushrooms for lunch. The woman is a soup-making genius; how lucky was I? She warmed up my leftover fish from the night before and made me a wonderful fried fish sandwich with lettuce, tomato, and tartar sauce on a buttered, toasted potato roll. She even cut up some lemon wedges. I asked her where she had learned to cook, and she said her grandmother and her mother had both been excellent cooks and had taught her. I could tell she was pleased that I liked her soups so much.

She'd made chicken breasts in a creamy lemon-garlic sauce with rice for my dinner. The chicken had artichoke hearts and sun dried tomatoes added to the sauce. It was already in the oven and all I had to do was turn it on. Anne Marie realized how much I loved her food, and I think she was showing off a little bit each time she made a new dish for me. She had already steamed what looked like a pound of asparagus. I was going to have to make more of an effort to find something to do since Anne Marie had all the home chores and all the cooking covered. She was doing an ever so much better job at all of it than I could have hoped to do.

My cell phone rang as Anne Marie was leaving. It was Detective Broderick calling to see if he could stop by later that evening. He said he wouldn't be able to come by until after dinner, and he would have the autopsy report in hand by that time. He wanted to ask me some more questions. I asked him if he had any information about the raft in my cove, and he said he would tell me about it when he saw me that night.

I turned on the oven to make my dinner, and Gaela and I watched another old movie. We fell asleep halfway through it and woke up after six o'clock. The chicken and rice were not overcooked in spite of the nap, and I had a glass of Pinot Grigio with the chicken and rice and asparagus. Anne Marie had cooked lots of asparagus, so the leftovers would make a delicious salad the next day. I was sure Anne Marie had wonderful plans for it. Nathanial was coming at seven thirty, so I warmed up some cider on the stove and put chocolate chip cookies on a plate. I was ready for my second visitor. In fact, it was the same visitor, just back for a second time.

Detective Broderick came to the back door tonight. It was still pouring rain outside, and the back door was closer to the road. He let me hang up his wet raincoat this time, and he was happy to have more warm cider and cookies. I offered to put a nice slug of rum or bourbon into his cup of cider, but he refused that. We sat down in front of the fireplace. Gaela greeted the detective. She was beginning to accept him as part of the household.

"The backpack you found on the beach did have a bomb in it." He wasn't going to beat around the bush blabbering about a lot of things that didn't interest either one of us. "You had already figured that out, so I decided there wasn't any point in not telling you about it. It looks like our body might be a 'lone wolf' bomber, a terrorist and probably a suicide bomber. We don't know what he intended to bomb, but we made the logical assumption that he intended to bomb something.

"We think the rubber raft that washed up in your cove was probably his means of transportation, his way of trying to enter the country. There was a second backpack in the raft, identical to the one that washed up on your beach. The backpack in the raft had more bomb-making supplies inside and was tightly wedged into a compartment in the raft. It's a miracle it didn't become dislodged and fall into the ocean when the raft turned over. The raft was almost completely destroyed by the rocks along the coast. If the second backpack had not remained wedged in the raft, we wouldn't have been able to link the two backpacks with one-hundred percent certainty. Being able to tie the two backpacks together allows us to tie the backpack on the beach to the ruined raft in the cove. We think the raft that ended up on your property was launched from a larger ship sailing off the Pacific coast. Our hypothesis is that the raft was intended to bring the young man with his bombs and backpacks from that ship to the United States mainland."

Broderick continued, "If he hoped to enter the U.S. in such a surreptitious and secret way, we can probably assume he was 'up to no good.' Of course, we don't know what his intended final destination was. We don't know what the targets for his backpack bombs were. We also won't ever know, unless more debris washes up on your beach or on someone else's beach, what other things of importance might have been in the raft. It looks like you are four for four in terms of clues. They all washed up on your property—the body, the backpack, the bombs, and the raft."

I was surprised, for several reasons, by the things he had to say. Nathanial had decided to be honest with me about what had been found. I'd heard about "lone wolf" terrorists which were becoming the "new" face of terrorism around the world, including in the United States. However, I'd not previously heard of any terrorists who'd landed on U.S. beaches bringing bombs with them. Not that it hadn't happened somewhere, but I'd not heard about it until it happened on my own beach and in my own cove. Maybe this kind of thing had already happened someplace in this country, and it had been kept out of the news for security or PR reasons. I also was surprised that all of the elements which had washed up on my property were connected. What were the chances of that happening? The Pacific Ocean was a big place. Would other things from the terrorist's rubber raft wash up on another beach nearby, or far away?

"This is all quite interesting, and it's also frightening. The thing that immediately comes to my mind and worries me is not the terrorist, his backpack, and the raft that washed up on my property. What worries me is the other rafts that set out to come ashore along the coast of the USA that didn't get destroyed in a storm. What happened to the ones which made it to shore and successfully landed with their passenger or passengers and their dangerous explosives? That is what I would be worrying about if I were investigating this whole thing and if I were Homeland Security."

"You are right on target with that one. We have not had a case like this before in Oregon, and the FBI and DHS are appropriately intrigued and concerned about the possibility that there might have been other similar scenarios. We are, for sure, worried about the rafts which did not get overturned and the terrorists who did not drown. Who knows how many of them might have already made it to land and continued on with their missions? Where did they land? What were they bringing into the country? What are their targets? We did have that bad storm which lasted several days, and it was fierce. The size of the raft our guy was using was never going to be a match for even the tail end of that typhoon from Japan. I'm surprised anybody with any knowledge of the sea or any way of following the weather report would send him over the side of a ship, into a storm, and on his way to try to make it to shore. Whoever made the decision to launch the raft made a bad one. They might have thought they were close enough, that the guy could make it to the beach. But no matter how close they might have been to shore, that raft was never going to arrive intact. We can only speculate about whether or not he is a real 'loan wolf' and not part of a larger organization. We don't have any way to know if this was a one-shot deal, one raft into the ocean, or if this is a bigger threat. Are there other rafts which have already arrived, and are there rafts that will be on their way in the future?"

I had questions for the detective. "Just out of curiosity, I'm wondering why you're willing to be so open with me about what is going on with all of this. I expect that everything you have told me is top secret, confidential information that civilians would never be allowed to hear anything about. This sounds like a story you would want to keep from the press. Why are you trusting me?"

"We know who you are, Ms. Linder. After the first time I met with you, I knew you looked like someone I had seen before. We looked into your background and found out that you are a famous writer who has written mysteries, thrillers, and spy novels under your pen name. You chose not to share that information with me when I mentioned you looked familiar, and I want to respect your wishes to remain incognito here in your new home on the coast of Oregon. However, it was your bad luck that the body and all the rest of it washed up on your property. Some of my colleagues and I discussed you and your history and your relationship to the circumstances of this case. We decided to tell you most of what we have been able to figure out in return for your promise of silence." Nathanial had an expectant and at the same time quite a determined look on his face. The set of his jaw made me realize he would not take no for an answer, not that I had any intention of refusing his request for my silence.

"So you know my pen name and my real name, and you also seem to know that I am trying to avoid being discovered in my new home and in my new life. Rest assured, I don't want to tell the press or anybody else about what I found on the beach. Who would I tell, anyway? I don't know anybody here except my housekeeper and my real estate agent, and now you, of course. I've texted with a person who will come to clean up my yard. But I have not had a chance to meet him in person yet. You have used the term 'we' in reference to those who are making decisions about what to tell me. I will not ask you to tell me exactly who 'we' are, but I trust that it is law enforcement authorities in general."

"We in law enforcement are willing to do everything in our power to keep your writing identity and your real identity out of this investigation. I know you don't want any publicity, and it seems pretty obvious that you are trying to 'hide out' as it were, here in Oregon. I respect your wish to remain anonymous. We've agreed not to divulge anything about you or your role in this. For our own purposes, we would like to keep everything about this event out of the news for as long as possible. When it inevitably gets into the press and the public domain, which we obviously hope it never does, we will not mention where the body was discovered or who owns the property where it was found. It is in the interest of confidentiality that you, as a somewhat well-known person, not be identified as part of the investigation. That would only heighten the fascination of the press and the public and make our job even more difficult. So you see it is in our best interest, as well as your own, to keep your identities out of it."

"I would appreciate it if you can keep it confidential. Of course, I would never have considered getting involved with the press or telling anyone anything at all about what has happened here. The last thing in the world I want to do is to call attention to myself or to what I found. One of the reasons I selected Depoe Bay and this area of the Oregon coast is that I'd heard there are other 'famous,' 'somewhat famous,' and even 'infamous' people who are also hiding out here. I've heard that the locals are happy to have us, as well as the exorbitant amounts of money we are willing to pay for the gorgeous real estate that is available in the area. That does not even begin to address how much the local people appreciate the outrageous property taxes we are delighted to pay. We, in turn, appreciate that they protect our anonymity with their silence. This area comes highly recommended because of its willingness to respect those of us who are attempting to 'get away from it all.'"

"Your sources, it would seem, are entirely correct. I had a sense from you the first time I was here that you didn't want to share with me that you are a well-known person. That's one reason I'm telling you everything. By the way, in the spirit of full disclosure, the autopsy hasn't been able to tell us very much. The victim drowned as far as the ME could determine. He was tossed around in the surf and has abrasions all over his body from striking the rocks and being pounded into the ocean floor as he was washed toward the beach. He may not have known how to swim. The timetable makes him a victim of the storm caused by the typhoon, again as far as we can determine. According to the DNA analysis, his ancestors are from Africa and the Middle East. We will never be able to give a name to our corpse. Considering the circumstances and the bombs he was carrying, that is not a tragedy. There will be no family to notify or any of those niceties usually associated with trying to find a name for the unknown victim of an accident or a drowning."

"I am sure you are investigating what ships were in the area around the time the ME thinks this bomber left an off-shore ship in his worthless raft. How far out to sea do you think a ship would have been, to drop him over the side? Given the size and condition of the raft and the weather conditions, what were they thinking? With all the satellites and all the eyes in the sky that the government has, I am sure you are finding answers to these questions. Could he have come down from the Canadian Coast? I am wondering if it's an organized group that sent this bomber out from the ship. Or, given the poor condition of the raft and the total disregard for the obviously terrible weather, could this be a group of incompetent stooges, amateurs who have gotten together to cause trouble? If it is the latter, he might have been one of a kind as opposed to one of several."

Nathanial stood up and said he was sorry that he had to leave. He had enjoyed our talk and felt certain that I understood what stakes were involved in this investigation. He wanted to talk with me at another time about what my housekeeper knew and what I thought she might talk about, that is, what she might "spread around town." He told me that someone from the Oregon State Police, the OSP, had gone to her house to question her and had asked her not to talk about anything she had seen or heard at your house because it was an "ongoing investigation." Nathanial said he thought that Anne Marie was a law-abiding, God-fearing woman. After the OSP had been to talk to her and had cautioned her, Nathanial didn't think, and I agreed with him, that she would breathe a word of anything to anybody. He thought she might not even be willing to talk about it with me, which was fine with me, I think. He said she seemed to be rather thrilled to be on the "inside" of the investigation and was eager to help keep law enforcement's secrets.

Nathanial said his goodbyes and, after putting on his still-wet raincoat, went back out into the rain. I was unusually tired after his visit this time. I admitted to myself that I was relieved the authorities now knew who I was. I didn't want to hide anything from the Oregon State Police, the FBI, Homeland Security, or anybody who needed to know. I was encouraged that they were willing to try to protect my identity and my wish to remain incognito. Gaela went out one more time, and I went to sleep trying not to think any more about our mystery corpse or the police investigation. I knew it would be front and center in my mind the next day, but I didn't have the energy to think about it anymore that night.

Chapter 4

Looking For Nothing

I slept later than usual the next morning and was dragging around my bedroom after I woke up. Anne Marie decided I needed a more substantial breakfast than usual and made a big plate of fried potatoes and bacon for me. I was happy to have the hearty food and loved the hash browns with onions. I was not up for a walk on the beach and asked Anne Marie if she would take Gaela for a short walk. I was certain she wouldn't go down to the ocean. I went back to sleep before they returned from their walk, and I slept through lunch.

Anne Marie left me a note that she had made an asparagus salad for my dinner, and she had also baked some biscuits for me. She suggested that I warm up the leftover chicken and rice. I was not feeling well and decided I would eat the salad and two of her biscuits for dinner. I thought I might be coming down with a cold or the flu.

I blamed my stuffy sinuses on the mornings I'd spent outside in the rain and the damp weather, wandering around the beach, and sitting on the cold, wet stones and pine needles while I waited for law enforcement to arrive to deal with my crisis of the day. Anne Marie didn't come to my house on Saturday or Sunday, so she would not be back again until Monday morning. I was on my own for the weekend. If I was going to be sick, I didn't want to have anybody around anyway.

When I woke up on Saturday morning, I had a bad sore throat and my body was aching all over. I knew I was probably coming down with something that wouldn't go away in a day. I let Gaela out the back door, and we went back to bed until noon. I didn't have an appetite and decided a cup of green tea would be therapeutic. I drank two cups of hot tea with honey and lay in bed thinking about the corpse, the backpacks, and the rubber raft. I assumed the authorities had taken away the remnants of the raft. I hoped they had.

I hadn't studied physics since I was in high school, but common sense goes a long way towards figuring things out. I had lots of common sense. I'd been thinking that the bomber's original destination probably had not been far from where he'd ended up dead—on my beach. I reasoned that the larger ship, which had dropped him and his small raft into the water, had been much closer to the shore than I'd originally thought. Or, if the larger ship had been located farther off shore, the raft had almost reached its destination when it had overturned and been ripped to shreds. The raft had to have met its demise close to the cove and the beach where the remains of it all had been found.

The coast of Oregon was rocky, and it would not be a stretch to imagine that a small raft would have been overturned and torn up on the rocks close to shore. The odds that the body, the backpack, and the raft would all end up on my property after a seriously violent storm were very remote, unless the small raft had been heading for my beach in the first place. I was beginning to think the raft had intended to land close to the spot where it finally washed ashore. The raft and its occupant had almost made it to the cove, if that was their original destination, and I thought it was. Mother Nature had intervened to upset the raft and the plan.

The Pacific is a big and boisterous ocean. The recent storm had been epic, or so I had been told. If the raft had overturned even a little bit farther out to sea, the debris would have been scattered and washed up over a much wider area. Because the three pieces of the raft disaster had ended up so close together on my property, I had to conclude that the intended landing location, as well as the location of the raft's actual destruction, had been close to, if not exactly on, my beach and cove.

Did this also mean that the bomber's target was close, or did it mean that someone in the local area had intended to meet the bomber? Someone would have had to meet him to transport him to his target, even if that target was nearby. The bomber had landed in the middle of nowhere, and I believe he'd come ashore exactly where he'd planned to come ashore. He just hadn't planned to come ashore dead.

He didn't have a car, and Depoe Bay was not a transportation hub. If no one had been meeting this "lone wolf," he would have had to hitchhike to some other place. This didn't seem like a hitchhiking situation. I was betting that someone had intended to meet him, and I was also betting that this someone was currently living close by, somewhere in the neighborhood of Depoe Bay. Since I didn't know anybody who lived here, how could I possibly figure out who that accomplice might be? I went back to sleep as my brain was tired and not operating on all its cylinders.

When I got out of bed in the evening, I decided I would feel better if I ate something and tried to raise my blood sugar. I warmed up the chicken and rice and finished the asparagus salad. Gaela was always solicitous when she knew I wasn't feeling up to par. Although I was hoping Nathanial and company were way ahead of me in their analysis of events, I wondered if I could search the internet to find out who owned the other half of my cove and the undeveloped property next door. That property was completely empty without a house or a road. In other words, it was the perfect place for a raft or boat to land secretly in an obscure location. I wanted to find out who owned that property and what the story was with the owner.

If I hadn't bought my house and moved in a few weeks earlier, there would have been two unoccupied properties side by side. My property would have been completely uninhabited, unused, and unnoticed. The cove would have been totally isolated. I tried to find out who owned the neighboring property by searching the internet. I'd looked up property ownership on the internet before, but properties are frequently owned, not by an individual, but by a corporation, an anonymous holding company, or a false name. I was not well enough to do anything serious that evening and decided I would resume my search when I was feeling better.

The next morning was Sunday morning. I was more rested, feeling better, and going a little stir crazy, so I opted to go to the diner for brunch. That decision turned out to be a big mistake. I'd forgotten about the after-church crowd. I finally got a place at the counter and decided it was too late for brunch. I ordered the diner's double cheeseburger and fries, and that made a great brunch for me. Afterwards, I decided to go for a drive with Gaela. She gratefully finished off the remains of my double cheeseburger while we explored the area.

Since we were already out and about, I decided to drive along the coast road to see if I could find an entrance off the main road that accessed the property next to mine. If there was such an entrance, it was well hidden and impossible to see. I couldn't find a road, and I couldn't find a mailbox. I would ask Anne Marie on Monday. She'd lived here all of her life and might know something about who owned the undeveloped acres. There had to be an address for somebody someplace, even if it was only an address for where to send the bill for the property taxes. It didn't look like the land had ever been farmed or built on or was even accessible from the highway except by walking through a dense pine forest.

I figured a young man with two backpacks would have no trouble walking through the woods from the beach to the road. I wondered if there was any place on the property next door where he would have been able to camp for the night. He might have brought his own food, but I didn't believe he had. I'd ask Nathanial if there was any food found in the bomber's backpack. If he hadn't brought food with him, where would he have found food, even if he'd found a place to pitch a tent? If he was going to eat in town in a public place, he would have to know English.

Depoe Bay was becoming more cosmopolitan, but a young man in his twenties who looked Middle Eastern and who didn't speak English very well would have attracted attention. Two backpacks would also have looked suspicious. I'd not yet been out to drive around the area and get to know the neighborhoods and towns on this part of the Oregon coast. Acquainting myself with a few of the local roads seemed like a good way for Gaela and me to spend the afternoon.

Around dinnertime, I found my way to the Oregon Coast Inn, a country inn that was a bed and breakfast as well as a restaurant specializing in comfort food. I wasn't dressed up, but who dresses up around here anyway? I put on a jacket I found in the car and decided I wouldn't cause a ruckus because of my wardrobe. It was early and the hostess was happy to seat me at a small table for two. I could tell she was curious about me as one might be when an older woman with a cane shows up dining out alone.

The menu was a blast from the past, and I decided on Sunday's special, the roast turkey dinner with all the trimmings. The trimmings included stuffing, cranberry sauce, mashed potatoes and gravy, sweet potatoes, and three green vegetables plus butternut squash. I love butternut squash. There were also homemade rolls and pumpkin pie. It was way too much food for one person to eat, even a person who has as excellent an appetite as I have. I took home leftovers for both Gaela and myself, and I knew I would come back here to eat.

The food was delicious, plentiful, and definitely comforting. They served roasted leg of lamb on Thursday night, and roast beef night was on Saturday. Gaela and I were in bed by nine-thirty. I was no longer the night owl I had been when I'd lived on the East Coast. Or maybe my body was still on East Coast time, and when I went to bed after nine o'clock, it mistakenly thought it was staying up past midnight.

Monday morning I was awake and drinking coffee before Anne Marie arrived. I told her I was recovering from a cold or the flu and had taken to heart the "stuff a cold" philosophy of healing. I told her I'd driven around on Sunday and tried to familiarize myself with some of the roads and other towns in the area. I asked her if she knew the neighbors on either side of me. I was careful to remind her that I wasn't yet ready to "get involved in the community" and therefore wasn't interested in meeting anybody, especially my neighbors. I told her I'd been curious about how much undeveloped land there was along the coast and wondered if it was government property or privately owned.

She knew what I knew about the land on one side of my property, that it was an environmental preserve of some kind, a joint venture between a private group and a government agency. Neither of us was exactly sure what either the name of the private group or the name of the agency was, but it was a pretty safe bet that the area on that side of my property would never be developed. There was some kind of endangered seabird which nested on the property.

A person or a group who cared a great deal about this particular bird or about birds in general had bought the property when it came on the market. In conjunction with government at some level, they had made it into a "preserve." I had known about that when I purchased my cottage, and having the conservation land on one side of my property had definitely been a selling point.

One of the reasons I had paid top dollar for my property was because of that "forever" protection. There would never be a housing development on that side of my house to block my wonderful view. Also, because my house was older, originally built in the 1950s, my property could not be designated as a preserve. It already had a house on it, and I was "grandfathered in."

I had been lucky to find my place and was lucky to be able to buy it. I'd paid a premium price for lots of reasons, and one of those reasons had been my desire for the remote, the obscure, and the lack of close neighbors—not to mention the spectacular views. I had insisted on a place that couldn't be seen from anyone else's house and a property from which I would not be able to see another house. For all of these reasons, my cottage had not been an easy property to find.

With way more foresight than any other state seemed to have had at that time, in 1910 the state of Oregon had designated large parts of its coast as state property. Oregon passed laws excluding development in these state-owned areas. There were still some properties that were privately owned. In recent decades, environmental groups all over Oregon and all over the country were buying up property along the coast to keep it from being turned into high-density housing. RV parks, older motels, and places with other "less desirable" uses were being gobbled up by "save the seabirds" organizations and other environmentally motivated groups. Developers were also bidding for the few good locations with views of the water.

Commercial interests and environmentalists, no matter where they're located, are always battling each other for access to oceanfront property. I had been competing with both—the people who didn't want to have any houses at all along the water as well as with those who wanted to fill every permissible inch of beach front with housing. I was thankful to have my own little cottage. It was a unique and special place.

Who owned the property on the other side of mine was still a mystery. Who owned the other half of my cove? Anne

Marie didn't know but thought it was owned by someone "foreign." Given her perspective on things, foreign could be somebody from Sacramento or it could be somebody from Abu Dhabi. Anne Marie said she would try to ask around and find out who owned it. I urged her to be discreet. She wanted to know if I was interested in buying it. I told her I didn't think so, but she shouldn't mention to anyone that I was asking. She seemed to like being in on a secret, so she was fine keeping her inquiries low-key.

I still wasn't up to doing much research and decided that taking a nap was a better choice. Gaela and I slept until lunch and then enjoyed some soup and a turkey sandwich that Anne Marie made out of my leftovers from the Oregon Coast Inn. She told me one of her sisters worked in the kitchen there and that it was the best place to eat for miles around. I agreed. After lunch I attacked my computer and the internet again and tried to navigate my way through the countless sites to find out who my next-door-neighbor was.

I was usually pretty good at finding out what I wanted to know, but most of the material I researched for my books was historical data and general information I could find on Wikipedia. Searching property records was tough going, and all I ended up finding out was that in the 1980s, at least part of the property next door had been owned by a Mr. Ellis Fong who at the time lived in Los Angeles. Learning about Mr. Fong was completely worthless information for my purposes.

I wondered if I was going to have to go to the Lincoln County Courthouse, wherever that was, to try to find out who owned the land. I didn't want anybody in the land records office or the tax office to have my name or ask me why I wanted the information. I didn't want it spread around town that someone was interested in finding out who owned that particular piece of the coast. I'd promised Nathanial I would keep a low profile, and I intended to do that. Maybe I could hire somebody to go to the courthouse to search the records for me?

Anne Marie had put a baked potato in the oven before she left for the day. She had microwaved some peas and made me a tomato and mozzarella salad which was in the refrigerator. The lamb chops were already in a broiler pan, and all I had to do was put the pan under the broiler, turn on the broiler, turn the chops over when the first side was done, and try not to burn them. Anne Marie had even found the mint jelly in the pantry and loosened the top for me. Sometimes my arthritic hands had a hard time with lids. Lamb chops were Gaela's favorite so I broiled an extra one for her. Anne Marie, Gaela, and I all agreed on the healing properties of lamb.

Gaela and I watched a Swedish movie with English subtitles and went to bed early. I didn't feel as if I were accomplishing much of anything these days. I was stymied in my search for the destination and intentions of the terrorist, and I'd not written anything at all. I hadn't even been able to find out anything about who owned the property next door. I'd learned my way around the area a little bit, but if I was trying to be a real recluse, why was I bothering to get to know my way around anywhere?

Chapter 5

Looking for Trouble

When I woke up the next morning, Anne Marie was already at the house squeezing my orange juice and making stone-ground oatmeal, the kind you have to cook for a long time, not the instant kind. It was October and the weather was cooler. The oatmeal with brown sugar and cream was heavenly. I felt so much better that I decided I might try to go to the Lincoln County Courthouse in Newport, Oregon that day.

I knew I had become somewhat obsessed about who owned the property next to mine and figured I was going to have to go to the courthouse to find the answers I needed. Because I didn't want anyone to know I had an interest in that property, I would have to go in a disguise and give a false name. I had to drive my car, but I could park it far away from the courthouse entrance. No one would know. This meant I would have to walk farther than I wanted to walk and would not be able to use my handicap sticker. But anonymity demanded all of these inconveniences. It would be painful, and I would not be able to use my cane.

I had a black wig to wear that nobody would think was anybody's real hair. I had a ridiculous muumuu and some dark horn-rimmed glasses to add to my disguise. It was too cold to wear flip-flops so hiking boots would have to do. There were lots of eccentric people in this area, and even though my outfit would draw attention to the weird woman who was wearing it, hopefully it would not draw any attention to the real me. I would wear eyeshadow and pancake makeup. It would be yucky, but it would only be for one morning.

I put on some of my disguise before I left the house but covered myself up with a raincoat. I didn't want my house-keeper to see what I looked like. I told her I wasn't going to take Gaela with me. That was the only thing that made her think there was something odd about where I was going and what I was doing. I took Gaela with me everywhere. Not taking Gaela was a part of my disguise. Anybody who knew me, and nobody around here knew me at all, would know that anywhere I went, I always took Gaela with me in the car.

I put the rest of my disguise in a cloth bag which would serve as my purse. I put a notebook and pen in the bag along with my cell phone. I stopped a little way out of town and put on the rest of my disguise including the wig, the makeup, and the glasses. It would be painful to walk a long way across the parking lot without my cane, but I needed to do it to keep my real self from being exposed. I parked as far away as I thought was necessary, limped through the parking lot, and finally made it to the courthouse.

The land records department was in the basement. I used a nasal twang and a higher-than-normal voice when I told the court clerk what I wanted. I had to fill out some forms to get access to the information, and I made up everything I put on the forms. I wondered if I could be arrested for bad paperwork. The clerk helped me look up what I wanted to know. I wrote down the name of the owner of the property and then asked where I could find tax records. I needed an address.

When I finally had everything I thought I could get from the courthouse, I struggled back to my car, trying not to act like I was as crippled as I really am. My knees were killing me. Finally, feeling completely worn out, I collapsed in the driver's seat of my SUV. When I was partway out of town, I pulled over to the side of the road to get rid of the more noxious parts of my disguise. I took off the nasty wig, and I was so glad to get it off my sweaty head. I knew I had to get rid of the makeup before I got back to my house, but I was so exhausted from the walking and the pretending that I almost decided just to go home as is. I did manage to get most of the makeup off my face and put my raincoat back on over the horrible muumuu outfit before I continued the drive back to my cottage.

When I got home, I hurried through the kitchen to my bathroom. Gaela had been predictably unhappy about being left behind, but she was super happy to see me when I returned home. I stripped down and put all the offending disguise items in the cloth bag. I washed my hair and my face and thoroughly scrubbed myself to eliminate any and all traces of the black-haired, made-up woman in the muumuu and hiking boots. She would disappear forever, never to be seen in the world again. I dressed in soft knit black pants, a turtleneck, and a sweater. The slippers always felt great on my feet, and after my "hike" through the parking lot and the courthouse, they were especially welcome. I was worn out and was more than happy to sit down to tuna salad sandwiches on whole wheat toast and a cup of hot apricot tea.

After my nap, I searched the internet to try to put together the information I'd gathered at the courthouse. It all boiled down to the fact that the ownership records and the tax records were a dead end. I'd been afraid of that, but I'd had to take the chance to try to find out what I could. The property was owned by a holding company with an officious sounding name. The address for the tax bills was a post office box in New York City. It could be that somebody was just trying to maintain a low profile for tax purposes or it could be that somebody had a nefarious motivation for obscuring the ownership of the property next to mine. I would have to call on one of my old East Coast private detective friends if I wanted to have any hope of finding out who owned the other half of my cove. My PI could find out who owned a particular post office box. I never asked him how he was able to find out the things he found out, and I didn't want to know.

I wondered briefly what Detective Broderick would think of the research I had done on my own. If there was a mystery, I wanted to solve it. But what the heck was I doing? What the heck was I thinking? This was completely out of my league. Lone wolf suicide bombers! Who was I kidding? This was none of my business now. It was a case that had become the business of law enforcement. I knew this in my rational mind, but I couldn't keep myself from thinking about it. Maybe it was because in "getting away from it all" I hadn't left myself with anything else to think about.

My mind kept turning over probabilities and more possibilities. I decided that the mystery corpse had been equipped with some kind of GPS, probably Google maps on his cell phone. I assumed he'd had a cell phone, and wouldn't that be a treasure trove if it could be found? I was sure it was now at the bottom of the Pacific Ocean. Furthermore, I concluded the GPS had worked until the storm had intervened to destroy the raft and drown its occupant. Why would he want to come ashore in an isolated cove near Depoe Bay? There weren't any military installations or high-profile targets around here. There wasn't even any public transportation. A small airport was located in a nearby town. I assumed there was a bus station in Depoe Bay, but I wasn't even certain about that. Somebody would have to have a car to go anywhere at all.

The thing Depoe Bay had going for it was its remoteness and obscurity, a good low-profile place to sneak ashore and make contact with somebody who could drive the bomber and his bombs to their important objective. This meant that there had to be one or more accomplices in the Depoe Bay area. I was convinced of it. Since I didn't know anybody here, how would I ever figure out who that might be?

There was no Middle Eastern restaurant here. There was no African restaurant. There wasn't even a Greek restaurant. I checked the phone book for foreign-sounding names, and I didn't come up with anything promising. So much for profiling. It wasn't getting me anywhere. Lots of people, myself included, no longer had landline phones and therefore were not listed in the phone book. I told myself to drop it as I was never going to be able to figure out anything on my own.

But I was not able to let it go like I should have. I decided I needed to ask Detective Broderick a few more questions,

questions he probably wouldn't want to answer. Why couldn't I just leave well enough alone? This could only be leading to one kind of trouble or another, and it was probably leading me into several different kinds of trouble. Maybe honesty would be the best way to get Broderick to talk and give me the information I wanted? If I told him my theory that the cove had in fact been close to the bomber's original destination, maybe even his exact intended destination, he might be more forthcoming with me.

The next morning, however, I realized I was suffering a relapse of whatever bug had attacked me the week before. I'd tried to bounce back too soon, and I'd been seduced by my own curiosity to go to the courthouse in Newport, Oregon to try to find out about the neighboring property. I should have taken an extra day to recover, but I hadn't. Now I was paying the price.

When I was younger I bounced back quickly from illnesses, but at my age, it didn't always happen that way. I had always been one to "push" myself to get on with things and get up out of a sick bed. Trying to change my ways, I stayed in bed that morning and let Anne Marie bring me a bowl of oatmeal. I went back to sleep, and she woke me up with a bowl of soup and a sandwich. I went back to sleep again and slept until the next morning. I hoped I wasn't slipping into being a depressed person who slept all day every day or who just stayed in bed all day every day.

The next day I made myself get up and eat my breakfast in front of the fireplace. I'd fallen in love with the oatmeal and the buttered toast Anne Marie served me on the cool October mornings. I decided Gaela and I would take a short walk back down the pathway to the beach. I didn't intend to go all the way to the ocean. We both needed exercise, and I especially needed to build myself up after being sick. We walked partway down the path until my knees began to hurt.

As we turned back toward the house, I glanced over at the uninhabited property next to mine. It jutted out into the ocean like my "point" did, but it was all high ground and covered with trees almost to the cliffs which dropped precipitously down into the Pacific Ocean. The property next door did not have an ocean-front beach. The only way anyone could access the point of land next to mine by sea would be by landing in the cove.

I tried to keep myself from thinking about "the mystery" in my life. I couldn't help but wonder if my purchasing the property where the cottage was located, as well as my ownership of half of the cove, had thrown a monkey wrench into the terrorist's plans. Had my recent move disrupted the intentions of the potential bomber who had hoped to land in the cove with two backpacks? My cottage and the land around it had been empty for many years before I'd bought it and moved to Oregon.

The house and land had been part of an estate, and because the heirs were unable to agree about what to do with it, the property had languished in limbo and been uninhabited for a long time. The cottage had been vacant for more than seven years when the heirs finally decided to put it on the market. The little house was antiquated and needed many repairs. According to my real estate agent, there had been a great deal of discussion among the heirs about tearing down the cottage. Because the house had been "grandfathered" in some way, a new residence would not be allowed to be built on the property. I wasn't sure exactly what the rules were, but Oregon was unusually protective of its oceanfront. I knew my cottage, as well as the property surrounding it, was something of an anomaly. Because the previous owners of the property realized they would be able to get a better sale price if they sold the land with a house on it, someone had made the decision to spend a substantial amount of money repairing and renovating the cottage.

What had originally been a sizeable three-bedroom house was made into a one-bedroom with a spacious, luxurious bath, a large walk-in closet, plus a small den or office. The sellers had decided to go for a high-end buyer and had opted for a high-end renovation. They had done an excellent job with it, and the small cottage had all the usual luxury finishes as well as its original charm. It had a new gas-burning fireplace, quartz counter tops, beautiful appliances, and a walk-in shower plus a whirlpool bathtub. It had a new roof and new cedar shake siding stained a perfect navy-blue color complemented with high gloss white trim. It was a classic. The reconstructed front porch was painted white and ran across the entire front of the house.

It had been an expensive renovation, and of course, the place also had a high-end price, especially for a one-bedroom cottage with an office that could be a second bedroom. The house had been on the market for more than fifteen months when I began my search. Because the property fulfilled all of my wishes and I could afford to pay the outrageous price they were asking, I was able to settle on the house quickly. The heirs were happy, and I was happy. With a few changes and additions and many gallons of paint, I was able to make the cottage my own.

But this property had been, for all intents and purposes, abandoned for almost a decade when I moved into it. The absentee owners of the property next door might have assumed, with good reason, that there would never be anybody living in the cottage. If it had been torn down, there could never be another house built on the site. If the heirs had not been able to sell the place to a rich, eccentric, one-bedroom plus an office customer like myself, the property might have sat on the market for another year or longer.

Today, as I looked over at the empty property next door, I was shocked to see someone walking in the cove. At first I couldn't believe my eyes. I didn't think there was any way to access the cove by land other than walking through the woods next door or by going across my property. Was there a hidden road I didn't know about? The Oregon State Police had accessed the cove by going through my property, with my permission, of course. Whoever was walking around the cove did not, thank goodness, look up in my direction. His head was down, and he seemed to be carefully searching the ground, the sand and rocks on the shore of the cove beach, and the surrounding area — as if he were looking for something.

The man was obviously inspecting the area, and he did not appear to have a vehicle of any kind with him. I figured he must have some kind of car or truck parked on the main road. He had to have walked to the cove through the pine forest. I did not want him to see me, although it certainly would not be impossible for him to find out who owned the other half of the cove, if he wanted to know that.

As Gaela and I hid behind a large pine tree, I called Nathanial Broderick on my cell phone and told him there was somebody snooping around the cove. I asked if it was law enforcement, and Broderick said it wasn't. I was too far away to see what the trespasser looked like, and Broderick warned me not to confront the man. I would never have considered doing that anyway. The detective asked me to stay where I was and observe the scene until he got to my house. I told him I would. Broderick hadn't asked, but I stepped out from behind the pine tree where I was hiding and took several photos and a couple of short videos on my phone. I sent them to Broderick's phone so at least he would have those, even if he didn't get here before the snooper left the cove. Gaela and I sat down on the damp ground once again. We waited. Gaela was not a barker, thank goodness, in spite of being a terrier and a small dog. I held her on my lap and hoped she would stay still and keep quiet until Nathanial Broderick arrived.

It seemed like it took forever before the detective appeared. The unknown "trespasser" had unfortunately given up on whatever he had been searching for, and he'd left the cove through the woods, no doubt going back to the main road the way he'd come. As far as I could tell he hadn't followed any established path, and I knew he hadn't left using my property.

When Broderick met me, he was disappointed but not surprised that the suspicious person was no longer in the cove. He was thankful for the photos and videos but scolded me for putting myself at risk to take them. I'd checked my watch when the mystery man left the cove. Before he'd arrived, Broderick had alerted the highway patrol for officials to be on the lookout for a person on foot. It seemed to me that it was past time to call in the troops and search the property. But I had to remember that law enforcement and Broderick were not as far along in their analysis of the mystery as I was.

As we walked back to my house, I told Broderick everything I'd observed that morning. Anne Marie had grilled ham and cheese sandwiches and a pot of homemade vegetable beef soup ready for me on the stove. She quickly made another sandwich for the detective. He was more than grateful for the food, especially for the hot soup which was exceptional. The soup was full of end-of-the season fresh tomatoes and fall vegetables, and Anne Marie had added some thyme and quite a bit of basil from my herb garden to the pot. It was so delicious!

I gave Broderick as good a description as I could of the man I had seen. He'd been too far away for me to see him clearly. Broderick had the photos and the videos I'd sent, but those had also been taken from quite a distance. My knees were aching, and I was tired from sitting on the cold, wet pine needles. These sitting-on-the-ground activities are not meant for an older person handicapped by arthritis. Broderick left, and I took a hot soaking bath in my luxurious jetted bathtub followed by a luxurious nap. I decided to eat out that night and try the Mexican place for something different.

I arrived late, for Depoe Bay I guess, and again had no problem finding a good parking spot. If somebody else had been driving me, I would have ordered a Margarita, but I passed that up this time. The special was cheese and onion enchiladas topped with chili con carne, and I decided to try it. It was on the borderline of being too spicy for me, but it tasted great. I had flan for dessert and placed an extra takeout order of the cheese and onion enchiladas to put in my refrigerator for another night's dinner. Gaela had gone with me to the restaurant, but she wasn't fond of Mexican food. She had leftover ham and cheese when we got home. It had been another big day, and Gaela and I slept well that night.

Chapter 6

Looking for a Troublemaker

The courthouse clerk made the call, as requested, to the phone number written on the back of the business card. She'd taken a two hundred dollar payment, or bribe if you looked at it another way, to report anybody who came into the courthouse looking for information about a specific property located on the coast outside of Depoe Bay. A very peculiar person had come to her office a few days earlier asking questions about that exact property. The clerk felt she should call the number and report the information, especially since she had already taken the money.

Aziz answered the phone when she called. He didn't give his name because he had to remain anonymous. He grilled her thoroughly about all the details of the inquiry and about the person who had come to the land records office. The clerk told him there had been more than one thing that was unusual about the woman who had been at the courthouse looking for information. The clerk reported that the woman's questions had been about only the one property. Sometimes real estate people came to her office fishing for properties to sell, wanting information about what properties were behind in their taxes or who owned properties next to ones the agent was listing, buying, or selling.

The clerk told the man on the phone she thought the peculiar woman had been wearing a wig and had tried to make herself look older than she was with makeup and terrible eye shadow and eyeliner. She said she thought the woman wearing the wig had pretended to have a limp. The affected and exaggerated limp added to the clerk's belief that the woman was trying to appear old. The muumuu and the hiking boots had made the woman's outfit even more outlandish. The clerk suggested that maybe the bizarre person who had come to the office was just an eccentric.

Aziz had never expected to hear from the woman in the county clerk's office. He was not happy that someone was snooping around, trying to find out who owned the property in question. But he congratulated himself for having paid the clerk the two hundred dollars to call him in case anybody did come to the courthouse asking questions. Now he had to figure out who this overly curious woman might be and try to determine how much of a threat she was. She could be someone who wanted to buy the property and didn't want to be recognized while looking into it.

Aziz realized immediately that the name, address, and phone number on the forms the mystery woman had filled out were all phony. This set off another alarm in is mind. He wondered how far a prospective buyer would go to obscure their interest in purchasing a potential property. On the other hand, he didn't think the mysterious woman's interest in the property could possibly have anything to do with him.

Aziz had quite a few reasons to be concerned. He knew from his informant inside the local sheriff's department that a body had been found somewhere on the beach, and that a few days later, pieces of a rubber raft had washed ashore. The young man Aziz had been expecting had failed to arrive and had failed to call, and Aziz was almost one-hundred percent certain the body that had been found on the beach was the missing soldier for Allah.

The Oregon State Police were handling the case because they had been the first to arrive on the scene after the 911 call was made. It wasn't exactly clear how law enforcement made decisions about when the OSP had jurisdiction over a particular case and under what circumstances the Lincoln County Sheriff's Department assumed control. The exact location where the body had been discovered was a secret for some reason, and no public announcement had been made about the discovery of a body. Police departments everywhere in the world prefer to deny the press access to any and all information about their investigations. Sometimes, however, when they have an unidentified body, they use the press to put out a description in the hopes of being able to put a name to an unknown corpse.

The OSP was heading the investigation and did not seem to care if this particular body was identified or not. Aziz thought that was odd and wondered if the OSP had somehow figured out that this particular corpse was something other than an innocent drowning victim. He didn't think it was remotely possible for investigators to suspect the corpse was that of a potential suicide bomber. But he wondered why they were not reaching out to the public to help identify the body. If the corpse was that of the jihadist, they could not possibly know its identity.

The jihadist had been told specifically not to carry anything on his person that could identify him. He could use his prepaid cell phone, but he was not to have any passport, maps, tickets, or other paperwork. He'd been told to cut all the labels out of his clothes. This was one of the first things all soldiers for Allah learn about security in the training camps, and Aziz felt confident the jihadist had not brought any identification with him.

The Oregon State Police had not revealed the information about the backpacks found on the beach and in the raft, so Aziz did not know that any backpacks had been found. He did know from his contact that the case had been turned over to the FBI and DHS. That was not good news at all. He realized, when he heard a body had been found, that in all probability it was the man he had been expecting. When the anticipated call never came, Aziz admitted to himself that the young jihadist had probably lost his life and his raft in the remnants of the Asian typhoon that had swept the Oregon coast the previous week.

Aziz had never imagined that any trace of the young man would wash up on any beach, especially not in Aziz's own town. He was shocked that the body and the pieces of the raft had been found so close to the area where the boy had originally been supposed to come ashore. He had almost made it to his destination. Worse luck that one law enforcement organization had found both the body and the raft. Aziz needed to find out more from his contact inside the sheriff's department, but that person seemed to be pretty much out of the loop in this case.

There were few Muslims employed in law enforcement organizations at any level. There were even fewer who were willing to do the work of Allah. Aziz wanted information from someone. He was angry that the weather had interfered with his plans which had seemed foolproof in the abstract. How could anybody have known there would be a typhoon that would ruin the carefully prepared attack on Satan America? It was bad luck, but perhaps Allah had a higher purpose for Aziz and his imagined brilliance. Aziz just had to determine what that was.

His calling from Allah at this time was to give logistical support to the "lone wolf" bombers and martyrs that ISIS had recruited to carry out attacks in the United States. Disaffected youth had traveled to Syria and other Middle Eastern locations to receive their training. The trouble with these jihadists was that, although their enthusiasm knew no bounds, they often were lacking in the practical skills they needed to fight effectively for the cause.

More and more young Muslims were trying to leave the U.S. to go to Syria and Iraq to train as jihadists. Many of these young warriors, however, lacked subtlety and sophistication, even in something as simple as their travel plans. Their parents often did not find out about these ill-conceived trips to Turkey, Somalia, or another Middle Eastern country until their offspring were already on their way to a jihadist training camp. Even the ones who made it to the camps and underwent the training were often not the cream of the crop and lacked the intelligence and other skills necessary to become successful bombers and freedom fighters.

The few who were able to pass the rigors of the training camps and were able to return to their hometowns in the United States, frequently did not seem to make good choices when they arrived home. Too often, they did something stupid and revealed their intentions by talking crazy or acting crazy when they returned—to Columbus, Ohio, for example. These enthusiastic but bumbling young people often didn't have a support structure to help them acquire the explosives, detonators, and other assistance they needed to carry out the missions for which they had been trained.

It was becoming increasingly difficult to get back into the United States after spending time in a jihadist training camp. It was almost impossible to smuggle any amount of plastique or other kinds of explosives into the U.S. unless one brought it in across an unsecured border. It turned out that significant support structures for logistics and weapons were required to make some of these "lone wolves" operationally viable. Muhammad Aziz was one of those who helped to man these below-the-radar but essential support networks inside the USA. His first effort to give assistance to a jihadist agent, Aziz's attempt to be somewhat "in the field," had not worked out. It had been a total failure, but it had not been his fault.

Organizers of jihad were trying to smuggle better-trained, foreign fighters into the United States by any and all possible means. They were entering this country all along the United States' non-existent border with Mexico. They were coming in from Canada. They were arriving in large numbers with the unvetted refugees from the war in Syria. They were being transported close to the Atlantic and Pacific coasts by larger ships and sent to shore in rafts.

The young jihadist, whose body had washed up on the Oregon coast and whose name Aziz had never known, had traveled aboard a Liberian tanker which was sailing up the west coast of the United States to take on a cargo of oil in Canada. The Jihadist had been hidden aboard the tanker during the voyage from Indonesia. The scheme to put the young man and the raft in the water was known to only three people on board the tanker. The jihadist had been supplied with a high quality GPS app on his cell phone, and he had been given the coordinates for an arrival location on the Pacific coast. While the tail end of the typhoon raged all around the tanker, the young volunteer for jihad had been off-loaded from the larger ship and set afloat in a small raft on the dangerous ocean waves.

His instructions had been that after landing in the small cove, he was to bury his raft in the thick brush of the woods on the empty property. Using his prepaid cell phone, the young man was to call his contact in the nearby town of Depoe Bay to let him know he'd arrived. The jihadist had initially been told that there was a small, unoccupied house on the adjacent property, and the young man was instructed to break into that house and stay there until he was contacted. The cottage had been empty for almost ten years and would have been the perfect place for the jihadist to stay while awaiting his instructions and his contact. He knew how to break into houses and how to stay hidden.

At the last minute, this place to hide had become unavailable because someone had purchased it and was in the process of fixing it up and moving into it. Because of the unavailability of a place for the jihadist to stay, Aziz's plans had been delayed to later in September. The delay in the timetable had put the operation at increased risk to encounter bad weather. That bad weather had become a reality with the arrival of the typhoon.

Because the cottage was now no longer abandoned and therefore was not available, Aziz had been forced to come up with an alternative place for the young jihadist to stay after he came ashore. Aziz had been ordered to pitch a tent in the woods for the young man. Aziz knew nothing about survivalist skills, and he had no idea how to put up a tent. Because the wind from the typhoon was so strong during the days prior to the jihadist's expected arrival, Aziz never had the chance to even try to erect the tent. The jihadist was supposed to be carrying the prepaid cell phone with him from the time he left the ship, and the phone's GPS would guide him to his destination. Aziz called this burner phone repeatedly to try to get word to the jihadist aboard the ship. He wanted to tell the young man that the operation should be aborted because of bad weather. The message never got through, and the jihadist's body had washed up on the beach a few days after the storm.

Aziz had been worried about the intensity of the typhoon, and when the young jihadist didn't call him back, he assumed that either the man had never left the tanker or had been lost at sea. Aziz had never expected the jihadist's body to wash up anywhere near the cove outside Depoe Bay, just yards from his original destination.

Aziz knew the one who would willingly sacrifice himself was supposed to be bringing plastic explosives and detonators, but Aziz didn't know how these were being transported. The detonators and timing devices were a special kind which would not set off metal detectors at Seattle's Space Needle. The plan was for Aziz to pick up the jihadist and drive him to Seattle. The young martyr would take his explosives to the Space Needle and set them off in a glorious bombing to damage the Seattle icon and to murder and maim as many civilian bystanders as possible.

Aziz felt it all would have worked beautifully once the jihadist had made his way to U.S. soil. It might have, and Aziz hoped he would have the chance to try again. Damn the woman who had bought the cottage and moved into it. She had ruined his timetable and forced him to delay the bomber's arrival. She had ruined the glorious tribute to Allah that Aziz had been so excited about.

Aziz worked as a waiter and bus boy at a popular seafood restaurant in Depoe Bay. The food at The Sea Dog was excellent, and the restaurant was a favorite with both locals and tourists. Aziz had come to the United States illegally more than fifteen years earlier. He had a fake Lebanese passport and a forged green card which allowed him to work. He liked his job at the restaurant. He got good tips, but more importantly, he could listen in to customers' conversations and stay up-to-date on all the local gossip. He'd become friendly with several of his co-workers and with local residents. Local law enforcement accepted him as a fixture in the well-known eatery. Aziz liked to bring his customers an extra-large order of fries, a free dessert, or occasionally a beer on the house. He knew the weaknesses of the regular customers. Alcohol was haram—forbidden. A strict Muslim, he never drank alcohol himself, but he knew whose lips could be loosened with a free drink or two.

Aziz's made-up story was that his family had been killed during a bombing in Beirut, and he had been brought to the United States as an orphan by a church group. In fact, Aziz was from Yemen where he had been trained as a jihadist. He had been planted in the U.S. as a sleeper agent to be called on one day to assist in causing terror in his adopted country. He had been sent to the United States by al-Qaeda and had been thrilled when the September 11, 2001 airplane attacks had been so overwhelmingly successful.

He sometimes wondered if he had been forgotten as he built and lived his cover identity in Oregon. He never let anyone know that he was a Muslim, and he never discussed politics. He had developed a dry sense of humor, and his English was quite good after living in the U.S. for so many years. He was a hard worker and was well-liked by his bosses and fellow workers, but he didn't socialize with any of them. He kept to himself and had no real friends.

Aziz lived in a studio apartment above a t-shirt store that was within walking distance of the restaurant. His life was a simple one. He prayed and read the Koran every day. Most of his meals came from the restaurant. He saved his money. He liked Depoe Bay in spite of the rainy weather and was always willing to work extra hours during the summer's busy season. He also was willing to work on the holidays American workers wanted as vacation days. He always worked on Christmas Eve and Thanksgiving Day. His willingness to work on these days made him popular with his co-workers.

Previously he had received his orders from al-Qaeda, but now he received orders from ISIS through the encrypted messages of social media. He had only rarely been called upon to do anything for Allah. Recently, his presence in the United States had become known to important people in the upper levels of ISIS. ISIS became a more active organization than al-Qaeda had been, and Aziz was thrilled to be a part of this new group that was always in the news and achieving victories for the caliphate. A former POTUS had called ISIS the JV team, and jihadists the world over were laughing out loud over that stupid remark.

Aziz had occasionally been asked to steal a driver's license, a passport, or a credit card. Usually, the request was for the ID of a person with a specific gender, age, and physical description. Aziz had learned to do these things in the restaurant without much difficulty, as women often left their purses hanging on their chairs. This made it easy for Aziz to get what he wanted as he leaned over to pour water or serve a plate of food. Men, too, hung their jackets over the backs of their chairs, especially in the summer, and it was easy to access the wallet if it was in a jacket pocket. Wallets in men's pants pockets were more difficult to reach, but given a few days, Aziz had always been able to come up with whatever had been requested.

He'd not been activated for anything major until a few months ago. Now ISIS was serious about attacking inside the United States, and his help was needed. Most resources were centered in and around the major Eastern seaboard cities and in the LA area. For some reason, having a sleeper agent available and willing in the Pacific Northwest suddenly became important to somebody. Aziz was always ready and eager to serve Allah.

Aziz was disappointed that his first assignment had ended in failure. It could have been such a great success. ISIS now was encouraging acts of jihad that did not include any escape plans. Westerners called these "suicide" attacks, but of course those who were unschooled in Islam did not understand what a great honor it was to die for Allah. Tremendous rewards awaited these martyrs in the afterlife, but Christians, Jews, and other infidels did not comprehend any of this. Aziz hoped to receive another assignment soon. He was ready to die as a martyr for Allah, if that is what Allah asked of him.

Chapter 7

Looking for Something to Do

My knees were still aching the next day, so Anne Marie gave Gaela her morning walk. I blamed my sore knees on the cold ground where I'd been sitting while I'd waited for Detective Broderick the day before. I wondered how much my reluctance to make more discoveries was influenced by the level of pain in my knees on any given day. Was I really in pain, or did I just not want to walk on the beach because I was worried about what I'd find? The beach was beautiful, and I loved looking at the ocean from my porch. The actual shoreline was a long walk from the cottage. Dead bodies and bombs on the beach were not something I wanted to find when I took a walk.

I finally decided I was going to have to start writing again. I loved to write, and even if the final product never entertained anybody but myself, I knew I had to get back to it. Research was almost too easy these days. I remember doing research for papers in my undergraduate and graduate school days. This long-ago research had involved hours and hours in the library with a card catalog. I missed that a little bit. Then it became possible to order any books I needed through catalogs I received in the mail. I would order them over the phone, and the books would be delivered to my door. Now with internet searches and electronic books, one never had to leave one's chair to have almost every bit of information in the world available at one's fingertips. No more trips to the library or the bookstore. It was ideal for a recluse. Why was I complaining? I decided I probably needed to eat out more often just to make myself get out of the house.

But Anne Marie's food was so delicious and better than most restaurants I could ever visit. It was difficult to make myself eat anyplace except at home. I decided I would try to eat more fish. Fish was good for me, and Anne Marie didn't like to cook fish. I would go to the seafood place in Depoe Bay for dinner tonight. I would order the salmon special I'd seen reviewed in the local throwaway newspaper. I had a plan. It was not a complicated plan, but it was a plan.

Just when I'd accepted that Anne Marie didn't like to cook seafood, she made a fabulous pot of seafood chowder for my lunch. She told me she liked to cook with shellfish. She said it was fin fish she didn't think she prepared very well. She would put fin fish into the soup, but she didn't like to fry it or broil it. She also didn't like to eat it. She said she didn't like to eat shellfish either.

Along with the steaming bowl of chowder, she made me a corned beef sandwich on rye with Swiss cheese, coleslaw, and Thousand Island dressing. Anne Marie said the corned beef was from a deli in Newport, a town south of Depoe Bay on Rt. 101 and the county seat of Lincoln County. Of course I knew where the county seat of Lincoln County was, but I couldn't let Anne Marie know I'd ever been there. She'd bought a pound of corned beef for me because she'd heard me talking about New York delis with Nathanial Broderick. How lucky was I? The corned beef sandwich could have come from the Stage Deli in New York City. Zero Mostel could have been sitting right next to me. And then there was the delicious seafood chowder. The weather was blustery, and it was getting on into the end of October. I had a second bowl of chowder.

I read and wrote all afternoon and decided I was much happier with a little bit of structure in my life. I knew the focus of my next book was going to be based on the "lone wolf terrorist" in the United States. Maybe I was right in the middle of the story here in my refuge, my hideaway. My focus on writing about this particular subject might have something to do with what had happened to me in the past two weeks. It was not too much of a stretch.

Now I had to start thinking like a "lone wolf terrorist" would think. I had to get inside the heads of these disaffected youth, these unhappy teenagers, these rebellious adolescents with nothing to rebel against except the society which gave them the luxury of rebelling. What a depressing bunch they were! Did I really want to try to get inside the minds of these narcissistic, immature, pubescent losers? Probably not, but it seemed essential in order to understand these young people and write about them in a convincing way.

Maybe I was too old to try to get inside the brain of a dyspeptic sixteen-year-old? Maybe I should write a "cozy" about yard sales in small towns someplace. But of course, that was not going to happen—not after finding a dead body on my own beach. In all the years I had been writing murder mystery novels, I had never seen a real dead body in person, except, of course, at the now rare open-casket funeral.

Anne Marie was curious that I was busy and working at my computer. I was happier. She said it was good for me to have a project that interested me. She told me the scuttlebutt around town was that I had been a famous writer who had just stopped writing one day. The reasons about why I had stopped writing were speculative, various, and downright silly. The rumors ran the gamut. I had become bored with writing. I'd been diagnosed with Alzheimer's. I was so rich I didn't need to do anything anymore. I'd fallen in love with a man young enough to be my grandson and had lived in Greece with him until he dumped me. I was living in Depoe Bay to get over my broken heart. I was living here recovering from a serious illness or a serious depression. No one seemed to know my nom de plume, which was a very, very good thing. Other gossip about me was that I was just an eccentric person with lots of money and a small dog; that I had been in a tragic car accident and was suffering from amnesia to the extent I had no memory of my former life; that I was hiding from an East Coast stalker who had threatened to kill me; and assorted other bizarre stories. None of these were true. Why couldn't anyone imagine that I just wanted to get away from my previous boredom and be bored in a different place? Why did anybody care about me anyway? I decided maybe I was weird.

I don't own a typewriter. Who even knows what a type-writer is anymore? I hadn't seen one in years. Anne Marie, bless her heart, had told everyone that she had rarely seen me use my computer and then only to search the internet.

This had been true up until today. She told everyone I could not possibly be a writer since I never wrote anything. I was delighted with her inadvertent misinformation campaign on my behalf. I confided in her that I had been a writer but that the words had left me. I was trying to get back to it, but I didn't want that information to be on anybody's radar screen any time soon. She understood that I wanted to be left alone and assured me that my secrets were safe with her. I believed her. She liked working and cooking for me. I was a big fan of everything she did. She loved Gaela, and Gaela loved her. We were doing fine.

Anne Marie told me the gardener I had engaged would be back this week. She knew him and approved of him and said he would also be discreet about my past. She said he was shy and didn't like to talk much. Thomas had taken care of the landscaping all the previous spring and summer and had brought the English perennial garden back from the brink. He had planted my herb garden to my specifications, so I already liked him and was indebted to him. He also loved hydrangeas. He was keeping my gardens under control and was responsible for maintaining them in their current beautiful state. He had prepared the yard and gardens for the fall before my arrival, and now that winter was looming he would come every month rather than weekly or more often as he had during the summer and early fall.

Anne Marie told me Thomas was proud of his work on the perennial garden and the herb garden and was thrilled that the pictures of the gardens, which my real estate agent had sent to me, had been the deciding factor in my choosing to buy the cottage. The yard and garden looked great. Whatever Thomas the gardener wanted to do had my vote.

By late afternoon, I decided I had done enough work at the computer and could leave the house to eat again. Gaela and I drove into town, and once again we had no trouble finding a handicapped spot in which to park in front of the Sea Dog. I couldn't resist having the shrimp cocktail again, and I ordered the poached halibut Oscar topped with Dungeness crab meat, asparagus, and hollandaise sauce. It was outstanding. The salmon would have been fine, too, but the halibut looked too good to pass up. I'd watched an order go by my table and had to have it. The halibut was delicious, and the asparagus was perfectly undercooked. I was certain the hollandaise was homemade.

I noticed that one of the waiters looked Middle Eastern, at least he looked that way to me. Here I was jumping to conclusions and profiling people. How politically incorrect was I? Good for me! I asked my waitress who the dark-skinned fellow was. I said he look so familiar to me, and I thought I had seen him years ago at a restaurant in New York. She told me he had worked at the Sea Dog for many years, for more than a decade. She didn't think he'd ever lived in New York. So much for that. I was enjoying every bite of the halibut, and I noticed that when my waitress talked to the swarthy waiter, he looked over at me. I waved my hand in a friendly way, and I admit it was a little bit strange. He would think I was just the eccentric old woman I wanted everybody to think I was. And, in fact, I felt that in fact I really was that eccentric old woman, so it wasn't hard to play the part. Gaela, like Anne Marie, doesn't love seafood, but she enjoyed the leftover rice pilaf that had accompanied my halibut Oscar.

Thanksgiving was coming soon, and I was planning a family reunion event at a hotel in Portland, Oregon. It was a fancy hotel, so my daughter Alison and her new husband were happy to join me there. Alison's two college-age kids from a previous marriage had both said they would also be in Oregon for the holiday. A second cousin of mine from Bend was joining us. At the last minute, my grandson, a sophomore at Bowdoin College, had received a much-sought-after invitation from his girlfriend to spend the Thanksgiving vacation with her family who lived in Portland, Maine. I was disappointed that he wouldn't be with us, but he would be having Thanksgiving in Portland, albeit a different Portland, on a different coast, and in a different state.

I was paying the bill for the hotel, for the spa days, and for the Thanksgiving Day dinner buffet which was supposed to be spectacular. The buffet and the spa were two reasons I had chosen this particular hotel. I was looking forward to seeing my family. They wanted to visit me in Depoe Bay but understood that my house there was too small for them to be able to stay with me. I was treating everyone for the Thanksgiving holidays instead of having them come to my tiny cottage and cooking a big turkey dinner for them myself. How ridiculous would that have been?

The fancy hotel in Portland was going to do the cooking as well as the clean-up. They would also wash all the sheets. I'd been to Portland before, and I knew there was plenty to do in that city to keep everybody happy. My daughter, my granddaughter, my cousin, and I would all be delighted to spend time indulging ourselves at the hotel's spa. It would be an ideal family reunion spot—with all the fun and festivity without any of the work. I could afford it, and I was more than happy to pay somebody else to do the holiday preparations and the cooking for me.

My daughter Alison had been divorced for many years, and I didn't think she would ever allow another man into her life. Just last year she had met a lawyer whose wife had died several years earlier. She seemed to really love this man, and he appeared to appreciate and adore her. I hoped she had not made a mistake. I didn't want to see her hurt again. More than anything, I wanted her to be happy.

Chapter 8

Looking for Information

Aziz was proud of the fact that he maintained a low profile in his job at the Sea Dog. He didn't draw attention to himself and did his best to fit in. It made him nervous that a customer, an older woman he did not recognize as a local or as a regular customer, had asked one of the waitresses about him. The woman had said he looked familiar to her, like someone she knew who worked at a restaurant in New York City. Aziz had never been to New York City. He worried because he did look Middle Eastern, and maybe this old woman just thought all Middle Easterners looked alike. He wondered who she was and why she had noticed him.

The restaurant was so busy in the summer that vacationing customers scarcely noticed what their waiter or waitress looked like. They only wanted their food as quickly as possible. The locals, on the other hand, had become so used to seeing Aziz working in the same job at the same restaurant over the years, they didn't notice him anymore. They accepted him as part of the scenery. He was used to being unremarkable and unnoticed. It disturbed him that a customer would pick him out and ask about him. He needed to find out who this woman was. If she was someone who was on vacation and was just passing through, it wouldn't matter who she was. She would be gone in a few days.

At the end of the evening Aziz went to the computer to see what he could find out about the woman who was asking questions. She had paid cash for her shrimp cocktail and halibut Oscar, so there would be no credit card information available. She'd left a nice tip. The only thing he had noticed about her that set her apart from the other old people who came into the restaurant was that she carried a distinctive and decorative blue and white cane. Lots of people came in with canes, but they were usually black or brown. Aziz assumed this woman would never come back to the restaurant, but he might ask around about her, if he could figure out what to ask. He stopped by the kitchen for the leftover food the cook always packed up for him to take home, and he left the restaurant to walk to his apartment. Ever since the typhoon had struck Depoe Bay, things had not gone well for Aziz.

A few nights later, Aziz questioned the waitress who had waited on the old woman with too much curiosity. Had she ever been in the restaurant before? A busboy standing nearby happened to overhear their conversation, and he told Aziz he had seen her in the restaurant at least once before. The busboy said she'd been in a couple of weeks earlier. He remembered her because she had ordered the Neptune Platter, a huge mound of fried fish and shellfish. He was surprised that the woman had been able to eat as much of the platter as she had. She'd asked that the leftovers be wrapped up so she could take them home, and he'd been the one to deliver the "doggie bag" to her table before she left. This was not good news for Aziz. This meant that the woman was probably living in town and was not just passing through. Maybe she was here for only a few weeks or wouldn't come back to the restaurant. If she ever did, Aziz wanted to be sure he was the one to wait on her. He needed to find out who she was and why she was interested in him.

Several days earlier, Aziz had ridden his motor scooter out to the cove where the jihadist had been supposed to come ashore. Aziz knew the raft had washed up somewhere in the area. Aziz had no reason to go to the cove other than his slim hope that the dead man who had been discovered on the beach had not been the jihadist. Aziz had not been able to find out anything from law enforcement about where the body or the raft had been found, but he admitted to himself that the unidentified body had been the young man he'd been expecting. Aziz made the trip to the cove just in case the jihadist had somehow survived the typhoon and come ashore. Aziz wanted to be sure there was no sign of his arrival in the cove. If he had by some stroke of luck landed there after all and had not been able to contact Aziz, Aziz had to be certain the man had not left any evidence behind.

Aziz had hidden his motor scooter in the brush beside the road and hiked to the cove. He had walked through the dense pine trees and thick bushes to reach the cove's beach. Every step of the way, he cursed the woman who lived next door. He'd had the perfect location for his operation, and then the cottage had been renovated and sold. Now there was someone living in it.

He hadn't found anything on the beach near the cove and decided the man in the raft had never made it ashore. Rain poured down on him as he made his way home on his motor scooter. He didn't mind the rain when he only had to look at it out the window of the restaurant or out the window of his room above the t-shirt shop. For someone who had grown up in the desert as Aziz had, too much rain was not a pleasant experience. Aziz was in a bad mood when he arrived for work that day, unusual for the cheerful Aziz.

Aziz had made some effort to get information about the case involving the body on the beach. Because the feds and the OSP had taken over the case, his local sources in the sheriff's department were not much help. He couldn't ask too many questions of his informants for fear of arousing their suspicions. The only thing he was able to find out was that the body had been found on a Pacific beach somewhere near Depoe Bay. It had not been found in the cove. There were several rumors about exactly where on a Pacific beach the body had been found. He could not believe his bad luck that the body had been discovered so close to the jihadist's intended destination. He had almost made it.

Aziz wondered what had happened to the supplies the man had been supposed to bring with him. He was to have brought his own explosives and everything else he needed to blow a big hole in the Space Needle and take out numerous Americans along with himself. Aziz wondered what had happened to the explosives and the other bomb-making components. He hoped all of that was now at the bottom of the ocean. He wondered if the new occupant of the cottage had been the one to find the body. He had heard the person who now lived in the cottage was eccentric and reclusive and never left her house. If it wasn't the person who owned the cottage, who had discovered the body? He needed to find out more about who lived on that property. He wanted to break into the cottage and have a look around, but how could he do that if the person never left her home.

A few days later, he decided to do some snooping and rode his motor scooter out to the woman's property. He had a hard time finding the driveway from the main road to the cottage and passed by it several times before he finally found the dirt road. It was almost completely obscured by scraggly bushes and shrubs. Whoever lived here certainly didn't want to be found. He wondered what USPS did about the mail and what FedEx and UPS and Amazon did about deliveries. Maybe whoever was living there never had anything delivered.

He left his motor scooter in the bushes and walked along the dirt driveway to the house. Without any street lights, it would be more difficult to make his way back out to the highway and more difficult to find his motor scooter after dark. On the other hand, it would be easier to trespass and look in the windows after the sun went down. He looked around the house and decided it would be better to wait until it was completely dark outside. When the person who lived in the cottage turned on their lights, he would be able to see inside the house.

When he looked in the window, he saw a woman, and she was old. He recognized her as the same woman who had asked about him at the restaurant. This was a surprise for Aziz. Why in the world would this woman have had any interest in him? The coincidence troubled him, and he couldn't come up with any kind of satisfactory explanation. Maybe she honestly had thought he looked like someone she knew? In New York there were so many people of so many nationalities, it was entirely possible that there was someone working in a restaurant there that looked like him.

He was just about to leave when the woman made a phone call on her cell phone. There did not seem to be a landline in the house. Aziz listened carefully with his ear up against the window. The old woman called the Oregon Coast Inn and made a dinner reservation for one person for the next night, Thursday night, for six o'clock in the evening. Aziz was in luck for once. He could return the next night while the old woman was at dinner and search her house. He saw the laptop computer and the printer on the desk in the office and knew he had to try to get into her computer to find out more about her. He needed to know if she had discovered anything on the beach, and he needed to know if this woman was up to anything that had to do with him.

Chapter 9

Looking for Information, Too

When Anne Marie arrived the next morning, she was happy to see me at my computer rather than getting ready for a walk in the damp air. She told me she'd heard something about the property next to mine. She said it was being sold, but she didn't know who the seller was or who the prospective buyer was. I was concerned because I was hoping no one would be able to build on that vacant land.

My cottage had been built in its current location more than sixty years earlier, and many oceanfront properties were no longer allowed to have houses built on them. I hoped this was the case with my neighbor's land. If it was being sold right now, so soon after the discovery of the body and the raft, it didn't seem as if the property was involved in any way with the bomber that washed up on my beach. I would have to have somebody look into it for me. I didn't want to return to the Lincoln County Courthouse to find out who the new owner of the property was. Maybe the seabird lovers were going to buy it for another sanctuary. That would suit me fine as long as they didn't have the ability to mess with my view or with my half of the cove.

Of course, I didn't know if Anne Marie's information was correct, but I told her I appreciated her keeping her ear to the ground for me. I told her I didn't think I wanted to buy the property next door, but if it meant new ownership would sacrifice my unobstructed view of the ocean and my cherished solitude, I would seriously consider buying it to protect my own property. She said she would try to find out who wanted to buy the land next to mine. She promised she would be circumspect when she made her inquiries.

I was roaring full speed ahead with my own made-up tale about the body I'd found on the beach. I hadn't heard anything from Detective Broderick and decided I would give him a call. He didn't pick up so I left a voice mail asking him to call me. I told him it wasn't urgent and to call when he had a chance. I told him I'd done some thinking and wanted to share some of my thoughts with him. That might or might not be enough to get him to call me back. He was a nice man and a polite one, so he eventually would call me back, later if not sooner.

Gaela and I didn't often take an afternoon walk, but today was going to be the last nice day for almost a week. It was going to begin raining again tonight. There was going to be a serious storm, and the forecast was that it would keep raining through the weekend and into next week. It was also going to be cold. I would probably stay inside for most of the storm, so I gave Gaela her second walk of the day. We went to the Oregon Coast Inn for their Thursday night leg of lamb dinner special. It was, like Anne Marie had said, the best place in the area to eat. I had a Dungeness crabmeat appetizer with garlic and butter. It was so good I could have skipped the rest of the meal. But the leg of lamb was medium rare and tender and delicious. I decided on the cheesy mashed potatoes with rich brown lamb gravy, peas, and asparagus. There were homemade rolls with hand-churned butter. Who churns their own butter these days? There was mint jelly. I ate all I could and had the leftovers wrapped to take home, some lamb for Gaela who waited in the car and the rest for my lunch the next day. I had the cherry pie boxed to take home. Full of a wonderful Oregon Coast Inn lamb dinner and tired, we made our way back to the cottage.

As I approached my driveway, I thought I saw a motor scooter pull out of my dirt road and turn onto the highway. That would be impossible unless somebody had been on my property without permission. That somebody would be trespassing. It was dark, and maybe I was mistaken about where the motor scooter had come from. It was already raining, and my driveway was difficult to see even in the daytime and in the best weather. That was intentional.

My entrance off the main road was narrow and crowded with dense brush. I wanted it to stay as hidden and as difficult to find as possible. I might have been able to see the tracks of a motor scooter on my dirt driveway if it were not pouring rain. Any tracks or traces of a motor scooter's presence would have been completely wiped away by the downpour. Why would anyone want to drive down the road to my cottage? What color had that motor scooter been? Was it local? Did this have anything to do with the body I'd found on my beach? Was I being paranoid?

Ever thankful for automatic garage door openers, Gaela and I pulled into my garage and put the door down behind us. The wind was supposed to be fierce and last for days, and I would probably not venture out until this storm had run its course. Anne Marie would be coming tomorrow if the weather was not too bad, and she always left me with plenty of provisions for the weekend and riding out a storm.

I'd had a generator installed in the cottage. Why not? I could afford it. If the electricity went out, I would have power. The typhoon, which had brought the body to my beach, had not taken out the electricity, so maybe I wouldn't need the generator. If I did need it; it was there. I'd done some research and found out that the storms in this coastal area were such that the power did go out, sometimes for days at a time. That's why I'd opted for the generator. It was powered by natural gas, so I didn't have to worry about refilling it with propane or gasoline. Cable TV lines had been laid underground, so if I wanted to watch TV, the generator would keep me in communication with the weather channel. Maybe the storm would not be as bad as predicted. In any case, I was ready for it.

When we walked into the house, I knew immediately that someone had been there. Gaela was sniffing around in the way she always does when something is different, when there are new smells to check out. I'd seen the motor scooter, and I was now certain that the person on that motor scooter had been in my cottage. I was furious and didn't know why I was so sure he had been here. Nothing was messed up. There were a few things out of place here and there, and I knew that because I have a keen memory for detail. I knew exactly where I put things, and I mean exactly. A few things were not precisely where I had left them. Whoever had been here had been extremely careful, almost perfectly careful, but not quite. Someone had been here looking for something.

I went immediately to my computer. I had passwords for everything and knew enough about computers to be able to find out if someone had tried to access my files. Someone had, but lacking the passwords, they'd not been able to open anything. I could also tell that whoever this intruder was had used a thumb drive to try to copy files from my computer. He had been unsuccessful in that effort as well. I wondered why the intruder had not just taken the whole laptop with him. The house had been searched, but it had not been vandalized. Whoever had been snooping inside my house did not want me to know he'd been here. It was infuriating and frightening to know that someone could get into my house, snoop around, and leave pretty much without a trace. I felt violated.

I thought about calling Detective Broderick again. He'd never called me back from the last message I'd left him. I decided I would call him in the morning. I was upset from the emotional distress of discovering my home had been invaded. I wondered how the burglar or the snooper or whoever he was had gotten into the house. I decided I needed a better security system and better locks on the doors and windows. How could I leave for several days at Thanksgiving if someone was watching my comings and goings? Unless somebody was watching my house, how could they have known that I would be out for dinner at the Oregon Coast Inn? How could they know exactly what time I would be returning home?

I had come to Oregon to get away to a safe, out-of-the-way life without complications. Now I was getting paranoid and for good reason. Why would anybody want to get into my house to look around, and why in the world would they have wanted to see what was on my computer? I wondered if the break-in could have anything to do with the fact that my property had been deserted for such a long time. Maybe the intruder was connected with the body on my beach? Did this have anything to do with my inquiry at the Lincoln County Courthouse? Had someone discovered who that odd woman was who had gone to the county clerk's office and researched the property next door? Why had somebody come into my house to snoop around?

I was exhausted, but the adrenalin was still pumping from the shock of the break-in and from my racing thoughts and anger. I took a long, hot bath and tried to calm myself. I was mentally making plans to have surveillance cameras installed on the inside and outside of my house the next day. I was so upset I'd almost forgotten there was a terrible storm coming. The surveillance cameras would have to wait a few days. I had an alarm system but must not have turned it on when I'd left that night to go to dinner. Sometimes when I was in a hurry, I forgot. I wouldn't be making that mistake again. I wanted to see the face of the person who had broken in to my house. I wanted a video of their snooping so I could press charges and put them in jail for a long, long time. I made some cocoa with marshmallows and finally fell asleep. Gaela knew I was upset, but she had bailed out for the land of nod long before I was able to join her there.

I had bad dreams that night. I dreamed that a man with long dark hair and a goofy Taliban beard had walked out of the surf of the Pacific Ocean and climbed up the path to my cottage. He was wearing a suicide vest and a black dive suit under the vest and knocked on the front door of my house. When I went to open the door, he pushed the detonator and exploded his vest. The sound of the explosion woke me up. I was drenched with sweat. The "explosion" in my nightmare had in fact been the loud, cracking thunder of the storm.

The early morning fog was thick and the rain was coming down in torrents. I couldn't see beyond my front porch let alone see the ocean. I was thankful I didn't have a basement and thankful I had tight windows and doors on the house. The wind was blowing as predicted, and I was still exhausted. I pulled the extra blanket folded at the foot of my bed up over me and went back to sleep. The storm was so ferocious I knew that Anne Marie would not be coming today. As I went back to sleep, I decided there was no real reason to get up until I was completely rested. It had been a rough night, and I was still shaken.

When I woke up for the second time, I realized the generator had started working. It was at the side of the garage and was somewhat noisy. I didn't mind trading off noise for being able to start my coffee maker and have hot water when the electricity went out. I made coffee and turned on the gas fireplace. Gaela went out for about thirty seconds and immediately came back inside. She was soaked from her short run in the yard, and I dried her off with a towel. She was as happy to be in front of the gas fireplace as I was. She cuddled up beside me on the couch, and I turned on the TV to watch what the weather channel had to say about the storm. It was still predicted to last for several days. No wonder people got depressed in the Northwest. It did rain a lot.

When I got hungry I made myself some French toast and sausages for brunch. I love my French toast which has a splash of pure almond extract in the egg and milk mixture. It tasted heavenly to me, and Gaela also appreciated it. I'd made an entire slice for her. After I cleaned up the kitchen from my cooking spree, I curled up on the couch to read. I changed the channel on the TV to the news.

Chapter 10

Looking at Terrorism

There was a breaking story on CNN and on Fox News about a "lone wolf" terrorist attack and bombing at a military installation in Southern California. In fact, there were two "wolves" involved in the attack. Driving an old truck, two young men wearing suicide vests and carrying automatic weapons had rammed the guard gates of a Navy SEAL installation on Coronado Island near San Diego. The truck had been powerful enough and going fast enough to breach the gates and run down one guard and injure several military personnel.

One terrorist had jumped out of the truck brandishing an automatic weapon. He began shooting indiscriminately at everyone and everything in sight. One of the terrorists lived long enough to explode his vest, and most of the injuries and deaths were from that explosion. The two screamed "Allahu Akbar" the entire time—until they died in a hail of gunfire. Fortunately, the military personnel at the Navy SEAL headquarters were armed and were able to kill both terrorists fairly quickly. Five people were known dead and twenty-two were injured, some critically.

Hearing about this event would have upset me terribly no matter when I heard about it, but now I couldn't help but wonder if the man whose dead body I had found on my beach had planned to do something evil, something similar to what had happened that day in Southern California. How had the Coronado Island terrorists come into this country? Were they Americans seduced by jihadist ideology and the internet promise of excitement and adventure? Had they traveled to the Middle East for training and indoctrination and then returned to the U.S. to do their evil deeds?

Or, were they jihadists from another country? Had they come ashore along the California coast? Perhaps in a rubber raft? Had they come across our open border with Mexico? Was there another bomber on his way with a backpack who intended to land in my cove in the future? Did these terrorists usually work in teams? What was the target of the man who'd turned up dead on my beach? I grieved for the dead in Southern California, for the brave men and women who keep this country safe, and for the cream of the military crop, our Navy SEALs, who were so highly trained and so dedicated. I was angry.

Subdued and sad, I puttered around my cottage for the rest of the afternoon. The TV droned on in the background filling in the details of the horrific attack in California. I wrote emails to my family and friends and took care of some bills and paperwork that had been piling up on my desk. I took a shower mostly because I didn't want to be one of those old people who stay in their night clothes all day and forget to bathe. I dressed in my uniform: black knit pants, a turtleneck, and a warm sweater. I watched the storm rage outside my windows and marveled at the power of Mother Nature.

I wondered about the kind of person who would be motivated to kill others without remorse and then to kill himself in the name of Allah. This behavior had never seemed to me like the kind of act any God would demand or reward. I thought about the differences, if there were any, between religious fanaticism and brain washing. It puzzled me that American teenagers, no matter how angry they were and no matter how confused and lost they might be, could become so radicalized over the internet with tweets and videos. What did I know about tweets anyway? I let Gaela out into the yard during a brief lull in the horrendous storm. My house was still operating under generator power.

My go-to comfort food had always been spaghetti. I was feeling down from the news and probably also from the low and still-dropping barometric pressure. I was sensitive to such things. I pulled a container of homemade sauce from the freezer and thawed it in the microwave, along with some homemade meatballs. I made myself a salad and cooked the spaghetti al dente. The Locatelli Romano grated cheese and some warmed up leftover garlic bread from the freezer completed the spaghetti feast I craved. My favorite comfort food cheered me for a short time, but the news was still depressing. Gaela loved spaghetti too. After we had eaten, she and I went to bed early.

I slept late again on Saturday. I realized I was beginning to get cabin fever. The weather had not improved much, and I decided it was better to stay at home rather than strike out in my SUV in the fog and unrelenting downpour. In spite of having four-wheel drive, I decided against going to the diner for brunch. It probably wasn't even open. With the bad weather, I knew I shouldn't consider leaving the house. Hadn't I decided that living in the cottage was my answer to getting away from it all? Was I now looking for ways to get away from the cottage? What was wrong with me? Was I never content with the current situation? I guess it was the artist in me that was constantly searching and wanting to find a new venue.

I made coffee and a cold sandwich for lunch and wished Anne Marie were here with a pot of hot soup. I had containers of her various creations awaiting me in my freezer. I looked at them and decided to wait for dinner to make up my mind. I was a mess. The news from California continued to be upsetting. More military personnel had died from their wounds as a result of yesterday's explosion. I was becoming quite angry now. The left-leaning loonies were calling for more gun control, as they always did. The right-leaning loonies were calling for more security at military installations and more scrutiny of mosques and Muslims.

I had my own opinions, quite apart from these political ideologies, since I'd had a terrorist with a bomb in his backpack wash up on my beach. Today I was tending to lean with the right-leaning loonies. I wondered to myself how it would ever be possible to monitor those who came to the United States on rafts and landed in obscure coves and other places along the hundreds of miles of our Pacific and Atlantic coasts. We pretended to focus on controlling our border with Mexico, but that had never been possible. What about the unguarded beaches of our two oceans? It was a sobering line of thought. I had no solutions, and I was afraid that no one else did either.

The word in the media was that our newest threat was ISIS which used encrypted networks over the internet to recruit, influence, and activate young jihadists. Why was it, with all of our expertise in computers in the United States and all the computer hackers in our midst, could we not hack back into their encrypted networks? Surely we were as skilled with electronic communications as some crazy desert rats living in Iraq who spent their time planning how to cut off people's heads and burn people in cages. It just didn't make sense that we couldn't hack into their stuff. They seemed to have no trouble hacking into ours.

Or was this some kind of PC crap which was running wild in the government and in the country these days? Maybe it wasn't that we couldn't hack into the terrorists' communications, but that somebody thought we shouldn't and therefore we wouldn't? I was sick of PC and the whole "word police" dance the feds and the media did as they tiptoed around trying to avoid offending some ethnic group or other. You couldn't say illegal alien; you had to say undocumented person. You couldn't say Muslim terrorist; you had to say radical extremist. Whatever happened to calling bullshit bullshit? A terrorist was a terrorist.

If somebody invoked the name of Allah and screamed out that he was killing in the name of jihad, he was a Muslim terrorist. Enough already with the PC bull roar! I realized I was getting pretty grumpy. I needed to calm down.

The California disaster, the news was now reporting, had been planned and carried out by two young Muslims from Minneapolis, Minnesota. They were part of the Somali refugee community there. One was a naturalized citizen of the United States who had been born in Somalia and educated in the U.S. His accomplice was also from Somalia. Terrorist #2 had never become a U.S. citizen and had recently traveled from Minneapolis to the Middle East through Turkey to some kind of jihadist training camp. The two had accomplished their murders in the name of Allah. I'd heard all I could stand to hear about Allah.

I did wonder briefly what Allah really thought about all of these atrocities being committed in his name. I decided that blaming these attacks on Allah was just a teenage boy's way of not taking responsibility for his own testosterone spikes, immaturity, and lack of good judgment. What was wrong with people? Didn't these bad boys' parents teach them the difference between right and wrong? I was getting old. The world I'd thought I lived in was disappearing. Bah humbug!

Why in heaven's name did the United States allow these airport-hopping teenage troublemakers back into the country after they had traveled to the Middle East? It was obvious these young men were not going to Turkey and on to Syria, Yemen, and Iraq to work on their tans or to see the historic sights. Why did we let them back into this country after they had spent weeks and months training in terrorist training camps? How hard would it be to lift or invalidate their passports? The hell with their civil rights! If they went to the Middle East to train to make war on the homeland, in my opinion, they forfeited their rights to hold a U.S. passport. I personally didn't think they should be allowed to reenter the USA. They should be returned to where they'd just been and not be allowed to come back into this country to cause trouble. But that's just me.

United States citizen or not, send them to a juvenile detention center. The powers that be in this goofball government were more concerned with protecting the right of these worthless terrorists than they were with protecting the lives of the rest of us who try to obey the law and do the right thing. The world was turned upside down these days. I was angry and sick of the whole incompetent business. Unless somebody "manned up" in this administration and implemented a policy change, there would only be more and more of this carnage. People would continue to die.

Why did we have all of these Somali people in Minnesota in the first place? Why did we need these refugees who lived on welfare and food stamps and Medicaid. They only got off their asses to do anything at all when they decided to turn around and literally bite the hand that fed them. Send them all back to someplace else other than here in this country. They should never have been here in the first place. I decided I needed to shut up — even when just talking to myself — and put my soap box back in the closet.

Chapter 11

Looking for Another Chance

Aziz used burner phones for the few personal calls he needed to make. He had been given a special satellite phone several years earlier and had been instructed to communicate with his handlers only with this special phone. Since he was a sleeper agent, no one was supposed to be suspicious of him. That meant no one would be listening in on or tracking his phone calls. Recently he'd been given a new satellite phone and told to destroy the old one. His new satellite phone would enable him to send and receive encrypted communications. The new phone was also smaller. Al-Qaeda's more violent and high-profile offshoot ISIS were ramping up their plans to hit the U.S. at home. The encrypted phone apps supposedly kept the NSA and FBI and others from eavesdropping on phone calls and from spying on emails and text messages.

Aziz had been in the U.S. long enough to know there was a great deal of electronic communications expertise in this country, and he had a hard time believing that the hackers at the NSA and other places could not crack the encryptions used by his fellow freedom fighters for Allah. He was always suspicious of whatever stories the federal government put out for public consumption. He kept his encrypted satellite phone and his personal prepaid cell phone with him at all times. He awaited the next message from his brothers in jihad and hoped that his failure to deliver on the last assignment would not disqualify him from being chosen for another mission.

He had emailed a lengthy and detailed report about the reasons his last mission had not been successful, citing the typhoon's role in the loss of the operative and his raft. Aziz had included the information that the young man, who had volunteered to sacrifice his life, had drowned and that his body had washed up on the coast. Aziz reported that there had been no identification of the corpse and assured his handlers that no one was suspicious. He had tried to report the facts in such a way that minimized his own part in the failure of the plan and maximized the influence of "bad luck" and weather. Aziz's superiors seemed to buy his explanation, but he was still waiting to be called on again to participate in another operation.

Just when he thought he might not be activated, he received an encrypted email that told him to be ready for another young jihadist who would arrive on the coast, again in a raft. Aziz wondered why they would risk repeating a scenario which had already turned out badly. In spite of Aziz's report to his handlers, he was aware that there were some suspicions about the corpse that had been found. Aziz wasn't making the decisions but felt it was too soon to repeat the exact same plan. He did not know if there was a new target or if it would be the Seattle Space Needle again.

Being called on to repeat the failed mission made him wonder how many jihadist sleepers his cause had in the USA. Aziz was in deep cover and had been in place before 9/11. He had to believe that the current president's enthusiastic policy of bringing more and more Muslim refugees into the country was an open invitation to jihadists.

If things kept up at this rate, one day Muslims would be in the majority in many cities. London already had a Muslim mayor, and Detroit and its suburbs were becoming more and more Islamic. Aziz could only dream the impossible dream that one day New York City would also have a Muslim mayor … just like London did. Was he completely out of his mind to hope for such a thing?

Aziz believed that it was only a matter of time before Muslims took over the United States from within. As more and more Muslims poured into the country, Aziz hoped that sharia law would replace the constitution. He hoped women would once again be forced back into their Muslim roles as second-class citizens, serving men as servants. Aziz believed, as sharia law instructed him, that women were intended to be subservient to men. The infidels would not know what had hit them. Some among the hordes of refugees that were coming into the country, especially from Syria and Somalia, would certainly be sleeper agents.

Sharia law is the ultimate misogynistic code. Many Islamic men love it. Many Islamic women, if they were allowed to speak the truth, hate it. But it was sharia law that guided the terrorists. Islam was not a religion of peace. In spite of the current world-wide attempts to clean it up and portray Islam as something it was not, it remained a cult that allowed men to stone their wives to death. Sharia law keeps women in slave-like positions. Sharia law despises infidels

     Sharia Rising

and teaches its believers, not only to take over the world, but to hunt down and kill those who do not worship Allah. Those in power in Western countries were currently pretending that Islam and sharia law were not dangerous. But the rest of the world that practiced other religions or did not practice any religion at all knew better. How was it possible that the whole world did not know the truth about Islam?

There were Iran's stooges Hamas and Hezbollah and Islamic Jihad that were always in the news. Al-Qaeda and ISIS were well-known everywhere. There was Boko Haram in Nigeria and al-Shabaab in Somalia. Abu Sayyaf spread terror in the Far East. The Taliban operated in Afghanistan. The Houthis were in Yemen, and the Muslim Brotherhood caused trouble throughout the world. These were just some of the countless Islamic terror organizations that operated across the globe. No other religion was as dedicated to terror. No other religion had the reach of the sharia warriors. The leaders of the United States might pretend that these groups did not exist, but ordinary citizens knew better.

Aziz was happy he was being called into service again, but it surprised him, given the utter failure of his last mission, that the new attack was to follow the exact same plan. That didn't seem smart to Aziz, but he was not a decision maker. He was an implementer, a helper, a foot soldier in the Army of Allah. He would do whatever was asked of him, even if that meant he was to be a martyr.

If only he'd had the use of that remote cottage. It was his bad luck that it had been sitting empty for years, and just when he needed it, somebody fixed it up and moved into it.

He didn't trust the woman who lived there and was afraid of what she knew about him. Ever since she had asked about him at the restaurant, he had been wary of her. His snooping through her house hadn't turned up anything useful in terms of satisfying his curiosity or allaying his suspicions. All of her computer files were password protected, and Aziz did not know enough about cracking passwords to get into any of the files. The password protection wasn't unusual. Most people protected their files with passwords. It was not an indication that she necessarily had anything to hide or knew anything about him. Aziz had tried to copy the files from her computer with a thumb drive, but that hadn't worked either. It probably didn't matter. The woman was old and crippled. What in the world could she possibly do to interfere with his plans? He cursed her frequently for living in the cottage.

Aziz was furious that he was again being told to put up a tent for the next jihadist who would arrive by sea. Maybe he could smuggle the young man into his own apartment and avoid the tent thing altogether? There was too much wind and too much rain on the Oregon coast to try to put up a flimsy tent. The people who gave him his orders mostly lived in the desert and thought tents were the solution to everything. He'd tried to tell them, but they continued to be enamored with tents. These people no longer lived in tents themselves, but they still seemed to believe that tents were a viable option. They had never been to Oregon in November. They didn't understand that tents didn't work in Oregon. Curses on tents! He would have to find a better place to house the next jihadist.

Aziz had also received word that the property with the cove where his contact was to arrive was changing hands. He was told this was not anything that would impact his plans. The real estate transaction was supposedly a move to make the ownership of the property even more obscure. The problem was that in the United States, by law, any property sales had to be printed in the newspaper. Property sales were public information. The name of the seller and the buyer would be published. But unless somebody was looking for it, it would never be noticed. It would be one more anonymous land transaction among hundreds of others.

The only person who might be interested in the sale would be the woman who owned the cottage next door. It was rumored that she had a lot of money. She might be keeping an eye on who owned the property because she wanted to buy it if it came on the market. She probably didn't want her view to be ruined and might want to buy up as much land as she could around her own place to keep potential neighbors away. Could she had been involved with the search of land records at the Lincoln County Courthouse a few weeks earlier? Aziz wished he could stop thinking about the woman in the cottage. She should not be a threat to him, and he tried to push her out of his mind.

Aziz had been trained to kill years ago during his jihadist training in the camps before he had moved to the United States. He'd not imagined that he would ever have a reason to kill anybody. He wondered if he would need an authorization to kill. Would a sleeper agent like himself be allowed to kill someone who got in his way? He didn't think there was any reason to risk killing the old woman, but it was always an option if she got too nosy.

Chapter 12

Looking for Comfort

I decided to take Gaela for a walk. I was so worked up I didn't care that I was going to have to walk in the rain or that Gaela would also get soaked. She hated the rain, but I needed to get out of the house before I threw something at the TV set. I pulled on my new oilskins and put a waterproof coat on Gaela. She knew what was coming when I put that coat on her, and she did not look forward to getting wet. It would be hell on my arthritic knees, and I would pay the price for my walk in the rain. We went out anyway. You couldn't see anything. The wind was fierce, and I could barely stand up against it. After about ten minutes, I turned around and came home. Gaela required considerable drying out, but I was just too angry to put on dry clothes.

We both sat in front of the gas fireplace and watched the rain come down. I was going to have to get out of the house for dinner. I'd not left the house at all since the intruder had been here. It was Saturday night, and the break-in had been Thursday night, just two nights ago. Was that possible? I had fretted and stewed about it so much, it seemed like I had been thinking about it for a month! My home had been invaded, and I felt as if I had been assaulted. In fact it had been my privacy that had been attacked and destroyed. This sense of being violated added to my anger. I needed a good dinner and I needed to see some other people. I didn't want to talk to any of them. I just wanted to see them. My efforts at trying to be a recluse were not turning out to be even remotely successful.

Gaela and I were finally dry when I pulled on my oilskins again and put Gaela in the car. She sniffed at my rain gear and was hugely relieved that I hadn't put her "raincoat" back on her. She knew she was going to get to stay in the safe and dry environs of the passenger seat of my SUV. I wasn't that hungry. I found I'd become so upset about someone trespassing inside my house as well as the bombings in Coronado and all that it implied, I'd lost my appetite.

At first I thought I'd go to the diner, but I decided fried food might take the edge off and soothe my discontent. We were going to the touristy seafood place, The Sea Dog. They had the most fried stuff on their menu, and now that the tourist season was over, parking in downtown Depoe Bay was not a problem. After all, I knew it was healthy to "eat more fish." I wondered if that admonition also applied to fried fish. It probably didn't.

When I walked into the restaurant, I noticed that the Middle Eastern waiter gave me a definite "look." He went up to the hostess Sand spoke to her briefly. I could tell that he was asking her to seat me at a table so he would be the one to wait on me. What was that all about? I'd asked about him when I'd been in here the last time, and maybe he was curious or upset about that. I decided I would be completely straightforward about my previous inquiry. He came to the table and introduced himself as Aziz.

"Hello, Aziz. I noticed you when I was in before, and you reminded me of someone I used to know who worked at a restaurant in New York City. I asked my waitress if you'd ever worked in New York, and she told me you'd worked here for years. Sorry about the mistaken identity. The waiter I remember from New York worked at Mama Leone's, an Italian place, and he was from Yemen." I was making up all of this chatter on the spur of the moment, and it was a total fabrication. I'd picked Yemen out of thin air, probably because it was one of the terrorist nations most often in the news right now, especially after its government had fallen into chaos a few months earlier. It was the first country to come to my mind, but I'd unknowingly and unexpectedly struck a chord with Aziz. He turned ashen when I said Yemen. He'd been smiling and fine up until that moment. He recovered his cool quickly. I had to give him credit for that, but something wasn't right. Now I knew he was from Yemen.

"I've never been to New York City, and my family is from Lebanon. I have been working here in Depoe Bay for more than fifteen years. You have me mixed up with someone else. Can I tell you about our specials today?" He seemed to want to get beyond the discussion of his origins and move on to the business of food. He was abrupt and bordered on being rude about it. He was being defensive, and this always raised my red alert radar. He was lying to me.

"Yes, tell me about the specials." He did and I ordered what I'd already decided I was going to have. "I'll have the large shrimp cocktail, a bowl of seafood chowder, and the fried fish sandwich with French fries. Can you bring me some extra tartar sauce and extra lemon wedges? And an iced tea, please."

"Coming right up with the iced tea and the shrimp cocktail." Aziz spoke good English, but he had an accent. I didn't know anything about distinguishing one Middle Eastern accent from another, but I knew I'd hit on something when I'd mentioned Yemen. I decided Aziz was definitely from Yemen, and he was lying about being from Lebanon. Why would he lie about that, and why in the world did it even matter?

Aziz didn't make small talk with me as waiters and waitresses usually do when they bring your food and refill your iced tea glass. I told him the chowder was delicious and just the right thing to have for dinner on a night like this. He gave me a perfunctory and forced smile when I complimented the food. I knew I had rattled him. He brought my sandwich and fries and put the plate down in front of me without a word. I reminded him about the extra tartar sauce and lemon wedges I'd asked for, and for just a second, he had an angry and hateful look on his face. He had messed up my order, in a small way to be sure, but it was a mess-up just the same. And I had called him on it. He was off his game. He knew it, and he knew I knew it. He brought catsup for the fries and the other things I'd asked for. He put them down on the table without a word.

His behavior was odd. If he'd just waited on me like I imagine he waited on all of his other customers, I wouldn't have been as suspicious as I was. The fact that he had specifically asked to wait on my table was the first curious thing he had done that evening. Now his obvious anger with me, for no reason, was puzzling. Something wasn't right with

Aziz, and I wondered how in the world I would ever find out what that was.

The fish sandwich was generous and hot and not greasy. I enjoyed my meal in spite of the hostility that emanated from my waiter. When it came time to pay, I paid in cash and left Aziz the same tip I would have left to anybody. I always leave twenty percent, and I gave twenty percent to Aziz. I put my money on the table and left the restaurant before Aziz came back to take my payment. It had been an interesting trip to eat seafood. It might be time to find out more about Aziz. Maybe I would order my seafood dinners delivered from now on. Trouble was, lukewarm fried fish was not a good thing.

I drove home in the wind and pouring rain. Gaela didn't beg for food as she is not a big fan of fish. She and Anne Marie had that in common. Gaela likes tuna from the can, but she doesn't like fried seafood. I was happy to see that no motor scooters were driving out of my driveway as I approached the road to the cottage. I'd have to keep my eyes open for that motor scooter. I was sure whoever owned it had been the person who had broken into my house and gone through the things on my desk. I hated that.

I checked the news and learned that two more people had died as a result of the terrorist attack in California. Many years before I'd thought maybe the Palestinians deserved some kind of state. I knew the story of how they had lost all of their land to Israel in 1948. I'd hoped there could be some kind of peace agreement that would at least give the West Bank and Gaza back to them if they would promise not to try to destroy Israel and would recognize Israel's right to exist. That was a long time ago. Now it was ISIS and the totally wacko Iranians. I had personally known two doctors who'd been born and grown up in Iran, and in my opinion, both of them were completely nuts.

The latest insanity was that the current administration in Washington, D.C. had found a way to attempt to put a jewel in the crown of the lame duck president by giving Iran the keys to the nuclear kingdom. This was serious business. The whole negotiating process had been lame from the beginning. A previous secretary of state had, unbeknownst to the American people, begun secret negotiations years earlier with the Iranians. The final agreement did nothing but reward Iran for its bad behavior.

One of the worst aspects of the terrible deal with Iran was the money Iran would receive as a "bonus" for signing the deal that benefitted them. The deal certainly didn't sound like it benefitted anybody but Iran. Iran would receive billions to use to finance terror around the world. I'd been trying not to look too closely at our country's recent unfortunate foreign policy decisions. It was hard to watch the disasters unfold, one after another on TV.

Now I was seriously worried about all those terrorist dollars Iran would have to spread around. And these were dollars that the U.S. had given to this terrorist theocracy. The Iranians were working on nukes that might reach the U.S., not to mention Israel. Once the Iranian crazies got their ICBM's up and running, who would know what to expect? Maybe the Israelis would take care of the Iranian problem. One could always hope.

I decided I wasn't going to turn on the news again for at least a week. We had sold out to the Iranians and to other radical extremists. But we all had to be careful not to call them Islamic terrorists in spite of the fact that they were exactly that. The president of the United States would not utter the words "Islamic terrorism" even though it was more than obvious that it was Muslim terrorists who had killed themselves and others in San Diego. I'd heard enough about all of the things done in the name of Allah. I was sick of it. And I'd had all the rude behavior I could stand from a Yemeni waiter who wanted to pretend he was from Lebanon. It was an insane world.

The next day was Sunday, so I was surprised when Detective Broderick called me and asked if he could come over later that morning. People in the West didn't pay as much attention to Sunday being a religious day of rest as people on the East Coast did. I told Broderick I had several things to tell him and would welcome his visit. I decided to thaw some of the cookies Anne Marie had made and frozen for me. I would warm up some of the cider that I knew he liked, and I would make some tea sandwiches. I didn't know if Nathanial Broderick liked tea sandwiches, but I did. They would be my lunch, and I made a bet with myself that Broderick would eat some if I put them in front of him. I spent the rest of the morning concocting sandwich fillings and cutting the crusts off of thinly sliced bread from the freezer. I guess I was bored.

Chapter 13

Looking for Redemption

ziz was so angry he could barely finish his evening shift. How could that old woman possibly know he was from Yemen? There was no way on earth she could know that. Since coming to the United States, he had never told *anyone* his true country of origin. He had never mentioned Yemen to a single person. It was impossible for her to know, so it had to have been a lucky guess on her part. Could she tell from his accent? He knew he still had an accent, but he thought his English was very good. She would have to be an expert in Middle Eastern languages to correctly place his accent.

Aziz was not only angry; he was also afraid. The woman who lived in the cottage was a smart one, even though she was old. She'd rattled him, and she had realized he was rattled. There was no way she could know that he had been the person inside her house. Or did she have security cameras he hadn't noticed? He had worn gloves and was confident he'd left no fingerprints. Maybe it was his motor scooter? Had she seen its color or the license plate the night he'd been leaving her house and passed her as she was driving into her driveway?

He was worried and feeling threatened. He knew he must make an effort to keep himself from becoming paranoid. Because he was so angry with her for buying the cottage out from under his nose, he had to avoid overreacting to everything she did and said. He didn't know what he should be doing next. He needed to focus on the upcoming arrival in the cove. The old woman and his worries about what she knew about him were a distraction.

The new jihadist would be arriving in one week. This time Aziz wanted his plans to go without a hitch. He would have it all worked out perfectly. He had decided to bring the young man to his house to stay instead of trying to pitch a ridiculous tent in the woods. The tent was a stupid idea, and it was much too close to the old woman's cottage. Aziz felt he could keep the boy hidden above the t-shirt shop until it was time for him to complete his mission. It would be so much easier than taking food all the way out to someplace in the middle of nowhere. Aziz wished he could find out more about what had happened to the first jihadist who had not arrived. He didn't want to make the same mistakes again, although he didn't think there was any chance that there would be another typhoon.

There was something about the old woman that continued to bug him. He decided she didn't really know he was from Yemen. There was no possible way she could know. But he had reacted when she mentioned Yemen. She'd noticed this, and Aziz realized she knew that some of the things she'd talked about had upset him. He was out of practice and needed to have some assignments to get back into the game. He'd grown sloppy and much too comfortable as a sleeper waiting to be activated.

Maybe he would have to kill the old woman. That would solve several problems for him, but he looked on that as a last resort. He had his plan in place to welcome the next jihadist, and now he just had to be patient, keep his "cool," and not do anything to draw attention to himself. He hoped the woman would not come into the restaurant again, and if she did, he was not going to be her waiter the next time. He had decided he was going to stay as far away as possible from her and from her house.

He was delighted, when he turned on his TV, that more deaths were being reported in California. His own mission to the Space Needle would have coincided with the massacre at the Navy SEAL facility. Al-Qaeda had been the master of simultaneous attacks in a number of different places around the world. The African embassy bombings in August of 1998 both had been executed within minutes of each other in Kenya and Tanzania. The brilliantly coordinated attacks on the greatest day of all in New York and Washington D.C. had been September 11th in 2001.

Apparently, ISIS was now attempting to copy this dramatic signature coordinated timing. If Aziz's jihadist had not drowned and died, Aziz would have been able to participate in another blessed simultaneous attack by delivering the young man with the bombs to the Space Needle in Seattle, Washington on the same day the attacks had occurred on Coronado Island in California. What a coup that would have been—to hit two places on the Pacific coast on the same day! Aziz was angry that he had missed this chance and that the weather had stolen from him his big moment to make history. He swore he would not fail a second time.

Chapter 14

Looking for a Motor Scooter

I brushed my hair, let Gaela out for a few minutes in the backyard, and assembled the food I'd made for Detective Broderick. I'd already eaten many of the sandwiches as I'd been making them, but there were enough left to make a nice-looking assortment—- tuna on wheat, watercress and cream cheese on white, cheese and tomato, and minced ham with celery, mustard, and chutney. I put the cookies on a plate and made sure the cider was hot. The detective was right on time and smiled as if he was happy to see me. He drank two cups of the cider. He ate all of the cookies and almost all of the sandwiches. He must not have a wife, and he must not know how to cook. He was always hungry when he came to my house.

I told Detective Broderick about my break-in the previous Thursday night. He was quite concerned, much more con- cerned than I thought he needed to be. He chided me for not calling him or the OSP or the sheriff's office that night. I explained to him that nothing had been taken as far as I could determine, and technically it had not been an actual break-in. The intruder had been able to open my door without breaking anything. If I were not such a stickler for detail and did not have this annoying videographic memory or whatever it was, I might not have ever noticed that anyone had been in the house. Whoever it was had been extremely careful not to leave any traces. Broderick said he would look into the ownership of the motor scooter. It was my only clue about the identity of the person who had invaded my home. I didn't have a license plate or even a color to help him trace the ownership of the scooter.

I also told Broderick about my interactions with Aziz at the seafood restaurant. He wasn't as impressed as I thought he should be by Aziz's reaction to my mentioning Yemen and Aziz's subsequent attitude towards me that evening. I specifically asked Broderick to try to find out more about him. I told him something wasn't legitimate about Aziz. I didn't know exactly what it was, but I was sure he was keeping some kind of secret. I could smell it. Broderick didn't trust my sense of smell as much as I did. He seemed skeptical but promised to look into Aziz. The detective had never heard of Aziz before I brought the waiter to his attention.

One time when I had been in the Sea Dog, I'd noticed that Aziz was quite chummy with a table of law enforcement people. The table was near mine, and the customers were yucking it up with their waiter. Aziz appeared to be close with several of them, even friends. I warned Broderick that I thought local law enforcement in the area knew Aziz because he cultivated acquaintances with them and catered to them when they came into The Sea Dog.

I'd tried hard to get Aziz on Broderick's radar screen, and I think I might have accomplished that—but barely. I urged Broderick to be discreet with his inquiries about Aziz. Because Aziz had been working in the same job for such a long time, his presence in town was a nonissue. I asked Broderick if he had ever heard of sleeper agents. He gave me a hard look and muttered something about stereotyping. When he left, I hoped he would at least make a cursory investigation into Aziz's background. The detective had resources I didn't have. At the very least, I felt I had brought Aziz to Broderick's attention.

We discussed my security arrangements and the usefulness of camera surveillance. I think Broderick had figured out that I was more interested in making sure my cottage was secure than I was in saving money. He said maintaining video cameras was expensive and should be set up to record only when I was not at the cottage. The recording on these cameras would be motion activated. We discussed the pros and cons of turning on the exterior system when I was sleeping or awake at home alone in the house, which was almost all the time. Increasing my security was getting more complicated. I was a recluse after all. Or at least I was trying to be. Nathanial Broderick said he would get back to me if there was anything he thought I needed to know. He did not say he would get back to me with the information I wanted to know. I would take what I could get, not expecting to hear back anything at all.

I was craving a steak dinner, so that night Gaela and I drove several miles south to a coastal town that was larger than

Depoe Bay. There was a steak house there that was supposed to be excellent. The rain was still coming down, but I didn't think there was quite as much wind. I ordered the Dungeness crab bisque, a Caesar salad, the two-pound Porterhouse steak rare, a loaded baked potato, a side order of asparagus with Hollandaise sauce, and an order of creamed spinach. It was not a vegan's delight, but it was all wonderful. Of course, I wasn't able to finish the steak or any of the rest of it. The leftovers would be at least tomorrow's lunch and dinner, and Gaela would have her much anticipated bone tonight. I always felt better after I ate rare red meat. This was strange to be sure and supposedly not a healthy thing, but it was so satisfying. I wondered if I were part vampire. I was sure I wasn't anemic.

I was ready for the storm to be over. It had not kept me completely inside the cottage, but the dampness now felt too cold. No one had been in my house when I returned that night after my steak dinner. I was looking forward to seeing Anne Marie the next day. I hadn't seen her since the day of the break-in, and I still hadn't decided whether or not I was going to tell her about it. I finally decided I would tell her about the motor scooter pulling out of my driveway but not about the fact that someone had been inside the house. She might know who in town owned motor scooters. I'd come to depend on Anne Marie for her cooking, her household management skills, her walking Gaela when I was not up to it, and her cheerful company. I was especially addicted to her soup magic, and I certainly didn't want to have her quit because she was afraid I had intruders or enemies.

The next morning, the rain finally stopped. Cold weather had definitely moved in. Gaela wore her heavy red plaid coat when she went outside, and I put on my warm clothes. The wind had picked up again, and it was starting to feel like winter. I wondered what winter here on the Oregon coast would be like. I had a well-insulated house and well-insulated windows, so I thought I would be fine. It wasn't like I had moved to Alaska. Coastal climates were supposed to be more moderate and temperate than areas farther inland. I would find out about that soon enough.

The sun was shining, but the wind velocity had definitely gone up another notch. It was a gorgeous windy day, one of the reasons I had chosen Depoe Bay, and I made myself get out there and enjoy it, whether I wanted to or not. We were just returning from our morning walk when Anne Marie arrived. She was also dressed in her winter coat. I could see some form of soup on my lunch horizon.

I worked at my computer and did some paperwork while I enjoyed the delicious smells that came from the kitchen. It smelled like chicken noodle today. I love chicken noodle. Anne Marie made the noodles from scratch. She rolled out the dough and hand-cut them before she added them to the soup. She also made me a steak sandwich from the leftover steak that was in the refrigerator.

Full of noodles and chicken and steak, Gaela and I took a nap and didn't wake up until the late afternoon. I was feeling restless again, but Anne Marie had left a wonderful curried chicken, broccoli, and cheddar cheese sauce casserole for my dinner. It had buttery breadcrumbs all over the top, and I couldn't pass that up. I decided I wasn't going back to the seafood restaurant any time soon. I found another World War II espionage movie on TV, and my Westie and I watched in suspense until the Nazis were foiled. Gaela and I made an early night of it.

Chapter 15

Looking for an Accomplice

My phone woke me up the next morning at eight-thirty. Most people who knew me knew not to call before nine, but apparently Detective Broderick hadn't received the memo. He asked if he could come by right away, that he had several things he wanted to talk to me about. I told him to give me twenty minutes, and I would be ready to see him. I showered and dressed and let Gaela give herself a walk in the fenced-in back yard.

Anne Marie had not yet arrived, and all I had to offer the detective was coffee. He looked around for Anne Marie, and I told him she never came to work before ten o'clock. I could see he was disappointed. He had no doubt been looking forward to something delicious made by the fabulous Anne Marie. When she did arrive, she squeezed orange juice for both of us and had hot buttermilk biscuits with butter and homemade raspberry jam and honey on a plate in front of the detective within a few minutes of her arrival. How did she do that? His smile and excellent good humor returned. The happier he was, the more likely he was to share information with me.

Broderick had news for me. "Aziz owns a motor scooter. It's an old one, and he's had it for years. You don't know what color the motor scooter was that was leaving your driveway last week, do you?"

"I don't know anything at all about motor scooters, but my fleeting impression was that it was dirty and old and not at all well taken care of. It didn't shine like a new one would, and the noise it made sounded clunky, like an older scooter would sound. I will bet it was Aziz. But why in the world would he want to break into my house on Thursday night? I didn't talk to him about his background and mention Yemen until Saturday night when I ate dinner at the Sea Dog."

"So you saw the scooter on your property Thursday night but didn't confront Aziz until Saturday?"

"I'd questioned my waitress about him the week before when she told me how long he had worked in Depoe Bay. I asked her if he had ever worked in New York. Do you think he broke into my house because of that? How could he have figured out who I was? Nobody knows me here, and I haven't used a credit card to pay for any of the meals I've eaten at The Sea Dog."

Broderick had more to tell me. "Not that many other people in the Depoe Bay area have motor scooters. Quite a few have motorcycles. Most of those who do own scooters and motorcycles also have cars because there's so much rain. Riding a motor scooter or a motorcycle in the rain is not a great option. Aziz doesn't own a car. His scooter is his only way of getting around town and traveling on the major roads to other towns along the coast. I'm betting Aziz is the guy you saw coming out of your driveway last Thursday night. Could you tell if anyone was riding with him?"

"He was alone. I'm certain of that." Even in the dark, I had clearly seen that there was only one person on the motor scooter. Detective Broderick seemed to relax a little bit—relieved that Aziz had probably acted alone and was riding alone on his motor scooter. Broderick was hesitating to tell me something. Of course I wanted to know what it was he was thinking of keeping from me.

"What else did you find out about Aziz? You know what I said about sleeper agents? I think he is probably from Yemen, and I think he has some kind of secrets he doesn't want anyone to know. He looked afraid when I mentioned Yemen. Why would he look afraid unless he had something to hide?"

Broderick didn't address my comment about Aziz looking frightened. "We think he could be from Yemen. We can't confirm that for sure. He has a green card that allows him to be here and to be legally employed. But the number on his green card is a non-existent number. His green card is a fake, and that makes me think he is also a fake. If he is a fake, is he here just to earn a living and enjoy being in the greatest nation on earth? Or is he a fake who is here for some nefarious purpose? There are millions of illegal immigrants who are here just to make some money or to get on food stamps and collect the other goodies we give away. Most of these illegals are jobseekers or freeloaders and have nothing to do with terrorism or crime or causing trouble. We don't yet have enough information to know which kind of fake Aziz happens to be."

"Given what you know about Aziz, do you think he has any connection to the body that washed up on my beach? I have lots of suspicions and several substantial theories that hang together pretty well for me."

"You aren't writing a book about this, are you?" Broderick looked and sounded suspicious. He deliberately gave me the eye of scrutiny. I tried not to look too guilty.

My answer was an attempt to be somewhat offhand. "I am making notes about all the things that have happened to me. I am a writer, and writers write things down. I stopped publishing books before I moved to Oregon. Don't worry about me, Detective." I tried not to think about my trip to the Lincoln County Courthouse in the ridiculous disguise. I wonder what he would think about that information-gathering field trip. He will never, and I mean never, learn anything about that escapade.

I had the detective's attention, and I continued. "I do have some theories about why the body, the backpack, and the raft all ended up on my property. The more I've thought about it the more certain I am that my cove, the cove I share with my next-door neighbor, whoever that might be, was the original destination of the backpack bomber. I also think he almost made it to the cove when his raft was overturned on the rocks just off shore. If his raft had been overturned farther out to sea, the body, the backpack, and the raft would have been scattered over a much wider area along the coast. The backpack and the raft would have washed ashore in different places—far afield from each other and far from where the body came ashore. I am sure about this part of it."

Broderick nodded his head in agreement as if my argument made sense to him. Of course it made sense. I knew I was correct about the bomber's original destination and how close he had been to shore when the raft went down. Detective Broderick was willing to give me some credit for my theories. "You make a pretty good argument. Common sense can apply when all else fails."

Now I was about to move into the speculative parts of my argument. "You know, of course, that this cottage was vacant for quite a few years before it was renovated and I bought it. I have suspected that our corpse, if he had survived his trip, may have been intending to come on shore and make his way to this house. Until a few months ago, it was a dilapidated and deserted small cottage that hardly anybody remembered was still standing. I think he was originally supposed to stay here, in what he believed was an abandoned house, until somebody made contact with him to help him get to the next step of his mission—whatever that mission was. I think my purchasing and moving into the cottage threw a monkey wrench into somebody's plans. Whoever might have intended for the bomber to stay hidden in my cottage had to go to Plan B. Then the unexpectedly powerful typhoon from Japan hit Depoe Bay."

I continued my speculations before Broderick could interrupt or shut me down. "If the bomber's raft came off a large ship or oil tanker which was sailing somewhere in the Pacific Ocean, whoever put him over the side might not have been closely monitoring or thinking about the weather on the Oregon coast. The captain of a large ocean-going vessel would always have to be aware of weather conditions. But maybe whoever put the raft over the side of the ship did it without the knowledge of the captain. Or perhaps the captain was such a Muslim zealot himself that he was willing to sacrifice the bomber for the work the young man had promised to do for Allah."

I continued with my theorizing. "The young jihadist should never have been set afloat in the ocean in the middle of a typhoon or when a typhoon was approaching. I can imagine that the local contact person might have tried to communicate a "no go" to the ship so the launch of the raft would be cancelled. Our corpse may not have had any idea that the tail end of a typhoon from Asia was going to interfere with his being able to bring the raft to the cove. We will never know why the jihadist was allowed to try to make it to land. " I had given the detective my best argument.

"So you really think our corpse had a local contact who was supposed to meet him and help him out?" Broderick wasn't challenging my comments … just confirming that he'd understood me.

"Yes, I do think that. He had to have had someone meeting him. There had to be somebody locally who was supposed to give support to the jihadist, even if it was just logistics like a place to stay, food, transportation, and directions to his target. Think about it. The young man arrives in a raft. He has no way of getting himself anywhere. He's not going to hitchhike, and he needs a place to stay. The local helper might even have been told to help the bomber with his explosives and/or to drive him to where he was supposed to set off the bombs. I don't know about that part." I waited because I wanted what I was hypothesizing to sink in with Broderick.

Then I continued with my most audacious leap in the analysis, "And I will bet you that if there is such a support person on the local scene, it is Aziz. I think he was sent here years ago as a sleeper agent to be activated when and if he was ever needed. I did a book on "sleepers" one time. The setting of my story was the Cold War. Sleepers might be sent to a location decades before any specific plans are in place for them. They move into a city or a town and establish themselves as part of the community, part of the wallpaper. Wallpaper, of course, is out of fashion now, but you know what I mean. You know all about this sleeper stuff anyway, I'm sure. These secret agents are sent out just to establish themselves in case they can ever be of use in the future."

I knew I was now speculating. "The sleeper agents might become active agents who will become the bombers themselves, or they may be the ones who steal the secret plans from a military installation. They might be the ones who strap on the suicide vests and take out a busload of school kids. Or, they might be in place strictly for support—to provide the actual bombers with a place to sleep, food to eat, American clothes, American money, a ride to the local train station, or to deliver them to the kill target. There are probably sleepers who are sent to places, live there for decades, and are never activated."

"I think your line of reasoning about sleeper agents is a valid one. There are probably a few left over from the Cold War who were put in place in this country to help the old Soviet Union. Now they are looking around wondering what in the world they are supposed to do with themselves."

I agreed with Broderick about the Soviet sleeper agents. "With Vlad the Bad in power in Russia and with him trying to reconstruct the old Soviet Union, these almost-forgotten sleeper agents may have work to do after all. They might be of use, if anybody remembers their names or where they are living and they aren't too old by now. But back to jihad. If there is anyone in Depoe Bay who was supposed to be part of a designated support network for our corpse, I think Aziz is at least a part of that network. This is pure speculation, but based on my interactions with Aziz and my somewhat superficial knowledge of what a sleeper agent is all about, I am betting Aziz is a sleeper."

"Of course, we have no proof whatsoever that Aziz is involved in anything. All we know is that he is not who and what he says he is."

"I thought Aziz was part of this before you told me his green card was a fake. And before you told me he owned a motor scooter. Furthermore, I think, and I am less sure of this than I am of all the other things I have said to you today, that whoever owns the property next door to mine may be connected to these events in some way. My reasons are not good ones, but how else would anyone have known about this extremely out-of-the-way cove? And who would know about what was, for many years, an abandoned cottage? I have no idea how you would ever find out who owns the property next to mine, but why would anyone select my small cove unless they had unusually specific knowledge about this area and knew precisely, and I mean precisely, where it was located. I will also bet our backpack bomber had a GPS programmed to bring him ashore right where the raft finally ended up."

"Well, I must say you certainly do have some theories, and I have to admit that your ideas are not wild and crazy. There is a certain logic to them the way you have explained it all to me. I appreciate your sharing your thoughts and hypotheses. But that is what they are, you know, just hypotheses. You are smart and analytical, and I know you can think like a spy or a criminal or a terrorist. I have been reading some of your books, and I have to tell you I've enjoyed them quite a bit. I don't usually read fiction. I am partial to biographies and history, but your stories are exciting and well-written. I have become a fan."

"Thanks, I appreciate that. I try to write my stories so they sound like history in the making. I don't think you are as into Aziz being a part of this mess as I am. But at least you found out that he's not who he says he is. Or at least his green card is not what he wants you to think it is. I do sense that he is angry with me and also a little bit worried about me. I wouldn't say he's afraid of me, just worried that I might know something about him—something he doesn't want anybody to know. I am absolutely sure he is hiding something. I am just not sure what that something is."

"You have always been so kind to feed me whenever I come to your house. Can I treat you to lunch at the diner?"

"I love the diner and greatly appreciate the invitation. I would love to have you treat me to lunch, but I think it is best if we are not seen together in public. I am still trying to maintain my anonymity. That won't last long now, I'm afraid, but I can still try. I don't want anyone to know I am talking to you or that I might have had anything to do with what you are investigating. You have done such an excellent job of keeping all information about the corpse from leaking to the public. I'd like to help things stay that way. Anyway, Anne Marie is the one you should be taking to lunch, not me."

Broderick left, and I felt a big sense of relief that I had prodded him with my various theories. I did worry about Aziz hearing that someone was asking questions about him. And I was concerned that he would figure out I was the one who was asking those questions. I was the one who had stirred his nest, and I was the one he would focus on if he tried to find out who was messing with his life.

Chapter 16

Looking for an Explanation

Nathanial Broderick's invitation to eat with him at the diner had sounded so good. I told Anne Marie I was taking Gaela with me and going to the diner for lunch. I love turkey, and because the diner roasts its own turkey breasts and because the hot turkey sandwich was on special that day, my order was decided before I ever picked up the menu. The hot turkey sandwich came with stuffing and mashed potatoes and loads of steaming hot turkey gravy all over the whole thing. There was broccoli on the side and a dish of cranberries. I saved some for Gaela. She likes turkey. We were both being thankful for the diner. After biscuits for breakfast and the ridiculously generous lunch special at the diner, I was ready for an afternoon nap.

Maybe I would have an epiphany about Aziz. Maybe what his role was in helping the bomber would come to me in a dream. I was sure he had meant to give logistical support to the person with the backpack. I knew the now-dead jihadist had been on a mission. What could it have been? Gaela and I slept until the late afternoon. It was windy and cold and definitely late fall weather outside. The sky was bright blue and the clouds were white and rolling across the sky. It felt good because it was not raining for once. Gaela and I took a leisurely walk. I needed to work up an appetite for dinner.

Two days a week, before she drove to my house outside of town, Anne Marie picked up my mail at a post office box in Depoe Bay. I paid most of my bills and did all of my banking online. I used email to communicate with friends and family and with Anne Marie. Occasionally there was some snail mail which was forwarded to me from Connecticut. My orders from Amazon were delivered to the P.O. box.

Because I had come to Aziz's attention, I was concerned that he would figure out my real name or my pen name. I'd already asked Anne Marie to be careful when she picked up my mail, and I reminded her of this on a regular basis. She thought I was just being extra careful about not wanting anybody in the town to learn who I was. But now, especially after the break-in, I also didn't want anyone following her back to my house or watching her as she went about her own daily routine. The last thing in the world I wanted was to put her in danger because she worked for me. The post office box was one of my few contacts with the outside world, with my former life, and with my real name and my pen name.

If Aziz wanted to know who I was, he could search the property tax records. He would find that my property was owned by a holding company which in turn was held by a family partnership under my mother's maiden name. He probably could find out my real name, but he would have to do some digging. I hoped he wouldn't bother with all of that.

As much as I liked seafood, I had decided not to go back to the restaurant where Aziz worked until the mysteries of the explosives in the backpacks had been solved and someone had been arrested. I was staying away. I didn't want to look at Aziz, especially since I believed he was the person who had broken into my house and gone through my office. I was afraid if I went back and had another conversation with him, I would say something rude or something that would make him angry. If it turned out that he was helping terrorists do bad things, I certainly did not want to get onto his bad side any more than I already was.

I went back to the Italian place that night and had spaghetti and meatballs, my comfort food. It was almost as good as what I made myself, and I always like to try other people's versions of my favorites. I like to eat out, and I always save a meatball and some spaghetti for Gaela. She loves Italian food and gobbled up the contents of the leftover doggie bag before my car was out of the parking lot of the restaurant. I hoped I wouldn't see any motor scooters exiting my driveway when I got home tonight. I wondered if I should get a gun. I'd never owned a gun, and I really am somewhat afraid of having one. Then again, there had never been anyone, as far as I knew, who had disliked me as much as Aziz obviously did.

I believed in the Second Amendment, but I also had reservations about a system that allowed people who shouldn't have guns to have them. I lived alone. I was old. I was not agile or fast on my feet any more. Someone had already been inside my house uninvited. I had discovered a dead body on my beach a few weeks earlier. I had found a backpack full of explosives on my beach the day after I'd discovered the body. Then I found a raft that was ripped to pieces along with another backpack which had probably also been full of explosives. I had confronted a Middle Eastern man that I believed could be a terrorist sleeper agent for some form of jihad. I doubted that the gun laws in Oregon allowed illegal immigrants with fake green cards to own guns. How crazy was I? Maybe what I needed more than I needed a gun was a moving truck to take my belongings back to the East Coast.

I decided I should try to start at the beginning of this whole thing. I would attempt to create a plausible scenario about what was happening from the moment I had found the body on the beach. This was sounding more and more like the idea for a book plot. There had been a terrible storm, the remnants of the typhoon from Asia. The weatherman had predicted it was coming. No one had expected the wind to be as strong as it had turned out to be, and no one had predicted that the storm would last as long as it had. Because it had lasted longer than expected, it had dumped more water everywhere along the coast.

The storm had brought a body to my beach. Twenty-four hours later, a backpack full of explosives and bomb-making supplies had washed up in the exact same spot. What were the chances that would happen if the two things were not related? A few days later, a rubber raft, which had clearly been torn apart by the storm, the rough waves, and the rocks off the coast, had appeared less than a hundred yards from where the body and the backpack had washed up. The raft held a backpack identical to the one I'd found on my beach. The three things were undeniably connected.

I took these facts and began my own speculation about how it had all happened. I surmised that the raft, carrying the bomber and his two backpacks and guided by a phone GPS, had intended to "make land" in the protected cove. Half of that cove belonged to me. The storm had interfered. Because of the weather, the plan should have been aborted before the jihadist had ever left the much larger ship at sea. Because of stupidity, or for whatever reason, the plan had been allowed to go forward. The young man's raft had been set afloat in the Pacific Ocean, and the raft had overturned on its way to safe haven, not far from the shore.

I could only assume that the young man and his deadly cargo had almost made it. I imagined that he was close to landing when his raft had turned over and over in the rough water during the storm. He may not have known how to swim. The water had been so turbulent, I doubted that even the best of swimmers could have survived in those stormy seas. Maybe the rough surf had broken the man's neck or battered him against the ocean bottom until he lost consciousness. Then he drowned.

Chapter 17

Looking for an Extra Bed

Aziz tried to focus on the future, on the upcoming arrival of the next jihadist. He told himself he had to let go of his anger and obsession with the meddling old woman. She was crippled and used a cane most of the time. What possible threat was she to him?

The next jihadist was arriving in a few days, and Aziz needed to have a place for him to sleep. Aziz had decided it wouldn't be convenient or comfortable to have someone staying with him. There wasn't room for more than one person to sleep or do anything in the one-room apartment above the t-shirt shop. Hopefully, Aziz's need for an extra bed would only be for a night or two. The jihadist would have a timetable for his attack. It was up to Aziz to provide whatever help the young man might need to make his mission a success. It was all for Allah, and Aziz was willing to put up with anything for his beliefs—except for putting up a tent in the woods or having someone stay with him in his tiny apartment. Aziz's assumption was that the new arrival was going to follow through with the previous plan to attack the Space Needle in Seattle.

What the media liked to call "lone wolf" terrorists came in all varieties and with all kinds of plans, large and small. Some were single individuals with a couple of guns who decided to storm a military recruiting headquarters. They would burst into these "soft targets" and start shooting people—as many as they could before they themselves were shot and killed. This always made the top story on the cable news shows. Soft military targets and law enforcement individuals were favorites with the single jihadist. Even the recent California killings which involved two men with suicide vests in an old SUV was a low-tech, high-impact operation.

Civilian targets were becoming increasingly popular with terrorists as evidenced by the couple in San Bernardino, Tashfeen Malik and Syed Farook, who attacked their co-workers at a holiday party. These efforts didn't require much planning, intelligence, expertise, or even firepower—especially if one was willing to die in the process. These are the blunt instrument terrorist attacks, perpetrated by the not-very-bright but dreadfully enthusiastic Jihadi Johnny and Jihadi Janey.

At the other end of the spectrum, there was the elaborate and well-coordinated plan like September 11, 2001. That of course was at the opposite extreme from a "lone wolf" attack. There were all kinds and levels of terror plots in between. There were the London, Paris, and Brussels attacks in Europe. The invasion of Muslim refugees over a period of decades into the European Union had proven to be an exceptionally dangerous and deadly problem for many countries. The current administration in the United States was in the process of inflicting a similar refugee disaster on the land of the free! The message was … come on in and blow us up!

The plan with which Aziz was associated was somewhat more sophisticated than the single gunman attacking a military recruiting office or a policeman in his squad car. There had not been many attacks on iconic sites in recent years in the U.S. Anything that involved more than a couple of people could be discovered more easily because of increased surveillance by law enforcement. Airports had heightened security to the extent that airplanes had been moved down on the list of targets for jihad. Jihadists had shifted their airport attacks to baggage claim and to the ticketing areas in the main entrances just off the sidewalk. These were open to the public without security or screening. Zaventem, the Brussels airport, had been a victim of just such an attack which struck the soft place, the unsecured, the unprotected ticket counter area of an international airport. No one would be expecting an attack on the Space Needle.

Aziz believed that the jihadist, who was probably going to carry out an attack on the Seattle tourist site, was trained in bomb making. He would prepare his explosives and would know how to circumvent the security systems which were in place at the famous landmark. Detonators and timing devices would not be made out of metal, and everything about the bombs would be built to pass without arousing suspicion through metal detectors. The young man would know exactly where to place his backpacks and set off his bombs for maximum effect. The suicide bomber knew he was making the ultimate sacrifice for Allah.

Aziz did not know anything about the latest bomb-making technology. He did not know if the jihadist would be constructing a "suicide" vest to wear into the Space Needle or if he would be making something that looked harmless which could be carried in a backpack. To cause maximum damage, he might use both of these means to deliver death and destruction to the infidels.

Aziz's job was to facilitate the work of the technical expert and martyr. Aziz knew that his own part in the overall plan was essential to making it a success. After the jihadist called Aziz's cell phone to let him know he had arrived on shore, Aziz planned to pick up the young man at the cove. They would bury the raft and hike through the trees to Aziz's motor scooter. Depending on exactly what time of day the man arrived, they might have to wait until after dark to make the motor scooter ride into Depoe Bay.

Aziz had not been able to solve the problem of how to get an extra bed into his small apartment. It would be impossible. Aziz would have to rent a truck to transport a mattress or a futon or whatever bed he thought would be sufficient. Aziz would need the extra bed only for a few nights, and it might be for only one night. What would he do with the bed or the mattress after the man left? Aziz had no place to store an extra mattress or a folding cot. Would there be more jihadists arriving for future missions who would have to stay with him? He thought about letting the young jihadist sleep on the floor in his apartment.

Aziz decided he would allow the jihadist guest to stay at his place. Aziz would move to a motel for a few nights.

Having the young soldier for Allah stay at his apartment seemed like the least conspicuous way to house the man. Looking at his dilemma from all angles, the motel option for himself seemed more and more attractive to Aziz.

It was settled. The jihadist would live in Aziz's apartment while preparing the explosive devices for his final mission. He would sleep there, and Aziz would bring him food and whatever else he needed. Aziz would stay at a motel. When everything was ready, Aziz would take a day off from his job at the restaurant. He never asked for time off, so he was sure his manager would allow him to have whatever vacation days he wanted. It was the off-season, and business was slow.

Aziz planned to rent a car from a company in Newport, Oregon, a coastal town south of Depoe Bay. Aziz had valid driver's licenses, to legally drive a car as well as to drive his motor scooter. Recently, he had rented a car and made the drive to Seattle and back just to practice the drive and become familiar with the highways and the streets in the city. He felt confident that his part of the plan could be accomplished without a hitch. He would drive the martyr to the Space Needle and leave him there to complete the operation.

After leaving the martyr in Seattle, on his drive back to the Oregon coast, Aziz imagined that he would turn the car radio to an all-news station. He would wait to hear the reports of the tragedy, the resulting shock and horror as the media of the Evil Satan America reported on the carnage the jihadist had inflicted. It would send his spirits soaring, Aziz knew, to finally have the chance to participate in such a significant way in the war against the infidels. No one in Depoe Bay or anyplace else in the country would ever know the part that Aziz had played. No one would ever suspect that the affable, friendly fellow who said he was from Lebanon had assisted in the tremendous act of jihad that would make news around the globe.

It did not matter to Aziz that no one would ever know of his contribution. The fact that he would continue to walk and work and live among the enemy and that they would know nothing of his greatness thrilled Aziz to his core. Aziz dreamed of the way he would feel. He almost wished he himself had been chosen to die in the attack, but he realized that he was being spared because he could be used again and again to help with other great attacks for Allah against the United States.

Aziz was Allah's servant, and whatever his faith required of him, he was willing to do. Well, except for pitching a tent in the woods which he felt was really more than even Allah should ask of him. It would take more courage to stay alive and continue to live his secret life than it would be to die a martyr. Aziz would make whatever sacrifices were necessary … almost … to serve.

Aziz worried constantly about all the things that could go wrong with his plans. He hoped the young jihadist would not stay with him for more than a couple of days. He worried that someone might see him bringing the young man into his apartment. He hoped the man would arrive at night. Ideally, Aziz would pick him up at night and have him secured inside the apartment before morning. Aziz would rent a car the day before they were to leave for Seattle. He would be sure that both he and the jihadist were inside the car and on their way before dawn the morning of the mission — before anyone in Depoe Bay woke up for the day.

A worst-case scenario that nagged at Aziz was the one in which the jihadist arrived in the middle of the day and would not realize that he needed to stay hidden. Aziz had heard that the woman who lived in the cottage had a little dog she took for walks all around her property. He worried that the woman and her dog would be taking a walk outside. Aziz was afraid she would look over and see the jihadist arriving, wandering around, or digging a hole to bury the raft. Worse, she might be walking in the cove and come upon the young man or the raft. That's all he would need to mess things up this time. The woman might see something or someone suspicious, and Aziz was sure she would immediately call 911.

Aziz realized he needed to get the man away from the cove as quickly as possible. The last thing he wanted was for the authorities to be alerted that somebody strange was in the area and to be on the lookout. If the jihadist arrived during the daylight hours, he might have to hide with Aziz in the woods and wait for darkness to avoid law enforcement. After sundown they could ride the motor scooter back to Depoe Bay without being seen.

Aziz prayed the woman would stay in her house and mind her own business. He realized he would have to alert the jihadist to keep himself and his raft hidden if he arrived at the cove during the daylight hours. He didn't think the woman's dog would bark in the middle of the night if it heard something out of the ordinary. There had to be noisy critters running around everywhere in the area. The dog would be used to hearing noises all night long. The jihadist's arrival should be a completely silent event anyway. Damn that old woman. If she hadn't moved into the cottage next door to the vacant property, he would have been home free. She was a thorn in his side no matter which direction he turned.

Aziz spoke Arabic and assumed his guest would also, but the guest probably wouldn't speak English. Aziz would have to keep the jihadist inside the apartment for the duration of his stay in Depoe Bay. He assumed the soon-to-be martyr would be compliant, but what if he decided on the night before he was to die that he wanted a night on the town at the bar down the street with bourbon and strippers? Aziz could always find something to worry about. He told himself he had to be sure the bourbon and strippers scenario did not happen.

He would babysit the jihadist and leave his apartment only after the man was asleep. If he decided he didn't trust him, Aziz could almost sleep on the couch. It was a tiny apartment, and the couch was just a love seat. No one ever came to see Aziz, so there was never any need to have seating for more than one person. It was not a couch that would make a comfortable sleeping place, but Aziz could sleep on it in an emergency. Aziz wondered if the young man would eat seafood. Maybe he was a vegetarian or a vegan? Aziz knew he had to remain flexible, but after the debacle of the typhoon, he was terrified of leaving anything to chance. He scoured his brain for any possible detail he had not anticipated. Damn that woman for taking the use of the cottage away from him. Everything would have been so much easier if she had never come to town.

Chapter 18

Looking for Proof

etective Nathanial Broderick was busy acting on the information he had discovered about Muhammad Aziz. The OSP and the FBI had decided to watch Aziz to see if he made contact with anybody unusual or if he did anything which seemed suspicious. Broderick was the leading and most aggressive advocate for the investigation into Aziz. That Aziz had a fake green card was a red flag for Broderick, but for federal immigration authorities, holding a fake green card only made him one of many millions of others who carried fake green cards so they could get jobs in the U.S. A fake green card did not, in and of itself, make a person a terrorist.

Furthermore, Homeland Security had become overly skittish about investigating anybody who had a Muslim-sounding name. Middle Easterners and Muslims in particular had become a protected class. The attorney general of the United States had threatened to investigate anyone who said something derogatory about a Muslim. These politically correct parameters were making all investigations into terrorism increasingly difficult.

Broderick finally got authorization to place a listening device in Aziz's home and to have someone monitor his cell phone. The detective didn't think there would be much to discover with these two monitoring devices because he was pretty sure that Aziz was not an active part of a larger network. Aziz fit the profile of the deep cover sleeper agent acting alone who was activated only occasionally, not the profile of a terrorist who conspired with others. Broderick did not think Aziz was a bomb maker, a weapons expert, or a martyr type. FBI profilers agreed with him.

Detective Broderick had pegged Aziz for the facilitator that he was, someone who handled the logistics and practicalities of assisting a jihadist who took the action to commit an atrocity. Aziz was in place to assist and give aid, not to blow himself up or use an automatic weapon. This would make Aziz more difficult to observe and almost impossible to convict of anything. He was the kind of Muslim extremist who is vital to the success of most terror attacks but who operates under the radar of law enforcement and the public. He was a peaceful Muslim, a good Muslim.

Broderick tried hard to convince his fellow law enforcement officers that Aziz's comings and goings needed to be monitored. He presented the argument that Aziz was in the country illegally and was nothing like the poor guy who had come over the border from Mexico to earn a few dollars. Aziz had been living here illegally for many years. Broderick and the FBI psychologist profiler painted a convincing picture of the sleeper agent, and they were able to demonstrate to their colleagues how Aziz fit this profile perfectly.

Broderick laid out his theory about why the dead body on the beach, the backpack on the beach, and the remnants of the rubber raft in the cove all happened to have come ashore in such close geographic proximity. He made the case that the person coming ashore with the bombs would have to have someone in the local area to assist him. Broderick made the argument that Aziz was probably that person. He told his colleagues that Aziz's motor scooter had been seen at night in the area of the cove.

The detective did not mention his suspicions that Aziz had broken into Abigail's cottage. There was no hard evidence of the break-in, no matter how convinced Broderick was that it had happened. He told his fellow law-enforcement officers that Aziz had made a big deal about coming from Lebanon and that Aziz's Lebanese heritage was a lie.

Aziz was going to be monitored but only electronically. A judge agreed to allow a tracking device to be placed on the motor scooter. Broderick was not able to get an informant as a waiter or waitress inside the seafood restaurant. But he was able to get an alert request that he would be notified if Aziz used a credit card to purchase an airline or train ticket, if he rented a car, if he made a reservation at a motel or a hotel anywhere, or if he spent a large amount of money on electronics gear or any amount on firearms. It was the best he could do. Broderick was now convinced that it was more than likely Aziz was the local contact for the young man who had drowned and been found dead on the beach.

Broderick was having a hard time convincing others to believe his hypothesis. Broderick didn't know, of course, if the death of the backpack bomber was a one-time shot in a rather amateurish terror plot with an unknown target or if there would be more young men on their way with backpacks full of explosives. The detonators and plastique explosives found in the two backpacks were real and convincing. Because nobody seemed to pay attention to fake green cards any more, the discovery of explosives in the backpacks was the only concrete evidence that kept the Aziz theory in play with Broderick's detractors. It was all they had, and Broderick's theory was the only one anybody had proposed.

It turned out that Aziz hardly ever used his credit cards or his motor scooter. Those who were watching Aziz were falling asleep waiting for him to do something. He kept to himself, and he went to work. He didn't have any friends outside of his colleagues at the restaurant and his customers there. He lived in a tiny apartment. To Broderick and to the FBI profiler, Aziz's lack of a regular life was evidence that he had a "higher purpose." They believed he could be waiting to be activated for an operation in the name of Allah. To other law enforcement officials, those who were less than convinced that Aziz was anybody special, he was just a guy who didn't merit much time or attention.

Just when it seemed that Aziz, after all, did not merit any attention, Broderick received an alert that Aziz had used his credit card to reserve a room at a local motel. The reservation was for three nights, and the name on the reservation was Aziz's own name. Broderick wondered if Aziz was making the reservation for someone other than himself. Broderick was puzzled since Aziz had an apartment where he had lived for years. Why would he need a room in a motel? The only reason Broderick could come up with was that Aziz was expecting company.

If another terrorist was coming to town, why would Aziz not keep him in his apartment? It didn't make sense, and it seemed to Nathanial Broderick that Aziz was taking a terrible risk to reserve a room in a motel for someone who might not speak any English. Broderick thought Aziz should be under surveillance for the duration of the period that included the motel reservation and for a period of time before and after that. Broderick didn't know how he was going to convince his fellow law enforcement colleagues that this needed to happen. A five-day or six-day surveillance required a lot of man power, and Broderick could not do it all by himself. He needed help and had not yet figured out how to get it.

The more he thought about Aziz and the motel room he had reserved, the more convinced Broderick was that another raft was going to arrive in the cove. He did not understand why the planners behind the first failed bombing plot would try the same scenario again. Good sense would suggest that they should vary their approach. Chances were there would not be a typhoon this time, but it was still terribly risky to drop a small raft over the side of a tanker and hope it made it to shore. The reservations Aziz had made at the motel at least gave the detective some kind of a time frame.

Chapter 19

Looking for a Master Planner

In spite of the fact that both of his parents were Muslims, Darius Marwan Abadi had grown up attending the Presbyterian Church. Darius was born in Cleveland, Ohio and lived all of his growing up years in a well-to-do Cleveland suburb. As a child, the name Darius had been difficult for other children to pronounce. So Darius began to call himself "Dee." Soon Dee became Dean, and when he entered the first grade, fellow elementary school students and teachers all called him Dean Abadi. His parents understood that this informal name change helped their son fit in. They understood his becoming Dean to others, but at home he continued to be Darius.

Dean attended the local public schools where he was an excellent student and had many friends. He got almost all A's in his academic college prep curriculum. He was tall and handsome, and he was on the football and track teams.

His parents' four-bed-room home was across the street from the large, popular Bethany Presbyterian Church. He had attended Sunday school at Bethany Presbyterian since he was eight years old, and when he was a teenager, every Sunday evening, he attended the Presbyterian Youth Fellowship meetings there. Dean's sister had been married in the church which was so convenient to their home. Dean had been an official member at Bethany Presbyterian since he was confirmed at age twelve.

Dean's father had been born in Syria, and his mother was from Jordan. Dean was named after his father, Marwan, who had lived in the United States for most of his life. He'd made a great deal of money in the bar and restaurant business. One of the secrets to his success had been the numbers racket he ran under the cover of his multiple legitimate businesses. Marwan was divorced when he returned to the Middle East looking for a second wife. He was a wealthy man in his forties and wanted children. He wanted a beautiful and well-educated wife, but he also wanted an obedient wife.

In the late 1930s in Jordan, Marwan was able to purchase a woman who met his specifications exactly. He negotiated with his future wife's family, and a deal was struck. Lujain was veiled, and it was customary that she remain veiled until after she was married. Marwan, however, wanted to see what he was buying, what he was getting for the enormous amount of money he had paid for his new bride-to-be. Determined to see if he was getting his money's worth, he peeked underneath the beautiful Lujain's veil. She was even more stunning than he'd hoped.

At age seventeen, Lujain was married to the wealthy Syrian-American and moved to the United States. Children followed in a few years, and Lujain was a wonderful mother and a wonderful cook. She was a good wife, but she also had an independent streak. Raised in a wealthy Jordanian family, she had attended a Catholic convent school where she learned, among other subjects, to read Latin and to speak and read French and English. Lujain was exceptionally smart. Although her family was Muslim, she did not practice her religion when she arrived in the United States. Marwan was a workaholic and spent all of his time tending to his businesses. He had no time for religion and could scarcely spare the time to be a father to the children he'd said he wanted.

Dean and his sister became Presbyterians because of the proximity of their home to Bethany Presbyterian Church and a quirk of fate. The minister at the Presbyterian church happened to pass by the Abadi's home twice every day as he walked back and forth from the rectory to the church. He noticed the two olive-skinned children playing in their yard, and one day he paid a call on Lujain. He told her about the fun things his church could offer the children and asked Lujain if she would consider sending Dean and his sister to Sunday school. She agreed and decided to send them, and they loved the church programs. Every June, they attended the two weeks of summer vacation Bible school offered by Bethany Presbyterian.

When the children's father realized they were regularly attending the Christian church across the street, he didn't pay much attention to it. If they were happy going there, it was all right with him. Religion was not a big part of Marwan's world. He regarded the neighborhood church as a kind of recreational center for his kids. Dean did not consider it odd that his parents never attended church with him and his sister. Many other parents among the Presbyterian faithful dropped off their children in the church parking lot for Sunday school on Sunday mornings,

Dean attended the University of Wisconsin and graduated with a dual degree in physics and electrical engineering. He was an excellent student, and he worked hard. Dean was popular and joined a fraternity. After graduation, he married a blonde, blue-eyed sorority girl. It was not a happy marriage. Pam was pretty and spoiled and always wanted her own way. She spent too much money and didn't know anything about taking care of a house. They divorced before any children were born.

After his divorce, Dean lived alone in an apartment in a Chicago suburb. He worked long hours at his job for a large construction firm. When he was offered a promotion and a transfer to Portland, Oregon, he accepted and made the move. It was when he moved to Portland that Dean began to question the Presbyterian religion and his commitment to Christianity in general. He knew his parents had been non-practicing Muslims, and he was curious about their religion. He wondered why his mother had so easily given up her children to the influence of the Presbyterian Church.

Dean first visited a mosque because he was interested, at an intellectual level, in learning more about Islam. Although both of his parents had been Muslims, he knew very little about their religion. Dean was greeted warmly when he visited the mosque. The imam took a special interest in him and invited him to his home for dinner. They became friends, and Dean became a regular at the mosque. He studied Islam and spent many hours talking with the imam. Dean read the Quran. His conversion happened slowly over a period of years, but he eventually found his spiritual home in the religion of his parents. He realized that his cultural background was Middle Eastern, and the foray into Presbyterianism had been purely happenstance.

A psychologist might speculate that Dean's attraction to Islam grew out of his subliminal search for a father. His own father was always working and had paid little attention to Dean when he was a child. Another analyst might say that Dean turned against the United States because of his disdain for and his rejection by the selfish, All-American, white-bread wife who had cheated on him. A Freudian shrink might say that his sexual ambitions had been replaced by spiritual ones. One might talk about long-suppressed anger and Dean's never being truly secure in his American identity. But Dean's reasons for turning against the country where he was born, the country that had given him the best it had to offer, would in reality be more complex than even a lengthy and sophisticated psychoanalysis would be able to explain.

When Dean turned sixty years of age, a new, young imam came to Dean's mosque. The new man's radical views captured and inspired Dean at a time in his life when he was vulnerable. Perhaps the young cleric represented for Dean, in some subconscious way, the son he'd never had. Perhaps Dean was in a late mid-life crisis and was looking for deeper meaning in his life? Perhaps Dean was looking at old age and wondering if he had yet fulfilled whatever dreams he might have had?

The Muslim religion had welcomed Dean and made him feel at home in a way that the Presbyterian church, Cleveland, the University of Wisconsin, and his cheating wife with the cute ponytail never had. Jihad gave Dean a purpose that his career in construction had not provided. Islam fed a desire he'd never known he possessed. It fed his soul and became his passion. Dean's middle-aged conversion to the religion of his ancestors became a late-in-life obsession with sharia law.

Dean developed a fanatical devotion to the goal of establishing the religious caliphate world-wide, including in the USA. For the first time in his life, he was a man with a mission and a reason for living. He was willing to die for Allah, and he would devote the rest of his days to bringing terror and chaos to the land of his birth, the land of the infidels, the United States of America.

Dean turned his brilliant mind, his life-long experience with physics and electrical circuitry, and his love of Islam to wreaking havoc on American non-believers. It has been said that those who convert to a religion become its greatest advocates, its most ardent disciples, its fanatics. Dean Abadi became that man. He was a convert to Islam, but in reality his religious roots went back centuries.

Chapter 20

Looking Forward to Thanksgiving

I was looking forward to seeing my family and celebrating the Thanksgiving holiday with them. We were going to do Face Time on Thanksgiving Day with my grandson who was celebrating in Portland, Maine. He was visiting his girlfriend's family so he was a happy young man, even without his own family around him. I was sure everybody at the hotel in Portland, Oregon would have a good time. They'd all claimed to want to see my cottage in Depoe Bay, but they took my word for it about how small it was and how much more comfortable they would be at the expensive Portland hotel. I had sent them many photos of my little house. I'd sent photos of the gardens and the magnificent views I had of the Pacific Ocean.

The best news was that the Portland hotel was dog-friendly. The West Coast was definitely more enlightened about how people feel concerning their pets. The hotel I had chosen did more than just allow you to bring your small animals into your room. They offered a "Pet Package" which provided dog walking and dog sitting, and even the food of your dog's choice. A dog walker would come to the room at a specified time, even early in the morning—like a room service breakfast. Your dog would be walked in a special area the hotel provided before you were even out of bed! When you went shopping or out for dinner, a sitter could come to the room to stay with your pet so he or she didn't have an attack of separation anxiety and scratch at the door or bark like crazy.

The provision of the "Pet Package" was the greatest thing I'd run into in a long time. I signed Gaela up for four days and five nights and was delighted to have the opportunity to pay the expensive doggie fee. It was such a great idea; why didn't all hotels offer such a service? People were willing to pay big money to be able to bring their dogs with them.

As excited as I was about seeing my daughter, my granddaughter, and the others, I hated to leave the Aziz investigation. I'd only be two hours away, and I'd only be gone for a few days. But I had a feeling something was about to happen. Broderick assured me he would keep me posted. But he was not in charge and was having a hard enough time impressing on his superiors that they should be paying more attention to the things he was telling them.

The hotel was wonderful and should have been for what I was paying per night for all the rooms my family occupied. They were happy, and we all loved the spa and the food. We had a great time, and the expense was more than worth it.

We had breakfast in our rooms. The women spent an entire day at the spa indulging in every possible service one could imagine, as well as some I'd never imagined. The chocolate body mask was a new one for me. It smelled delicious, but what in the world could it possibly be doing for me? I did wonder. I had the best haircut of my life and decided maybe I was going to have to drive to Portland in the future to allow Tabitha to style my hair on a regular basis.

We met in the bar every night for drinks. We took a limo to a famous seafood place. The limo had been my idea. It was expensive, but we all wouldn't fit into one taxi. Nobody had to drive, and I wasn't walking. It was fun, and I got lots of extra points for thinking of the limo. The Thanksgiving Day buffet at the hotel was everything it had advertised itself to be. Turkey with all the trimmings was there along with roast beef, ham, shrimp, lobster Newberg, smoked salmon, and a thousand other temptations. There were salad stations, a sushi station, and table after table of desserts. It was truly an extravagant, beautiful, and ridiculous display of gluttony, and we loved every minute of it.

We laughed a lot and enjoyed meeting my grandson's Down East girlfriend via Zoom. I decided I liked Alison's new husband more and more. I'd worried about her decision to marry again after her first marriage had ended badly. She'd been happily single for many years. I was concerned that she might be too set in her ways to share her life with anyone again. My new son-in-law was smart and very funny. He adored my daughter, and he seemed to like me pretty well. We developed a rapport and found we enjoyed each other's company. I was glad he had joined our family Thanksgiving and glad he had married Alison. She deserved to be happy, and I decided this man could make that possible.

I listened carefully to everything my granddaughter was willing to tell me about what was going on in her life. It was a great family reunion. It had worked out better than I could have hoped, and it was more than worth the enormous expense. Even Gaela had enjoyed her stay at the hotel. I loved my new haircut and had Tabitha, the hair genius, on speed dial. Life was good. After many hugs and extended goodbyes, Gaela and I drove home to Depoe Bay.

I'd not heard from Detective Broderick and was anxious to know what was going on with the investigation. I had no rights or privileges to know anything at all, except that a lot of the events had occurred on my property. I was more involved than I should be, but I couldn't help myself. I'd been writing about this kind of drama for years, and now these things were happening right in my own backyard. Or was it in my own front yard? I sent Broderick an email asking for updates.

Anne Marie had been watching over the house while I was gone. She'd made several trips to the cottage to check on things and had even come after dark a couple of times. I'd never told her about the break-in since I'd rationalized there wasn't anything much to tell. She'd been happy to make some extra money to keep an eye on my house for me. I'd had an unexpectedly fun Thanksgiving but was ready to get back to my familiar routine as a recluse. The night we returned home to Depoe Bay, Gaela and I slept soundly and a long time.

Chapter 21

Looking for Rafts

The weather during the first week in December was unusually mild, and it felt more like September than just three weeks before Christmas. Dean Abadi was keeping a close eye on the Weather Channel. He didn't need a repeat of the Japanese typhoon and the disasters that storm had brought to his earlier plans. His overall timetable had been delayed, but it looked as if everything was coming together this time. Two rafts, three heavy pieces of cargo, and three people would arrive at the cove in Depoe Bay this week. Safe passage depended on calm seas and not much wind.

Dean had been negative about Aziz from the beginning. He felt Aziz had more than outlived his usefulness to the cause. He wanted Aziz out of the picture. Aziz would know nothing about the rafts and the other things that were arriving in the cove. He would learn about only one person. Aziz had been told to expect his guest within a certain thirty-six-hour window. In fact, the rafts, the cargo, and the people Dean was focused on would arrive almost two days before Aziz was expecting anybody. Dean Abadi and the young Imam Muhammad Muhammad were personally going to Depoe Bay to meet this group. It was that important.

From his law enforcement sources, Dean had learned that Aziz was under surveillance. He was certain Aziz was completely unaware that he was being watched. Dean and the imam had informants in the highest echelons of several national intelligence organizations as well as in local law enforcement offices. Dean and the imam were worried that Aziz had been compromised. Aziz's failure to meet the Space Needle jihadist had not been his fault, but the truth was that he had been an agent-in-waiting for too long. He had not exactly "gone native," but he had lost his edge.

In his own mind, Aziz might be as committed to jihad as he had ever been, but he was not as careful as he should have been. He had made mistakes and had forgotten his tradecraft. Furthermore, tradecraft had changed, and Aziz's skills were more than outdated. The training of the cadre of soldiers who now fought for Allah around the world was much more technical and weapons-oriented than it had been when Aziz had done his training many years earlier. Aziz could not hope to be even a peripheral and insignificant player in this latest and most important plan. Aziz was expendable.

There were many in Portland who could be called on to help, in large ways and small, with Allah's work. Dean had easily obtained a dark green Ford panel van large enough to transport a John Deere Gator. The green van was parked in Dean's garage. It would not be used until the night of the operation in Depoe Bay.

Dean and the imam made a trip from Portland to Depoe Bay to check out the site where they would rendezvous with their young jihadist brothers and sisters who would arrive by raft. On this preliminary run, they used a car that had been borrowed from a friend of a friend's Hispanic gardener. The license plates on the gardener's car were stolen. The car could never be traced back to the mosque or to either of the men who were in the car. Dean and Muhammad had both worn wigs and worker's clothes on their drive southeast from Portland. With surveillance cameras at every gas station and stop along the way, they wanted to be sure no one was able to recognize them.

During their preparatory visit to Depoe Bay, they decided that on the night of the pickup in the cove, Dean would stay with the van and the imam would drive the Gator and keep the rendezvous with the arriving jihadists. Leaving an empty van on the side of the road was not a good idea, especially if local law enforcement was keeping an eye on the property. If the police or another car stopped to see why the van was parked alongside the road, Dean could drive away and come back later. The men had fashioned a ramp so that the Gator could easily exit the van and just as easily drive back into it after their people and their cargo had been retrieved.

Dean knew, because he had done his homework, what would be required to transport the jihadists and their valuable supplies to the van which would be parked on the paved public road. Dean knew about the woods and the fact that there was no road between the cove and the main highway. The lodgepole pines in the woods were very close together in some places. Dean and the imam walked the woods and plotted a course so the Gator was sure to be able to fit between the trees. When in doubt, they measured the distance between the trees. They marked their path with iridescent chalk on the tree trunks. The chalk marks would show the imam and his Gator the way on the night the rafts arrived, but these chalk marks would be gone with the first hard rain.

Dean Abadi and Imam Muhammad Muhammad would personally oversee both the arrival of the technicians in the cove and the next phase of the operation. Dean was staying in touch with his people on board the tanker in the Pacific. They were supplied with satellite phones which afforded much better reception than ordinary cell phones could provide.

Chances of discovery were greatly reduced if the young people arrived after dark. These travelers were equipped with night-vision goggles because they planned to arrive in the cove at night. Aziz had thought his ancient motor scooter and a rented Ford Taurus were adequate for the job he'd been asked to do. Dean was disgusted with the sloppy and short-sighted Aziz.

Aziz had not adequately prepared for the last arrival. He had not considered the obstacles he might confront, and he was not dependable. The cargo which would arrive in two days was too valuable to be left to a slacker like Aziz. Dean and the Imam had made a detailed and careful plan; they were well-prepared and intended to be successful. Amateur night was over; the professionals were now in charge.

The night of the operation, Dean and the imam again put on their disguises. They observed their previous precautions and guarded against any undue attention that might be drawn to their van. They arrived in Depoe Bay before midnight and easily found their way back to the property along the Pacific Coast. The imam put on his night-vision goggles because he would be driving the Gator 625 4X4

XUV through the woods in the dark. The weather report was good, and the chalk marks on the trees were still in place. The imam had been practicing how to operate the Gator, and he felt confident that he could find his way through the woods and down the embankment to the shore of the cove.

Chapter 22

Looking for Cargo

The weather was perfect, and the Pacific was as smooth as glass. It was cold, but there was no wind and no rain. It was a rare night for December. The trip from the Liberian tanker to the cove near Depoe Bay would be an easy run. Dean felt that Allah must be smiling on their preparations which would ultimately culminate in an event to honor him.

They stayed in touch by satellite phone. Dead spots for cell phone reception occurred everywhere near the ocean and in the wild. Equipment that provided good communication was worth the extra planning and the extra expense. The jihadists were ready on board the tanker, and the pickup team was in place. The operation was a go. The three young people and their valuable cargo were lowered in rafts over the side of the ship and down into the ocean.

Besides the jihadists, only four other people aboard the tanker were in the know about the plan. No one else knew anything unusual was happening on the ship that night. The two rafts were lowered just as lifeboats would be lowered if there were an emergency. The transfer was silent, timely, and without incident. Headed for a deserted beach in an obscure cove of the Pacific Ocean, the two men and one woman followed their GPS directions to the rendezvous.

The imam drove the Gator, which successfully made the trip through the woods and down the embankment to the meeting place. The chalk markings on the pine trees had been vital in guiding the Gator through the pine forest. On his satellite phone app, the imam was able to watch the progress of the two rafts as they moved through the ocean towards the cove. Each of these rafts was equipped with a small outboard motor. He spoke with the people in the rafts frequently and talked them through their journey to shore. The imam was thankful for his night-vision goggles. It was completely dark that night. There was no visible moon and no other ambient light along the seacoast. When the rafts and their occupants had arrived safely, the imam gave directions about handling the precious and dangerous cargo.

They unloaded the footlocker from the raft directly onto the back of the Gator. It was large and awkward and took three of them to make the transfer. The two large suitcases weighed almost fifty pounds each. These two bags went onto the back of the Gator next. The imam and one of the young people secured the cargo with heavy duty bungee cords for the rough ride up the embankment and through the woods to the van that was parked along the main road. Two of the jihadists let the air out of the rafts and stuffed the deflated rubber boats around the secured cargo. Both outboard motors that had powered the rafts were also loaded into the gator.

The previous plan to bury the rafts had been rejected. Authorities were already looking at the cove because of the : last failed attempt. It was decided that the rafts and motors needed to be removed and discarded elsewhere, not buried. Law enforcement would love to find evidence buried near the cove. They were not going to find that evidence this time. The team grabbed their backpacks, and ten minutes after they'd arrived on the shores of the USA, they were leaving the cove.

It was slow going up the incline. The Gator had a powerful engine and great traction. But the bank was steep and the ground was soft from the recent rains. The three young people ended up pushing the Gator up the slope as it labored under the weight of its cargo. But in the end the Gator was up to the task, and once it was on level ground the three passengers from the rafts climbed aboard the 4X4. Traveling over fallen branches and piles of pine cones made for a rough trip, but the Gator was an amazing vehicle. It successfully made its slow and measured journey through the woods. The Gator's engine was loud, but who would hear it in the middle of the night in the middle of nowhere? Who would wake up and hear the drone of the engine as it traveled through the dense forest? Even if someone happened to hear the Gator, who would know what was making the noise or bother to do anything about it? The imam stayed in touch with Dean who was waiting in the van. Constant communication was the key to a successful result.

The back doors of the van opened, and the ramp was quickly set in place. The four riders from the Gator pushed it up the ramp and into the van. The rear doors of the van closed, and in a couple of minutes, the Gator, carrying its world-altering cargo, was secured inside the van and on its way. Well-planned and well-executed, it had been a nearly perfect maneuver. It had taken less than two hours from the time the Gator had first left the main road on its way to the cove until the van and its passengers were on their way back to Portland, Oregon.

Allah would be pleased. The return trip to Portland was without incident, and the van parked unobserved in the enclosed garage next to the mosque. The Gator's cargo was unloaded, and the passengers from the raft were shown to comfortable accommodations in the mosque. Dean was home asleep in his own bed before the sun came up.

This important part of the intricate operation had been completed two nights before Aziz had been expecting someone to arrive on the shores of the cove. If Aziz was under surveillance, the people watching him would have completely missed the earlier arrival of the rafts. To be watching Aziz was to be watching a red herring, a diversion, a distraction. Aziz could not know, of course, that he had been demoted from being a real player in the scheme of things to being a small red fish.

Early the next morning Aziz received a text on his satellite phone that he was not to go to the cove to meet his contact. He was told he was to go instead to the bus station in Newport, Oregon where he would pick up the arriving jihadist. The man was to arrive on the bus from Portland the following afternoon. Aziz was confused by his new orders, but he followed them exactly and picked up the young man at the bus station in Newport. The contact spoke Arabic. Aziz told the jihadist he was going to stay at the apartment above the t-shirt shop. Aziz would be staying at a motel.

The man frowned when Aziz mentioned the motel. The expression on his face became downright disgusted when he realized Aziz would be driving him to Depoe Bay on an old, rusty motor scooter. Aziz told the new arrival, whose name he did not know, they would be renting a car to make the trip to Seattle. This made the young man furious. He lit into Aziz about using a credit card for the motel and for the rental car. Aziz tried to reassure him that using a credit card was not a problem. Aziz did not like for his decisions to be challenged. This young person was a martyr for Allah after all and would soon sacrifice himself. Aziz, confident in his self-importance, reassured himself that he would live on to guide the next martyr to his fate.

It was not dark yet, but Aziz drove the new arrival to his apartment. Aziz knew he was taking a risk, but he was anxious to get the man inside. The man carried only a backpack. Aziz told him he was not to go outside the apartment and was not to speak to anybody. Aziz asked him what he wanted to eat. When the man said he did not want anything to eat, Aziz left him and went to his job at The Sea Dog. Aziz assumed the man would spend his time alone putting together the explosives for his mission in Seattle.

Aziz had been given some rudimentary explosives training many years before, but by now he'd forgotten almost everything he'd learned. Bomb-making technology had changed, just as everything else had changed. Aziz knew he would not be any help in preparing bombs for the attack. Aziz was annoyed with the young martyr who had arrived on the bus. Several things were wrong with the man, including this last-minute change of plans. None of it made sense to Aziz, and he felt strongly that something was "off."

Chapter 23

Looking for the Train Station

After his work shift that day, Aziz drove his scooter to Newport to pick up his rental car. He had called ahead to reserve the Ford Taurus with Budget Auto Rentals, and he'd used his own credit card to hold the reservation. When he used the credit card, Detective Nathanial Broderick was notified. Broderick dropped everything and drove to the Budget lot in Newport. He showed his credentials and questioned the rental agent.

Broderick was allowed to look at the car which had been reserved for Aziz. He surreptitiously placed a tracking device on the car. He had a tracking app on his phone and would be able to see in real time exactly where the car was at every moment. Broderick would not need to follow Aziz and keep his rental car in sight to know where it was going. Broderick would follow Aziz's car from a distance. The tracking device he'd placed on Aziz's scooter let Broderick know it had made a trip to the bus station in Newport. Neither Aziz nor the scooter had gone anywhere near Abigail Linder's cove.

Aziz left his scooter at the Budget lot. He would pick it up after the trip to Seattle, when he returned the Taurus. Aziz told the man who was staying in his apartment that they would leave before dawn the next morning. They both had disposable cellphones purchased exclusively for this operation. Aziz parked the Ford Taurus in the parking lot of the motel. It was filled with gas and ready to make the drive the next day. Aziz was energized and even excited. Making contact with the martyr had been disappointing, but the personality of one who was willing to die for Allah was not Aziz's problem. His job was to deliver the martyr to his target.

The next morning before dawn, Aziz picked up the jihadist. They began their drive north from Depoe Bay. They had been traveling less than thirty minutes when the young Jihadist told Aziz that the plans had changed. Aziz was told he was not going to drive the man to Seattle at all. The new plan was that they would go to the train station in Portland, Oregon. Aziz protested that these had not been his instructions. The jihadist was insistent. He told Aziz to call his controller if he did not believe the new plan was valid. Aziz did not want to contact his controller and decided he would go along with the new orders.

Aziz was not happy for more than one reason. He rarely drove a car, in part because he was not confident about his driving skills. Because he hardly ever drove, Aziz was not a good driver. He had a driver's license, but he didn't own a car. More importantly, Aziz was somewhat familiar with the route to Seattle and the Space Needle. He'd done a trial run to Seattle in a rental car to practice driving to the Space

Needle. But Aziz was not at all comfortable driving to the Portland train station. He didn't know this route. Now that the plan had changed, Aziz was in a bad spot. He did not know where he was going. Fortunately, his jihadist passenger had a GPS app on his phone and was able to give Aziz directions. After many wrong turns on the confusing and complicated Portland interchanges, they finally arrived at the train station. The jihadist told Aziz to drive the car into the nearby parking garage.

When they reached the parking garage, the jihadist directed Aziz to an out-of-the-way parking space. Just as Aziz turned off the car's ignition, the jihadist drew a gun out of his jacket pocket and shot Aziz twice in the head. There was a silencer on the gun, so no one heard the shots or saw what happened. The jihadist took a cloth from his pocket and wiped down everything inside the rental car he thought he might have touched. He collected his backpack and locked the car with Aziz's body inside. The young man who would not be a martyr today, exited the parking garage. He hailed a taxi in front of the train station. He returned to the mosque and reported to the imam that Aziz would no longer be a problem.

Two days before Detective Nathanial Broderick had followed Aziz's Ford Taurus to Portland, he had received a lengthy text from Abigail Linder with photos of her cove. She was concerned about something that had happened there the night before. She had discovered a disturbance in the cove's terrain that made it obvious someone had been there and something had happened there. Broderick had passed along the information from Abigail to his superiors. He had urged them to investigate what had happened in the cove. But Broderick himself chose to continue to pursue Aziz and whatever he was planning.

The route Aziz had taken to the train station parking garage had been confused and indirect. Broderick wondered if Aziz was trying to shake anyone who might be following him or if he was just lost. Broderick was delighted when the tracking device on Aziz's car indicated that the car had stopped. Broderick decided he would not drive into the parking garage but would watch for Aziz to come outside. Aziz could be meeting someone inside the parking garage, or he might be meeting someone who was arriving on the train. There were a number of possibilities as to what Aziz might be doing in the train station parking garage and what he might do next.

Broderick could not know at the time that Aziz would never do anything again. Broderick could not know that the small dark man wearing a backpack, who exited the parking garage and hailed a taxi in front of the train station, was the man he should now be following. It was not until the next day that Nathanial Broderick learned Aziz was dead. A passerby had seen Aziz sitting in the driver's seat of his car, slumped over the steering wheel, dead from gunshot wounds to the head. A 911 call brought the Portland police to the scene. The trail Broderick had been following had gone cold. But Aziz's murder definitely got the attention of others in law enforcement and energized the investigation.

Chapter 24

Looking for a Motive

I hadn't heard from Detective Broderick since before Thanksgiving. I'd called a couple of times and left brief messages. He hadn't called me back. Maybe he had a girlfriend? Gaela and I had taken advantage of the unusual early December warm weather. Each day we walked a little bit. Some days we walked more than other days. Sometimes we made it all the way to the beach, but most of the time we didn't make it that far. I always took my binoculars and always looked long and hard at the cove, just to be sure there wasn't anything going on there. Every morning I looked, and every morning the cove looked exactly as it had looked the morning before.

Imagine my shock one morning when I looked at the cove through my binoculars and saw that the beach and the ground on the steep embankment going up from the beach were all torn up. The dirt was gouged out in quite a few places, and there were deep tire tracks clearly visible in the soft soil. Something and somebody had definitely been on the property next door. A vehicle with wheels had been in the cove and had dug deep ruts into the ground. It looked as if someone had been trying to drive a utility vehicle up the hill from the cove into the woods.

I didn't need the binoculars to see the obvious damage that had been done to the ground. Who had been in the cove? What kind of vehicle could have driven there and then driven away? I took several pictures with my cell phone. I even climbed a little ways down my own embankment to get a better view of the way the dirt in the cove had been churned up. I sent the photos to Detective Broderick with an email describing what I'd seen. Since I'd been keeping a daily watch on the cove, the disturbance had to have happened the night before.

I didn't hear back from Broderick right away, and that was unusual. Because of the photos I'd sent to him and the messages I'd left that it was important he contact me, I'd expected an immediate call back. Maybe he was on a case? Maybe he was on vacation? Maybe he had decided not to tell nosy me anything more about what he was doing? Finally I received a one-word text that said, "Thanks." That was it? I guess he was too busy to send me a more detailed reply.

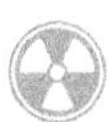

When Gaela and I went out later that day, it was obvious I'd grabbed Broderick's attention with my photos of the destruction in the terrain around the cove. He or somebody had sent an army of technicians to investigate the area. The cove had become a hive of activity. Techs were dressed in hazmat suits, and that certainly aroused my interest. What was that all about? I tried to figure out what was going on, and I tried to find Detective Broderick in the crowd of people who appeared to be mostly on my property. Broderick wasn't there, but it seemed everybody else was. My curiosity was out of control, and I hoped that soon I would hear from my friend in the OSP with all the details. Was he ignoring me?

I'd had enough of the sunshine and unseasonable spring weather. It was December. Christmas was coming, and what had happened to winter? Where were the wild winter storms and the wind that Oregon had promised? I wanted to have an excuse to sit in front of the fire and eat seafood chowder. It seemed as if my housekeeper Anne Marie cooked for the weather. She'd made me a spinach salad for lunch yesterday. It was delicious, but where were the hearty dishes of the winter solstice? I knew someday she was going to make shepherd's pie and beef simmered in onions and wine ... when it finally got cold enough. I was longing for her mashed potatoes with cream cheese. Bob Evans was great in a pinch, but cream cheese in mashed potatoes was the food of the gods.

I hadn't been back to The Sea Dog and hadn't thought too much about Aziz, but I was anxious to know what was happening with the investigation. I'd slowed down on the story I was writing. I'd wanted it to be based on my own adventures and discoveries, but in the absence of any real facts or information, I tended to give my imagination free reign. Since I hadn't heard anything lately, there wasn't any new material from the real world. I knew the tire tracks I'd seen in the cove had raised the stakes, and I wanted to hear from Detective Broderick in the worst way.

Just when I thought everything had come to a standstill, I finally got a call from Detective Broderick. He thanked me for my photos of the cove. He told me that he had sent a team to take imprints of the tires and look at the disturbances to the area. But I already knew that. I'd seen the team as they'd been doing their work. But, the detective said we needed to talk. He said he had news to tell me. He sounded stressed and was not his usual cheerful self. Something had happened.

I told him to come for lunch. Anne Marie was making beef barley soup with mushrooms. She would also serve turkey and bacon club sandwiches with Swiss cheese and Thousand Island dressing because the Detective was coming. She knew he loved her cooking, and she liked to please him. She put some chocolate chip cookies in the oven.

When he arrived, Detective Broderick had dark circles under his eyes. He tried to smile when he greeted Anne Marie and me, but you could see his heart wasn't in it. He looked as if he hadn't slept in days. The creases in his forehead were more pronounced. We sat in front of the fire to eat lunch, and he had two bowls of soup and an enormous club sandwich. He also had some potato chips and ate five cookies. If he had a new girlfriend, she wasn't cooking for him. I could tell he had something he wanted to say to me, but he was trying to delay talking about it. After he'd finished all the cookies, he got to the point.

"Aziz is dead. He was murdered in the parking garage next to the Portland train station. His body was found yesterday."

I was shocked and didn't know what to say. Who could have imagined that Aziz was important enough that anybody would want to murder him? "Was he mugged? What was he doing in Portland? Was he in a car when he was murdered? I didn't think he drove a car."

"He was in the driver's seat of a rental car when he was shot in the head. He was shot twice in the head which is more like an assassination than a mugging. I don't think it was a mugging. He'd had a passenger with him in the car, and we think whoever was in the car with him is the person who killed him." Broderick went on to explain to me about the notifications he had received when Aziz had used his credit card to rent a motel room and then to rent the Taurus from Budget.

Broderick told me about the tracking devices he had placed on Aziz's scooter and on his rental car. He told me how he had followed Aziz to the parking garage at the Portland train station. "I made following Aziz a priority. One reason I haven't been in touch is that so much has happened in such a short period of time. I was not able to participate in the investigation at the cove because I was following Aziz to Portland."

"So the case is hot again … as a result of Aziz's murder?" I was shocked by the news that Aziz was dead, but it seemed as if Broderick's emphasis on following Aziz had turned out to be important.

"I'm sorry to say that the trail that involved Aziz is officially cold. Or at least it has taken a turn in a different direction." The detective sighed and finally continued. "Except for those of the dead man, there were no fingerprints in the car. The car was wiped clean. We have no idea who Aziz's passenger was. We're pretty sure Aziz picked up the mystery passenger at the bus station in Newport the day before he was killed . We have some video of Aziz and someone else from the bus station. Aziz apparently put the guy up at his own apartment and rented a motel room for himself for one night. That's how I knew Aziz was on the move. I was notified when he put the motel reservation on his credit card."

"If this mysterious person stayed in Aziz's apartment, couldn't you get some fingerprints or some DNA or something from the apartment?" I almost interrupted Broderick with my obvious question.

"The man was extremely careful. He didn't leave a single fingerprint that we could find. It's like he was a ghost staying in Aziz's apartment. However, he did leave traces of something while he was there, and this is what has put everybody, including DHS and the FBI, on high alert."

"What did he leave in the apartment?" I couldn't imagine what he might have left that would finally get the authorities to sit up and take notice of Aziz. Too late, though, since Aziz was dead.

"When we investigated Aziz's murder, we found minute traces of radioactivity in his rental car. Subsequently we also found traces of radioactivity in his apartment." Broderick paused and looked to see my reaction to this startling piece of information. "Radioactivity is the last thing anybody expected to find. Testing for radioactivity has recently become a routine part of our screening at a crime scene. With the growing threat of terrorism and increasing fears that ISIS will get hold of material to make a dirty bomb or even a real nuclear weapon, we have developed better ways to test for traces of radiation. Remember the old-fashioned Geiger counter that alerted authorities when something was radioactive? Our equipment has come a long way since the 1950s. Our capabilities always included a way to detect if radiation is present ... in a suitcase, in a storage container, in a room, on a ship, on a person, or wherever."

I was stunned to hear about the radioactivity. My eyes were wide and my jaw literally dropped. I was unable to get my mind around what Broderick had just said. I was silent while he continued.

"Now we are able to tell, after the fact, if nuclear material has been present in a place, even if the actual radioactive item is no longer there. Anything radioactive gives off gamma rays or alpha rays in varying quantities. To be able to detect the tiny particles of this residue that have been left behind requires a super sensitive detection device called a dosimeter. These days we routinely bring a dosimeter to all crime scenes, although we have never before had anything show a positive. That is, we never had a positive reading until we tested Aziz's rental car. Then we also had a positive reading in his apartment. Of course, radiation is everywhere around us all the time. We'd never use the dosimeter to find radioactivity in the radiology department of a hospital or in a dentist's office. We already know there is radioactivity in places like that, and it is supposed to be there. Our dosimeter device is designed to pick up minute traces of radioactivity in places where it isn't supposed to be."

Broderick continued. "You are surprised. Believe me, so was I. So was everybody. The traces found in the car and the apartment were so small—almost undetectable. We didn't find any positive readings in Aziz's motel room, so Aziz was not the source of the radioactivity. Our hypothesis is that the person Aziz picked up at the bus station and took to his apartment had been in contact with something radioactive. We don't know when he was in contact with the radioactive material, but we think it was not long before Aziz took him to his apartment. Likewise, we think the passenger who had been in the car where Aziz was murdered left traces of radioactivity behind. The obvious conclusion is that the person in the car was the same person who stayed in Aziz's house."

I still was speechless … unusual for me. So many questions were swirling in my head, but I couldn't find my voice.

Broderick had lots to tell. "It could be that whoever drove to Portland with Aziz works with radioactive materials, in a hospital or in a radiology office, for example. However, that is unlikely. People who work with these dangerous materials on a regular basis wear special lead aprons to protect them from the radioactivity. The bottom line—whoever murdered Aziz had recently been in contact with something that was radioactive.

"We didn't initially check the cove for radioactivity, but after finding it in Aziz's apartment and in the rental car, we are back at the cove now with our dosimeters. Technicians from the FBI are, as we speak, checking the cove and the woods to see if there are traces that anything radioactive passed through that area. We don't expect to find any evidence of radioactivity in the cove. Aziz never went there. The action in the cove occurred almost two days before Aziz picked up his jihadist at the bus station. As far as we can determine, that contact came on the bus directly from Portland. Aziz did not pick him up in the cove. We don't expect to get any positive readings on the dosimeter near the cove, but we're checking it out anyway.

"I also wanted to tell you that during our original investigation at the cove, we took castings of the imprints of the tire tracks that tore up the sand and dirt. We believe Aziz was connected in some way to the man whose body washed ashore on your beach, but we don't know if these new tire tracks in the cove are connected to Aziz. We wonder why the MO changed and why Aziz picked up his contact at the Newport bus station, rather than in the cove. Our videos of the bus station might yield something through facial recognition software, but if that guy is not already in the system, we won't have anything. Of course, we will enter his face from the bus station videos into that database anyway, in case he turns up some place in the future."

I finally found my voice. "Wow! That is quite a lot of news. I don't hear anything from you for ages, and all at once you have an almost unbelievable story to tell me. Is there enough radioactivity involved to be dangerous to people or animals?" I was concerned about Gaela digging in the ground and uncovering something she shouldn't.

"Even if we were to find something radioactive at the cove, it will undoubtedly be a much smaller amount than you would get in a dental X-ray. Nothing to worry about at all. But you can imagine that any time radioactivity shows up, even a small amount gets a lot of attention from everybody. That's where we are now."

"I appreciate the update, Nathanial. I continue to keep your confidences and hope you will find a way to follow this through to its conclusion. If I can help, let me know."

"It helps me to talk to a person who writes about and unravels mysteries," Nathanial smiled at me, his first genuine smile of the day. "Things become clearer in my own mind as I talk them over with you. With your observation that some kind of vehicle had been driving around in the area of the cove, you gave us the information that sent our investigation there. Because you had been walking by the cove every day, you were able to tell us the exact night it all happened. We are lucky it didn't rain and destroy the tracks before we had a chance to cast them. Thanks to you, we learned about all of this right away after it happened. I will let you know what comes of today's investigation into the radioactivity."

Broderick smiled at me again. "At least you won't have to worry about Aziz letting himself into your house in the future." Detective Broderick thanked Anne Marie for the delicious lunch. She had wrapped an extra sandwich and more cookies and put them in a paper bag for the detective to take with him. He was most appreciative. I wondered if the man ever ate anything except what he ate when he came to my house. He did know there was a diner in town, so I knew he wouldn't starve.

The many new pieces of information Broderick had just reported to me put an entirely new spin on the mystery. If Aziz had been the point man in Depoe Bay and now he was dead, what did that mean? If he'd picked up his contact from the bus station and not from the cove, did that mean the person who had handled the radioactive materials did not come ashore from the Pacific? Did he come from somewhere in the United States? I knew the emergence of homegrown jihadists was on the rise. These bad boys and girls were the newest concern for law enforcement and intelligence organizations.

Who had shot Aziz, and why? Had he made his superiors angry? Who were those superiors? Had he shown incompetence? Was he a loose end? Was he a threat to a larger plot? Did somebody think he would reveal something he wasn't supposed to reveal? And most importantly, what did the traces of radioactivity mean? Did the people who killed Aziz have some kind of nuclear weapon? If they had one, what did they intend to do with it? My brain was going crazy processing the new information I'd heard that day. I wasn't able to put it together in any rational pattern. I now had more pieces of the puzzle, but I didn't yet have enough pieces. Or maybe I just didn't have the right pieces.

I took Gaela for a walk to the beach. I needed to clear my head, and I was curious about what was going on in the cove. There were still a few crime scene technicians milling around, and I wondered if they had found any radioactivity or anything else that would move the investigation forward. Broderick had finally convinced the FBI and other agencies to show an interest in Aziz and in this case. Now Aziz was dead. Surely the discovery of radioactivity in several locations would motivate more law enforcement people to pursue the investigation. It had already brought the feds on board.

The late afternoon weather was getting colder, and it looked like a storm might be on the way. Gaela and I hurried back to the house and turned on the gas fireplace. Anne Marie had made Italian meatballs with beef, pork, and veal for dinner. It was my mother's recipe. They are the best meatballs in the world. A saucepan of homemade spaghetti sauce was on the stove, and a pot of water, complete with EVOO and salt, also sat on the stove. There was a beautiful artichoke and romaine lettuce salad in the refrigerator. Gaela loves spaghetti and so do I. We decided not to think about the case for a few hours and settled down to enjoy the fire and our Italian feast.

Chapter 25

Looking for Winter

A wild winter storm had begun to batter the Pacific Coast, and I was loving every minute of it. Freezing rain was mixed with snow. It was so extraordinary. I wish I had the artistic ability to paint the scene outside my windows. Gaela didn't like going out in it and was happy to wear her red winter coat when she went to the backyard for just a few seconds. We spent a lot of time in front of the fire, and since Detective Broderick's last visit, I was spending more time in front of my computer working on a fictionalized account of the real intrigue that was happening all around me.

Detective Broderick braved the storm to come by again today with an update about the radioactivity the crime scene techs had found in the cove. I had to give the man credit for his efforts to keep me informed. The facts were being collected in dribs and drabs, and it seemed that whenever there was something of importance to tell, Broderick made an effort to come to the house and give me a report. Could that have anything to do with Anne Marie's delicious cooking?

When he came to the house this afternoon, Broderick said he wanted to give me an update, but he had to leave soon to attend a meeting. I could see he was disappointed to have to turn down an invitation to stay for dinner. Anne Marie had almond flavored sour cream cupcakes in the oven, and the aroma from heaven filled my cottage. She had a bittersweet chocolate glaze melting on the stove. The chocolate glaze would be poured over the cupcakes as soon as they came out of the oven. The chocolate soaked into the warm cupcakes, and oh my! Anne Marie made the mistake of describing the cupcakes to Detective Broderick. Anne Marie told him to come back later to get some of the exquisite pastries.

Anne Marie had made a pork roast for my dinner. She had also made mashed potatoes and gravy, an apple and pecan salad, and sauteed French green beans. It was a wonderful winter meal. I'd invited Detective Broderick to join me for the pork roast because there was way too much for me to eat, even considering the leftover roast pork sandwiches I would have for future lunches.

Before he left for his meeting, I'd asked him to come back and have dinner with me. I thought the poor man would swoon when I told him what the menu was going to be. He said he would love to have dinner, but he had to drive that night to Salem, the capital of the state of Oregon. Broderick was truly crushed to have to say no to sour cream cupcakes with dark chocolate glaze and a pork roast dinner. He finally left saying he was already going to be late for his meeting in Salem. Did I imagine that he was salivating as he went out the door?

In addition to the news about the radioactivity, Broderick had shared with me more news about the disturbances in the soil of the incline going up the hill to the woods opposite my cove. When I'd sent him the photographs of the damage to the terrain, the investigation had taken on more importance and received more attention from law enforcement at every level. As the drama of the investigation played out, I was keeping my eyes open and reporting things to Broderick when something didn't seem right. I think he was more willing to keep me updated about what was happening in the case because of the things I had discovered and related to him.

Today he told me they'd identified the tire imprints in the dirt as those from a John Deere utility vehicle. The treads which had left the tracks were consistent with the tires on a 4X4 heavy duty Gator that could carry more than a thousand pounds in its cargo hold. There were several models of these utility vehicles that resemble small tractors, and they all use the type of tires which had been identified. To take the trouble to acquire such a specialized vehicle and drive it through the woods indicated that significant planning had taken place. Something of great value had been transported from the cove, through the woods, and to the road.

The most important information was that more traces of radioactivity had been found in the dirt around the cove. The level of radioactivity on the beach and in the woods was significantly greater than the amounts found in Aziz's apartment and in his rental car. Something heavy and radio-active had been brought ashore. If it had not been for the radioactivity that was discovered alongside the tire treads, law enforcement would probably not have paid as much attention to this location.

There had been a myriad of shoeprints in the dirt of the cove as well, and the crime scene technicians concluded that there were four people involved in whatever had occurred there in the middle of the night. Investigators had been able to determine that there were probably three men and one woman who had participated in the arrival and transfer of the radioactive material and whatever else they had transported in the Gator.

The authorities had tracked the path of the Gator through the pine forest from the cove to the road. This had been done by following the trail of radioactivity that the Gator had left in its wake. But the road was where the trail stopped abruptly. The obvious conclusion was that when the Gator reached the road, it had been loaded aboard another vehicle and driven away from the scene.

Because of my observations, law enforcement knew exactly what night the activity in the cove had occurred. It would be useful to find out what large ships had been sailing off the Oregon Coast that night. Was it possible to find out that kind of information? The mysterious people and their mysterious cargo had come from someplace in the Pacific Ocean. Where exactly had they come from?

Knowing the night the arrival at the cove had taken place also made it possible for law enforcement to check security videos and find a possible route for whatever vehicle might have delivered and picked up the utility 4X4. Not many vehicles of any kind came down the paved road near my house. If a security camera of any kind happened to record a truck or a van on my road that night, there might be a lead to the 4X4 and the radioactivity.

Investigators could only guess at a precise timeline, but at least they had the correct night. The arrival of the radioactive materials in the cove and its transport via the Gator had to have occurred while it was dark. Broderick had shared with me his theory that he thought whoever had transported the radioactive "thing" had made a mistake. It was obvious that a great deal of planning had gone into the operation, but for some reason, there had been no attempt to smooth over the deep ruts in the dirt of the embankment and the tire tracks and footprints in the sandy cove. This suggested to Broderick that the operators of the Gator had little experience with the way a utility vehicle could tear up soft terrain. He also knew, from looking at the ruts in the sand and dirt, that the Gator had been carrying an exceptionally heavy load.

Broderick was convinced the operation had occurred at night and that the perpetrators had been in a rush. If the people driving the Gator had been able to see all the tire tracks and footprints they'd left behind, he thought they would have made some effort to cover up the mess they'd made. If they'd not been in such a hurry, they might have taken the time to notice their telltale tracks and smooth over the evidence. They had ignored all that, either because they hadn't noticed it or because they had been pressed for time. Broderick hoped that the traces of radioactivity that had been discovered in the cove as well as the information about the Gator would lead to something useful. But that night, Broderick was stumped, and he'd intimated that his colleagues were also stymied.

Chapter 26

Looking For Christmas

*I*t was a couple of days before Christmas, and I was beginning to wonder if my decision to spend the holidays alone had been a mistake. I'd done the big family reunion thing at Thanksgiving and part of trying to be an eccentric recluse was to avoid all the Christmas hoopla. I'd driven the Christmas train full speed ahead through most of my adult life. I'd outdone myself year after year. I'd overdone the season with enormous holiday parties and elaborate meals, fresh boxwood garlands, and handmade gifts.

Eventually, it had become an onerous time of year that I'd begun to dread. It was my fault; the dread was entirely of my own making. I had so raised expectations among my family and friends, and for myself, that I'd made it impossible to compete with myself and win, let alone enjoy anything. I had become Super Santa beyond belief. It takes weeks to make more than one hundred loaves of cheese bread, distribute it to friends and neighbors, and mail it to relatives throughout the country. I'd had to go cold turkey to break myself from the whirling Christmas dervish I'd become. Now I was thinking how lonely I might be on Christmas Day.

Christmas Eve was going to be fine. I no longer attended church regularly, but I had always enjoyed attending Christmas Eve midnight mass. I loved singing Christmas carols and lighting candles as the congregation sang "Silent Night." Before the church service, I was going to treat myself to a seafood dinner at The Sea Dog. Although I didn't think I could legitimately claim any Italian ancestry, I thought the Italian tradition of eating seven fishes on Christmas Eve was a tradition I was meant to observe. Now that Aziz was dead, I felt I could return to the Sea Dog as often as I wanted. I already had my reservation and was thinking about what I would order. Would I dare order seven different seafood items? I guess one big fried seafood platter would go a long way toward covering that tradition.

I'd heard there was a fabulous Christmas Day buffet at the hotel outside of town. The Depoe Bay Hotel Pacific was well-known and expensive. Their buffet sounded promising, and I'd made a reservation. I had never eaten at the Pacific, but I'd heard the food was wonderful. I wanted to try it and thought I would have a good time. I'd long ago gotten over being self-conscious about eating out alone, but this would be Christmas Day. I didn't want any pitying looks in my direction as I hobbled back and forth to my table for one with heaping plateful after heaping plateful from the buffet table.

My daughter was planning to spend Christmas in Connecticut with her new husband's family. My granddaughter would be in Old Lyme with her mother. They had invited me to join them, but it was too far away. My Bowdoin grandson was going to Portland, Maine again. It seemed this young woman was someone very special. Everybody was going to be spending Christmas with somebody they loved, and so was I. Gaela and I would open our stockings and our presents together on Christmas morning. Then we would get all dressed up, or at least I would get all dressed up, and we would go to the Depoe Bay Hotel Pacific.

I'd ordered my gifts over the internet—wrapped and delivered for an additional fee which I was more than delighted to pay. I'd asked everyone what they wanted and sent them what they'd requested. Then I sent everybody money. Money was always a popular gift. I sent an outrageously expensive, already-sliced organic ham to the Old Lyme, Connecticut crowd and to the Portland, Maine crowd.

I'd bought gifts for Gaela and gifts for myself and had them sent to me. Where was Amazon when my daughter was little? I remember driving hundreds of miles one year to try to find the exact doll that everyone was asking for. I loved Amazon. It was a recluse's best friend. I ordered everything I needed, and a lot I didn't need, from Amazon. Bless them. They hardly ever got it wrong.

I'd been so wrapped up in worrying about my own holidays, I had almost forgotten to wonder if Detective Broderick had anybody with whom to spend Christmas. Maybe I should invite him for tea or soup on Boxing Day or something? Anne Marie was coming to my house the day after Christmas although I'd offered to let her have the week off. She would be happy to make food for Nathanial, so I decided to call and ask him over for lunch on Boxing Day.

Nathanial Broderick had probably never heard of Boxing Day. Most Americans don't know what it is unless they read British novels which refer to this day-after-Christmas holiday which is celebrated by our English-speaking friends across the pond and maybe in Australia and Canada. Broderick was free the day after Christmas and said he'd love to come for lunch. Anne Marie was going to make something special.

I'd been in Oregon for three months, and I loved living on the coast. It was beautiful and wild. I loved my house and garden. I loved my housekeeper and her amazing cooking. I loved the restaurants in the area. The whole recluse identity I'd thought would be so appealing … well, that was somewhat questionable. Whether or not I was making a success of living a solitary life was still to be determined. Things had happened.

I'd found a dead body on my beach. Then I'd found a backpack with a bomb inside it on my beach. Then I'd found a beaten-up raft in my cove with another backpack bomb inside it. It wasn't what I'd planned, but real life never turns out as one has planned. And what would I have done with myself, my time, my brain, or my imagination if all this hadn't happened to me. Would I have died of boredom? Probably! The fact was I loved the excitement of being involved in a mystery. I'd spent years writing about mysteries, and I had loved doing that. Now I was involved in the real thing. It was all happening on my doorstep, and I loved being involved in the real thing even more.

I'd gone to church on Christmas Eve, and it had been a lovely service. I'd sung my heart out during the Christmas carols, and that had been good for me. I still remembered all the verses to the old favorites, and the Episcopal Church where I'd attended the service was still, thank God, singing the old favorites. I wasn't feeling at all sorry for myself because I'd decided to celebrate Christmas without my family.

I'd had an email from my granddaughter. She said she was having a great time in Connecticut. She told me her new stepfather's family was lots of fun. She said they were eating well, and there were many gifts under the tree. They had received the ham, and everyone loved it. What more could one ask of Christmas? We did some Zoom on Christmas morning, and I felt in touch with most of the people I cared about. I was once again thankful I hadn't attempted to put on a Christmas extravaganza, the ridiculous uber celebration I had produced year after year in the past.

I'd purchased chocolate croissants and some Canadian bacon for my Christmas morning breakfast. These were two foods which were expensive and somewhat difficult to find. I considered both these purchases to be indulgences but splurged because it was Christmas. Gaela wasn't allowed to eat chocolate, but she could help me eat the Canadian bacon. We enjoyed our breakfast and had a short walk. It was cold and blustery, but Mother Nature had decided to give Depoe Bay a break in the rain department for Christmas Day.

My reservation at the Hotel Pacific for the Christmas buffet was at two o'clock. I got dressed up and decided to put on lipstick. It was Christmas after all. I had a wonderful black cashmere dress with a scoop neck. Scoop neck dresses are usually not the first choice for older women, but I had my family pearls to wear which always distracted from any neck wrinkles that might otherwise be seen. I wore a red silk scarf and my long leather coat. My bright red lipstick matched the scarf. Yes, it was Christmas. What a fashion plate I was! Gaela and I drove to the Depoe Bay Hotel Pacific. I was lucky and got a handicap parking spot. There were lots of cars in the parking lot, so that meant the food was probably going to be unusually good.

I loved the buffet and ate until I was way past full. I had my leftovers wrapped for Gaela. Wrapping leftovers is not really de rigeur at buffets, but I was old and left a big tip. The food was already on my plate, so they let me take it home without a fuss. The buffet had been ridiculously expensive anyway. One small bag of leftovers was the least they could do for me. I was sated and tired. Gaela loved the leftover roast beef and Yorkshire pudding I had brought for her. We took a long Christmas nap when we got home.

I hadn't heard my phone ring, but when I woke up I saw that Detective Broderick had called. Didn't he know it was Christmas Day? If he was calling me on Christmas Day, he must not have any kind of personal life at all. I called him back and told him I was looking forward to seeing him at noon for lunch on the 26th. I knew how much he loved Anne Marie's cooking. When the detective came for a meal or a snack, she always went the extra mile to show off a little bit for him.

Chapter 27

Looking for Anything

*I was surprised at how delighted I was to see Detec-*tive Broderick when he showed up the day after Christmas. Had he become a friend of mine while I wasn't looking? He seemed genuinely happy to see me, too, and he was even happier to see Anne Marie in the kitchen. He brought each of us a bouquet of red and white roses. How sweet was that? Anne Marie had tears in her eyes when he handed her the flowers. She was truly touched. I was too.

Nathanial Broderick made a nice speech when he presented us with the flowers. "I knew I needed to consult with Abigail Linder. She often has a novel (pun intended) way of looking at a mystery. Just as importantly, she has a housekeeper who can cook like a Cordon Bleu angel. It is always fun to visit Abigail and Anne Marie."

Anne Marie had made turkey and wild rice soup, and it was a meal in itself. Rich with celery and onions and fresh thyme, the soup was a work of art, culinarily speaking. She'd also made Dungeness crab salad sandwiches. The crab salad was a new recipe for her, and the Russian dressing she'd mixed with the crab meat was her own homemade special sauce. It had little bits of minced red onion, sweet gherkins, and Worcestershire sauce in it, and it was incredible. She had gone all out for Broderick today, and he loved it. He ate every bite and had second helpings of everything.

Anne Marie brought out a moist almond sponge cake with whipped cream icing for dessert, and Broderick literally groaned when he saw it. The cake had toasted sliced almonds on the top and in between the layers. Nathanial groaned again when he took his first bite. It was a wonderful day for food. I guessed he had not had any kind of special Christmas dinner or he would not have been able to eat as much as he had on the day after Christmas.

The last time Detective Broderick had been at my house, he had been discouraged and even downright depressed. He did not seem quite as down when he'd arrived for lunch today. After we had eaten, he brought me up to date on the Aziz murder and his still-fruitless search for the people involved with the radioactivity. He told me he had nowhere to go in his efforts to find Aziz's killer. His attempts to trace the people with the Gator and the radioactive materials were likewise going nowhere. Even the FBI, with all of their resources, had come to a dead end. Broderick didn't know much of anything new that he had not known about and reported to me the last time we'd talked. I could see he was continuing to feel frustrated about his lack of progress. The man literally lived for his work, and when work was not going well, he was way too dejected.

We talked about the Gator and the imprints its tires had left in the sand of the cove and in the soft ground of the embankment going up from the cove. We both saw this as perhaps the only mistake the people involved in this undertaking had made. Broderick told me that the probable make and model of the Gator had been determined from the tire tread imprints left in the soft sand and dirt. These markings had been sharp and distinct, which indicated that the Gator could be new. Or it might just mean that the tires on the Gator were new.

Broderick felt strongly that the Gator had been purchased for the specific purpose of ferrying people and materials through the woods from the ocean cove to the road. Somebody had known what they were doing when they purchased the Gator. It was the perfect vehicle for the job, and Broderick was betting the Gator was now sitting in someone's garage someplace. Its usefulness had come to an end—at least until the next bunch of jihadists arrived in a remote location.

Broderick prided himself on being able to find a pattern in a case from just a few clues, but he was not able to put things together on this one. He knew it was an unusually important case. With radioactive materials involved, everybody ought to think it was an unusually important case! The Gator pickup at the cove and the transport, which had ended up with the complete disappearance of the Gator and its contents, had obviously been extremely well planned. A lot of careful forethought had gone into that part of the operation. Whoever was behind this had covered their tracks almost perfectly. Except, they obviously and mistakenly had left quite a few of their tracks behind.

Broderick had one dead guy in a parking garage in Portland and some Gator tracks in a cove in Depoe Bay. He had radioactivity in both places so he knew they were connected. He just didn't know yet exactly how all the pieces fit together. He needed a fresh approach, an epiphany, anything. He hoped I would be able to provide the inspiration he was looking for.

I was going to do my best for the detective. I'd been thinking. The facts and my own imagination had been rolling around in my head, and I'd come up with several ideas. In my mystery novels, it was usually that one mistake the perpetrators of a "perfect crime" made which eventually solved the case. The mysterious group and their radioactive cargo had arrived at night. Because it was dark, among other possible reasons, none of them had noticed that the Gator had left tell-tale tire tracks behind. If these people had seen the mess they'd left, I was certain they would have done something about it. I told Broderick he needed to pursue the clue of the Gator's tires. When I made this suggestion, he looked at me as if I had three heads. I knew he was thinking he'd already spent too much time gathering information about the Gator and its tires.

Then I told him he had another clue … the murder of Aziz. I told him I didn't think he had given that aspect of the case enough thought. He told me he'd thought of nothing else day and night since Aziz had died.

"You have a murder at the train station in Portland, and you have Gator tracks in a cove near Depoe Bay. We know Depoe Bay and my cove were a destination for the previously discovered dead body, the tattered raft, and the backpack bombs. Now we have another group arriving in the same exact place. What is so special about this particular place along the Pacific Coast? There must be hundreds of coves which would be suitable for a small raft to come ashore. I think you need to find out who owns the property next to mine. Who is the owner of the other half of my cove? Who owns those woods?"

I continued with my analysis. "The people who brought the Gator through the woods to the cove were confident they would not be trespassing on some unknown person's property. They knew they could travel freely back and forth from the road to the cove. They knew they could do whatever they wanted to do in the cove, at least in their half of it. They knew they could come and go at will on the land and through the woods next to mine. Why pick this location in the first place? Why would they be confident that no one would object to their presence or accuse them of trespassing? If you find the owner of this property, if indeed it is possible to find that information, you will be adding to your clues. It may be another dead end, but it might help." I admitted to myself that I was much too eager to know who owned the property next to mine. I hoped Detective Broderick would find out that information for me.

"We will probably never know why Aziz was sent to Depoe Bay. Why was he sent as a sleeper agent to this small town so many years ago? He did a remarkable job of 'fitting in' here in spite of his accent and his Middle Eastern looks. But why was he sent here in the first place? He was sent here such a long time ago." Broderick was focused on Aziz's decision to make his home in Depoe Bay.

I personally didn't think we would ever know why Aziz had come here, and I almost interrupted Broderick to bring him back to the point at hand. "I don't think this is a useful line of inquiry. My theory on Aziz is that he was sent here to establish a cover for himself. I think his handlers pretty much forgot about him. Maybe the group who was running him has changed. We know that al-Qaeda was operationally strong prior to 9/11. Now ISIS seems to have taken over as the superior terrorist force in the Middle East. This may have something to do with the death of Bin Laden and the fact that al-Zawahiri is now quite elderly and in poor health. Has al-Qaeda of yesteryear ceded its leadership role in terrorism to ISIS?"

Broderick tended to agree. "I have speculated in my own mind that Aziz was considered a liability by this group that has the Gator and whose overseas compatriots arrived most recently. Maybe they felt Aziz had gone native or had lost his edge for jihad. It is obvious that he was support staff. He was not a bomb maker or a suicide vest kind of operative. . His training, whatever that might have been, occurred more than fifteen years ago, before 9/11. His training was out of date, and Aziz himself was out of date."

Broderick continued. "I am sure these new jihadists are quite a bit younger than Aziz, more the ages of the terrorists in Paris and Brussels and the ones in San Bernardino. Aziz was deadwood. It was bad luck and not his fault that the typhoon in the fall took out his backpack bomber. If the weather had not intervened to destroy that plan and the operation had turned out to be a success for him, he might have proven his value. Maybe his new handlers would have kept him on."

I added my two cents and agreed that Aziz had become a loser for the cause. "Aziz made a mistake by using his credit card to rent a motel room and a car. He should have stayed in his own apartment with the person he picked up at the bus station. Even if there wasn't room for both of them and as uncomfortable as that might have been for Aziz, he should have found another way to house his contact. Or he should have moved to a larger place if he knew he was going to have to accommodate fellow jihadists. The old motor scooter was his only means of transportation until he used his credit card to rent a car. He was operating on a shoestring and wasn't thinking along the lines of how present-day jihadist operations are run. Money is no object for jihad these days. They have all that oil money, and they raise funds through a thousand bogus 'charitable' Muslim organizations. And then they have hawala which not only circumvents the IRS, it also helps to avoid scrutiny about what frauds they are perpetrating, who they're stealing from, and what terrorist organizations they are funding. Aziz was an anachronism, and he had to go."

I had thought a great deal about the contact who had arrived on the bus from Portland. "When you think about it, sending somebody from Portland on the bus to meet with Aziz was taking a ridiculously big chance. It seems obvious to me that the only reason that person came to Depoe Bay was to get Aziz to drive to the Portland train station so he could be murdered in the parking garage. The contact became involved with Aziz so the two of them could drive to Portland for the hit. The murder had to happen in a city, a place where the death could be blamed on a mugging."

Then Broderick told me something I didn't know. "We have pursued facial recognition software on the man who arrived on the bus, but we can't match him to anybody in any existing database." This was the first time Broderick had mentioned they'd run the bus rider through their facial recognition software. I'd been wondering if they had tried to identify Aziz's guest and killer that way.

I tried to get Broderick to think beyond the considerable technical tools he had at his disposal. "I think that young assassin is now quite well hidden. You will not find him going out to the bars and clubs in Portland. He is being kept under wraps somewhere while he is working at something or just being held in reserve for whatever his mission is going to be. Given what we know about everything, where would you guess Aziz's killer is being harbored? He may or may not speak any English, so where would he be able to hide out so he did not have to go out in public for any reason? People have to buy food to eat. People have to have a place to sleep, and they have to wash their clothes. According to the analysis of the footprints, there are four of them. These four need a place to stay that has plenty of room. It won't be a hotel or a motel. They can't use credit cards. Think about it."

Broderick had paid attention to my argument. "A mosque! Or a private home! And because there are four of them, I will bet they are living at a mosque someplace! That is where Aziz's killer is staying. At least that's where he and his cohorts are staying for a while. I'm sure of it! They may have already moved on from Portland, but I'm sure you are right about this. Unfortunately, with the current administration in Washington, D.C., we have to keep our hands off all mosques. This president has filled his administration with Muslims, and they will not allow surveillance or investigations of mosques, even the ones that are known to be extremely radicalized. The head of the CIA is a Muslim. Can you believe that? How did that happen? It's a real problem, and the FBI has been told not to go near mosques. The feds know there are certain troublemakers they need to keep their eyes on, but they can't get close to them. Mosques in the U.S. are more protected right now than they have ever been. It's impossible to get a search warrant for a mosque. The federal government has been adamant that no mosques will be searched or investigated. The U.S. attorney general has a hang-up that Muslims are being discriminated against, even though it's mostly Muslims who are trying to kill us. There will not be any warrants asked for or issued for any of these places, even with just cause. It is not going to happen. It's the strangest policy I have ever encountered in my entire law enforcement career. My friends in the FBI are being completely blocked in all of their terrorism investigations. Of course, these people are going to hang out and hide out in mosques. They know they are untouchable there. Mosques in the USA are our version of Europe's 'no go zones.' It's completely absurd and very dangerous." Broderick spoke with disgust and was clearly frustrated.

He continued. "I remember a few days after San Bernardino, the kooky couple's neighbors said they thought something untoward was going on in Tashfeen and Farook's garage. Packages were being delivered all the time, and people were coming and going at all hours of the day and night. It was definitely suspicious activity. After the fact, people were outraged that the neighbors didn't speak up about their suspicions and call the authorities."

Broderick was remembering things from the past that had disgusted him. He was on a roll. "Then, just after the San Bernardino attacks, the United States attorney general said her 'greatest fear' was that Muslims were going to be discriminated against and singled out for scrutiny and suspicion. Her greatest fear was not that there might be more terror attacks on the horizon or that people might hesitate to call authorities if they saw suspicious activity in the future. Oh, no, her greatest fear was that somebody might say something against a Muslim, even a suspicious Muslim.

"Of course not all Muslims are terrorists. But the extremist Muslims, the terrorists, want to destroy our culture and kill as many of us as they can. How many Hindus or Buddhists or Seventh Day Adventists have been attacking cafes and theatres and Christmas parties lately? Please! After San Bernardino and the failure of the neighbors to do anything about their suspicions, we are being urged to 'see something; say something'—but not if it's about a Muslim. The feds will be all over you if you call authorities about or cast any aspersions against suspicious Muslims. The world is looney tunes!!" Broderick sighed and put his head down. I was as discouraged as Broderick about where the world and my country were heading. It was absurd beyond belief!

"So, our latest arrivals are probably hiding out in a mosque in Portland unless they've already moved on to someplace else. We have to speculate that some imam in Portland is or was giving shelter to these jihadists who have radioactive materials in their possession. You would think that the radioactivity thing alone would motivate Homeland Security to want to track down these people. But if they are in a mosque, they are untouchable. We will never know if that mosque is contaminated with radioactivity. I don't know where to go from here." Nathanial Broderick was terribly disheartened.

"Do you have access to membership lists from any of the mosques? Is there any way you could find out who in the Portland area has bought, in the past year or two, the exact model of Gator you are looking for? If you could compare the mosque membership lists with the list of those who have purchased Gators, there might be a possible match between mosque membership and a Gator purchase. To look at mosque membership would currently be a politically impossible thing to do. Could you get the information some way other than going through the FBI?" I was trying to be helpful, but I realized in many ways that Nathanial's hands were tied.

"It's just that so many of the president's appointments to important positions have been Muslims. He's comfortable around Muslims. He's not as comfortable around Christians, and he wants to talk about the Crusades and how terrible Christians have been down through the ages." Nathanial knew he was saying things he was not allowed to say, but he knew I wouldn't turn him in. "I don't know if there is any other way I can get the mosque membership lists. I can probably get the Gator purchases list through the FBI. I just can't tell them what other list I am matching against the list of Gator owners. If I told anybody I was looking at mosque membership, my investigation would be shut down in about five seconds. But it might be worth a try."

I'd run out of ideas, too, for now. "That's the only thing I can think of. These people who came into the cove from the Pacific Ocean in the middle of the night and rode the Gator through the woods aren't in the country legally. You can be sure they are keeping as low a profile as they possibly can. I doubt if they are still in Portland, but I will bet you anything, they stayed hidden at a Portland mosque for some period of time during their journey. How else could they exist without ever using a credit card? They've never rented a car or bought anything at a grocery store or gone out in public. It's too bad you can't take that Geiger counter, or whatever you are calling it these days, around to the various mosques in Portland to find out if there are traces of radioactivity in any of them. As sensitive as you claim your machine is, I imagine it would be able to pick up some traces that these people had been there, even if they're gone by now. At least you could identify the mosque where they'd been staying. Then you would know which imam to watch."

Detective Broderick's eyes lit up. I could tell something I'd said had given him an idea. I knew he was sharing more information about this case with me than he was supposed to share. The case had to have a top-secret classification because of its radioactive materials aspect. I was flattered Broderick wanted to discuss things with me. I hoped some things I'd said had jogged his brain and suggested a new path for moving his case forward. He seemed more upbeat when he left my house than when he'd arrived. Part of that was the food Anne Marie had made for him, but I hope he might have thought of something new because of our discussion.

I was unhappy that the case had hit so many dead ends. The restrictions on following good leads burned me because so much was politically forbidden. It's a good thing I was old and dabbled in law enforcement only through writing novels and through my friend Nathanial Broderick. It was a good thing for all concerned that I wasn't a member of law enforcement. I was too independent and too much of a rebel to ever have considered such a career. My associations with crime were strictly of the fictional sort. At least, they'd been fictional until I had moved to Depoe Bay and been thrust into the middle of a real-life criminal investigation because of my discoveries on the beach. Crime in reality was exciting, but crimes in novels were much easier to control … and to solve.

Chapter 28

Looking for Access

Through a series of shell corporations, Dean Abadi had purchased an events planning company based in the Cleveland, Ohio area. The *Let Us Entertain You* group had an excellent reputation and arranged all the most important events in the community. They did the expensive bar mitzvahs and bat mitzvahs in Shaker Heights. Everybody wanted them to do birthdays, anniversaries, and every kind of party short of weddings. They would do wedding showers and baby showers, and they would plan and organize a rehearsal dinner, even on the beach of Lake Erie. But they drew the line at weddings. They worked with the best caterers in the Cleveland metropolitan area, and they were booked months and years in advance. *LUEY* was an exceptionally profitable business.

Let Us Entertain You had done many events at the Quicken Loans Arena, commonly referred to as "The Q." Everybody associated with the multipurpose arena in downtown Cleveland knew *Let Us Entertain You.* They were a first-rate company. They were a familiar fixture on the local party scene and had organized and put on countless breakfasts, lunches, and dinners before and after sporting events at "The Q." They organized large receptions for hundreds of people, and they arranged small, intimate gatherings for twenty in the luxurious skyboxes. They would be way too busy during the Republican National Convention in July. In fact, before the end of December of the previous year, they were already fully booked for the convention in the upcoming summer.

Dean had been well aware of the reputation and popularity of the events planning company when he'd bought it. He had made the long-time owners an offer they could not possibly refuse. After the papers were signed, the older couple, who had started the company many years earlier, would be able to retire in grand style. They'd never in a million years imagined that their small company would grow into such a hugely successful business, let alone that they would be able to sell it for millions of dollars.

They signed a non-disclosure agreement when they sold the company. The new owners, a nameless and faceless LLC which could never be traced to a real person, said they did not want current and potential customers to have any doubts about the continuity of the quality of the services the company provided. They wanted customers to feel confident that the high standards the previous owners had always insisted on would continue. This made sense to the sellers, and they agreed to abide by these conditions and maintain their silence about the sale for one year. No one knew the company had changed hands and was now under new ownership. No one knew who currently owned *LUEY.*

Even the numerous employees who worked for *LUEY* were not aware that the business had new owners. The company's success over the years had led to the hiring of more and more people. The organizational structure had become quite complex as layers of decision-making and multiple new services were added to the growing enterprise. Payroll checks would continue to be issued in the name of the business. Nothing had really changed when ownership had been transferred to one of Dean's LLCs with its generic and meaningless name. *Let Us Entertain You* continued, without a pause in their bookings, to conduct business as usual.

As early as March, *Let Us Entertain You* was gearing up for the multitude of events it would be organizing for the Republican National Convention at the Quicken Loans Arena in Cleveland in July. They were hiring extra people and had leased additional office space. *LUEY* would be in charge of putting on multiple events during the Republican Convention. The most important night, of course, was the final evening after the candidates were chosen and the party came together to show unity and enthusiasm for itself. "The Q" would be packed as Republicans listened to a final evening of speeches.

Every convention wanted to outdo the conventions of previous years, and this convention was no exception. *Let Us Entertain You* was responsible for the balloons, the tickertape, and the hoopla that would surround the nominee's speech on the final night. The balloons were going to be better than ever this year. It was rumored at *Let Us Entertain You* that someone in the company had invented a new air-circulating machine to keep the balloons floating in the air throughout the finale of the convention.

Thousands of red, white, and blue balloons would be dropped from the ceiling as usual. In the past, when the helium inside the balloons had lost its power, they sank to the ground and sat there on the floor in piles for people to step on and kick out of the way. A few people would pick them up and pop them. Sometimes, the helium filled balloons floated to the ceiling of the building and got stuck there in the rafters of the structure until they popped or died a slow death from loss of gas. Everyone loved balloons as long as they were kept inside, but the helium-filled orbs, whether they were going up or down, didn't stay in circulation for very long.

Supposedly, somebody at *LUEY* had figured out a way to keep the balloons floating in the air during the merriment of the convention's final night. Balloons would still be falling to the ground, but they would not gather and remain in bothersome clumps on the floor. The technology was a closely held secret, but employees knew that special machines were being brought in to keep the air blowing and the balloons circulating. It was going to be a wonderful and innovative surprise.

Chapter 29

Looking for Opportunity

*T*he Wells Fargo Center at 3601 South Broad Street in Philadelphia was more than twenty-five years old. From July 25th through July 28th, the center was scheduled to host the Democrat National Convention which would nominate its party's candidate to run for president of the United States. The deck was stacked in favor of the party's preferred contender, and the DNC had done everything they could do to structure a win for their "chosen one."

The Democratic Socialist representative from a New England state turned out to be unexpectedly popular. He was giving the designated Democrat nominee an excellent run for her money. But everyone with an ounce of sense knew that party politics and the Democrat machine would ultimately prevail. The home girl would be nominated and would run, even if her campaign took place from a jail cell with her wearing an orange pantsuit. It would all be happening for the world to see in downtown Philadelphia in the middle of the summer. It would undoubtedly be terribly hot in July in the city which was home to the Liberty Bell.

Philadelphia had been welcoming conventions of all kinds for many years. One of the most famous and infamous was the American Legion Convention that had been held at the Bellevue-Stratford Hotel in July of 1976, more than forty years earlier. Scheduled to coincide with the celebration of the United States Bicentennial, the American Legion had whooped it up in Philly in 1976, from July 21st through July 27th. When the convention ended, the legionnaires left Philadelphia for their hometowns all across the United States. Then the legionnaires began to die.

The first indication that something serious had happened was when a number of relatively young, healthy men who had attended the convention began to pass away from pneumonia or unexpected heart attacks. Because these seemingly random deaths were occurring in isolation in states throughout the country, it took a while before a pattern emerged. It took even longer for the cause of these unexpected and unexplained deaths to be traced to the air conditioning unit on the roof of the Bellevue-Stratford Hotel in Philadelphia.

The deadly disease, when it was finally detected and described, was given the name Legionnaire's Disease. The link among those who died of this mysterious illness turned out to be that they all had attended the American Legion Convention in Philadelphia. They had all stayed at the Bellevue-Stratford Hotel. *Legionella pneumophila*, a newly discovered bacterium, had been bred in the air conditioning system of the hotel.

The bacteria that causes Legionnaire's disease thrives in the mist that is sprayed from air conditioning ducts and can infect an entire building. In Philadelphia in 1976, these bacteria spread their deadly spores throughout the air conditioning system of the Bellevue-Stratford and into its hundreds of rooms. Many conventioneers were infected; some died.

Philadelphia in July can be a miasma. Air conditioning is absolutely essential. The bigger the assembled crowd, the more cooling power is required. Imam Muhammad Muhammad had lived in Philadelphia before moving to the mosque in Portland. He knew all about Philadelphia's July weather, and he knew all about the Wells Fargo Center. He had been in Philadelphia when the Wells Fargo Center was a new facility.

The imam knew that HVAC systems are critical for large summer gatherings. He also knew that they do not last forever. Most people don't think much about an air conditioning system, and everyone assumes it will work as it is supposed to work. The HVAC system is ignored and taken for granted—until it goes on the blink. Once the AC quits, it becomes not just the most important crisis of the moment; it becomes the *only* crisis of the moment.

The imam knew what to do. He had not been in Philadelphia in 1976, but he had studied what had happened at the fateful American Legion Convention. The imam had, through a series of anonymous and faceless limited partnerships, purchased an HVAC company that specialized in providing industrial-sized portable air conditioning systems for large gatherings. He knew with absolute certainty that the twenty-year-old HVAC system in the Wells Fargo Center would fail during the last week of July at the Democrat National Convention. He also knew with certainty that those who ran the center would not be able to repair the AC in time for the last day of the convention.

The imam had made sure that the only company which would be able to provide the back-up air conditioning required to cool the Wells Fargo Center for the convention's finale was Emergency Cooling and Heating, the company he now owned. Emergency Cooling and Heating, ECH, was based in Cherry Hill, New Jersey. The imam had all the bases covered. He just had to wait for the July heat. Even an unexpected cool spell in Philadelphia would not ruin his plans.

Chapter 30

Looking For Cesium

The young Pakistani man had heard the siren song of ISIS. Zohran traveled to join the caliphate with other sharia warriors to fight for Allah. He was one of many who had left their homes and families behind and signed on for jihad. At the training camps, he had not distinguished himself above the others, and he often struggled to keep up with the demands of the rigorous physical training. He desperately wanted to stand out and was willing to sacrifice his life to be a martyr for the cause. He read the Quran every morning and prayed five times a day. He was doing everything he could to prepare himself to serve. He had great enthusiasm. He even had passion. He just did not have the skills. It made him furious that he might turn out to be a mediocre soldier for Allah.

One day, an ISIS deputy called Zohran aside and asked him about his family. Someone in the ISIS organizational structure had discovered that Zorhan's father worked at a nuclear power plant in Pakistan. Zohran's superior questioned him closely and took him to meet with three other important high-level ISIS warriors. The committee asked many of the same questions his superior had asked. They wanted every detail that Zohran could give them. They asked him quite a few questions he couldn't answer. The bottom line was they wanted to know if Zohran could get into the Pakistani nuclear power plant where his father worked. ISIS wanted Zohran to steal the power plant's nuclear waste.

Zohran's family lived outside Karachi, and his father worked as a night watchman at KANUPP-1, where the Karachi nuclear reactor was located. Zohran's father was not allowed to talk about his work with anybody. He was not supposed to tell his family about the layout of the place where the reactor made the energy that kept the lights on in Karachi. He was not permitted to talk about the power plant which produced nuclear waste as a by-product of the fission of nuclear reactions. Zohran's father's workplace was top secret. But everyone, no matter what their occupation, talks about what goes on at work. Everyone tells their families what they do all day at their jobs. This is human nature and is to be expected. Consequently, Zohran knew a great deal about KANUPP-1 and how the facility operated.

Zohran was nervous because he knew he was not supposed to talk about his father's work. He did not want his father to lose his job. His younger brothers and sisters needed to eat. Zohran told the ISIS interrogators he didn't think he could get into the facility. He explained how tight security was and how many steps were required to obtain a security clearance.

The ISIS operatives were smart. They knew Zohran wanted desperately to please and to be a success at the training camp. They knew he had weaknesses, and they knew they could manipulate him with ridicule and praise. They would work on him until he began to see that he could do their bidding. Zohran was transferred to more comfortable living quarters, and the quality of the food he was given improved. His superiors were preparing him and softening him up for a special mission. They hoped to convince Zohran that he could indeed undertake an assignment of the utmost importance for the caliphate. They told him his mission had the potential to change the world forever. Zohran was to have the chance to serve Allah in a dramatic and unique way.

The ISIS team was eventually able to persuade Zohran that he could accomplish the mission. When he became enthusiastic enough about it, the strategists turned him over to special instructors who worked with him to teach him how he could steal the radioactive waste from the storage pool on the grounds of the nuclear reactor that employed his father. They walked him through every step of the operation he would have to undertake. Zohran practiced what he was to do over and over again until he thought he could do it with his eyes closed. He knew he was being given special treatment and was being groomed for this important undertaking. It thrilled him and frightened him at the same time.

Zohran was sent home to Karachi. He knew exactly what he had to do. He was no longer ambivalent or afraid. He had become a zealot and drew his confidence from his commitment to rebuilding the caliphate and establishing Islam and sharia law throughout the world. His family was shocked when Zohran arrived home driving a small, dirty, dented pick-up truck. They all knew he could not afford to purchase a vehicle on his own—even a truck as disreputable as the one Zohran was driving. Everyone wondered how he had been able to buy the truck.

One night after his family was asleep, he stole his father's security badge. Zohran undertook his mission on a night when his father was not scheduled to work. Zohran applied makeup to his face in the way the ISIS operatives had taught him to do. Zohran already had a striking resemblance to his father. Except, of course, Zohran was twenty years younger. To make himself look older than he was, Zohran was shown how to use clothes and makeup. Even Zohran was surprised, after he had altered his appearance, how closely he resembled the photo on his father's security badge. They could be twins.

Zohran would not have to go inside the reactor or do any of his father's job. The security badge was just to get him past the gate and into the vicinity of the reactor's nuclear waste storage pool. Zohran's father drove an ancient motorcycle with a sidecar. His father constantly worked on the motorcycle to keep it on the road. It was always breaking down, and parts for the old vehicle were hard to find. On the night he was scheduled to steal the nuclear waste, Zohran took his father's motorcycle. The guards were used to seeing his father, so Zohran was confident his appearance at the gate of the nuclear reactor would not raise any eyebrows.

Zohran gained access to the grounds of the nuclear reactor without a problem. Pretending to be his father, he explained to the guards that he had been called in to work because one of the night crew was sick. Zohran's father had been called in many other times to take over for someone who could not work their hours, so his unscheduled appearance on the old motorcycle during the night shift was not unusual. Zohran had studied site plans of the facility. He was able to drive immediately to the storage pools, the location of the prize he had come to steal. Zohran had practiced, with his instructors at the training camp, what he was going to do during the next few hours. Being on the actual site of the nuclear reactor was intimidating, but Zohran knew what was expected of him.

The rods Zohran was going to steal were waste from the nuclear reactor. Used nuclear fuel is a troublesome by-product of the nuclear energy industry. This nuclear waste consists of small radioactive pellets stacked inside air-tight cylindrical containers made of steel and lead. These fuel rods of nuclear waste are stored and protected at reactor sites in steel-lined concrete pools filled with water. Nuclear waste at KANUPP-1 is held in storage pools kept at the reactor site. Zohran's assignment was to steal twenty of the rods from the storage pool.

A special lead-lined steel container had been built to hold the rods Zohran lifted out of the pool. The container had been sized to fit perfectly into the side car of his father's motorcycle. Zohran secured the motorcycle so that no one would be able to see it while he was loading it. Because his father was a night watchman, Zohran was familiar with his father's routine and the way he conducted his rounds. Because he knew how his father did his job, he knew how to avoid discovery while he was stealing the valuable rods out of the cooling pool. Zohran knew the night watchman's schedule for this particular area and was able to work around that schedule.

It was necessary for Zohran to go into the water. He carefully lifted each rod, one at a time, out of the storage pool. The rods were heavy, but Zohran had been building up his strength as part of his training for the mission. Zohran could retrieve five rods before the night watchman again made his rounds of the storage pools. After he had carried five rods to the sidecar and secured them, he waited patiently until the watchman completed his inspection. As soon as the man had moved on to his next location, Zohran lifted five more rods, one at a time, from the water and carried each one to the motorcycle's sidecar compartment. Before the watchman returned to his rounds at the storage pool, Zohran would have hidden himself again. As soon as the watchman completed his rounds in the area, Zohran was back in the water, liberating more rods.

Zohran did not know that he was exposing himself to deadly radiation every time he went into the cooling pools. When he had asked his ISIS superiors if he would be in any danger from the radioactivity, they had lied to him. They had failed to tell Zohran how dangerous his mission was and that it was in fact a fatal one. Each time Zohran went into the water, he exposed himself to more deadly radioactivity. His handling of the rods was even more toxic.

Finally Zohran had secured twenty of the pellet-filled cylindrical storage rods in the special lead-lined container of the motorcycle's side car. He closed and sealed the container. It was only then that the radioactivity was sufficiently contained, and Zohran was safe from further exposure. By the time he was on his way off the grounds of KANUPP-1 on the motorcycle, he already had been exposed to multiple lethal doses of radioactivity. He just didn't know it.

Zohran drove the motorcycle away from the grounds of the nuclear reactor. No one had stopped him as he left KANUPP-1 with his sidecar full of radioactive rods. Security was used to seeing Zohran's father and the old motorcycle. The guards just waved to Zohran as he moved his treasured hoard out of the facility—right under their noses. As Zohran left the grounds of the nuclear reactor, the motorcycle labored under its heavy load. Zohran was worried the motorcycle wouldn't make it back to his house. It was still dark, and his family was sound asleep.

In spite of the weight of its cargo, the motorcycle made it. When he arrived at his home, Zohran transferred the heavy lead and steel container from the side car of the motorcycle to the back of his pickup truck. His ISIS controllers had anticipated that, once the side car's container was filled with rods of nuclear waste, Zohran would not be able to lift it on his own. They had fashioned a kind of winch for the back of Zohran's truck that enabled him to lift the heavy container out of the motorcycle's sidecar and into the back of the pickup. The ISIS planners had tried to anticipate every contingency.

Zohran parked the motorcycle where it always spent the night, just inside a small lean-to shed attached to his house. His father might be surprised that he had to fill up the motorcycle with more gas than usual this week. But the bike was so old and consumed such huge amounts of oil and gasoline, Zohran's father might not notice the difference. Zohran was exhausted from his night's work. It had been physically demanding to climb in and out of the cooling pools so many times and carry each rod to the motorcycle. He wanted to go to sleep, but there was one last part of his mission that needed to be completed.

Zohran drove his truck to the rendezvous point. He was early and had to wait for the other truck to arrive. Three men arrived in another rusty and decrepit pickup truck which could have been a clone of the one Zohran was driving. These men had their own mechanism that made it possible for them to lift the lead-lined container from Zohran's truck into the back of their own. Zohran had delivered the precious rods and had fulfilled his assignment perfectly. He wondered what his reward would be when his superior heard that he had successfully obtained the canisters of nuclear waste. He hoped that taking these risks, which he had been more than willing to do, would bring him praise from ISIS. He hoped that jeopardizing his father's job and his family's well-being would make Allah pleased with him. He felt he had accomplished an incredible feat for the caliphate.

As soon as he had delivered the container carrying the radioactive pellets in the lead lined rods, Zohran was no longer of any value to ISIS. He had accomplished his task and was now a loose end. There would be no gratitude or praise for his sacrifices. There would be no reward for his service. He was now a liability, and his father was also a liability. His family was an unnecessary problem for the operation. These insignificant players, in this most critical of missions, were expendable. Their continued presence on earth would not be tolerated. Zohran and his pickup truck disappeared. They would never be seen again. A terrible fire engulfed Zohran's family home the next night. Everyone who was sleeping in the house died. All loose ends were taken care of.

The container, for which Zohran and his entire family had paid the ultimate price and which held nuclear waste in the form of pellets of cesium encased in metal rods, would begin its long, circuitous, and convoluted journey from Pakistan to Indonesia. The container in the back of the pickup was covered with animal dung. An old, dirty canvas cover was thrown on top. Who would want to search such a cargo as the truck made its way across the mountain passes? The truck was driven by two bearded men who each had an AR-47 under his seat. It was a truck filled with terrorists' gold.

If anyone was ever able to trace the truck that was carrying the load of nuclear waste that had been stolen from the nuclear reactor in Pakistan, they would be puzzled about why the truck did not proceed directly to the port of Karachi and load its cargo onto a ship. Pakistan has India as its neighbor to the east. India and Pakistan have not always been the best of friends. Pakistan has Iran as its neighbor to the west. Pakistan is primarily a Sunni Muslim country. Iran is primarily a Shia Muslim country. Since the revolution in 1979, Iran had become an outlaw nation in the world. To the north of Pakistan are the war-torn nation of Afghanistan and the disputed territory of Kashmir. It was possible to drive to China, but where would one go from there?

The truck carrying the cargo that Zohran had died for began driving west toward Pakistan's border with Iran, but the old pick-up would stop before it reached the theocratic Islamic state. The truck drove 472 kilometers along the Makran Coastal Highway from Karachi to Gwadar. Gwadar is a deep sea port on the Arabian Sea. In an effort to do the unexpected, the truck carrying the nuclear rods from the Karachi reactor was going to leave Pakistan in a different way. It would eventually reach its final destination, but it would have been too obvious if the truck had driven directly to the port of Karachi. In Gwadar, the old truck spent two days parked in the garage of a private home. On the third day, the yacht, which would transport the priceless nuclear waste on the next stage of its journey, arrived in the Port of Gwadar.

The transfer took place at night, and the billionaire owners of the yacht had no idea that anything radioactive was being loaded on board their luxurious sea-going home. What they also did not know was that the man who had captained their yacht for the last ten years was a committed supporter of radical Islam. No one would have suspected that this British-born former commander in the Royal Navy had become a fanatical follower of Allah. His Muslim parents had left India when the country was divided in 1948. They opted to relocate to London rather than live in East or West Pakistan. The captain of the yacht had been born in London and had lived there all of his life.

Deep inside the hold of the yacht, next to the cases of vintage wines and the crates full of tins of caviar, the steel and lead container with its dangerous cargo from KANUPP-1 rested safely. It would remain there for the next four weeks as the yacht made its leisurely way from Gwadar, Pakistan to Jakarta, Indonesia. When the yacht reached Jakarta, the yacht's captain would oversee the transfer of the steel and lead container to the hold of a Liberian tanker which was heading to Canada. The captain's mission for Allah had been to shepherd the valuable cargo through one stage of its journey and on to the next. He did not know where its ultimate destination was, what its ultimate intended use would be, or what was in the container. He knew it was important and would ultimately be used to kill infidels. He was willing to do whatever he could in the service of Islam.

The container holding the deadly pellets would cross the Pacific Ocean on the tanker and reappear on the West Coast of the United States. The journey would continue. The radioactive material, which had been stolen from a nuclear power plant in Pakistan, would make its final appearance more than a year later at the Quicken Loans Arena in Cleveland, Ohio. Radioactivity would sneak into "The Q" like a silent and subtle specter. Once inside, it would work its way into the air and disburse its insidious poison throughout the convention hall. Only a few would have any idea what had slipped through security until it was way too late.

Chapter 31

Looking for Something to Sell

*I*n 1978, *Walter Reed Army Medical Center had a* thyroid scanning machine in its Department of Nuclear Medicine. The machine required a component of radioactive material. Americium, a man-made radioactive isotope, was essential to the scanning process. It was encased in lead to protect the doctors and technicians who operated the machine. The nuclear medicine department was staffed by active duty military personnel and civilian employees. Almost every one of these people was devoted to healing and to serving his or her country. Walter Reed was the Army's showcase military teaching hospital located in the nation's capital of Washington, D.C. The people who were talented enough to be chosen to work in this facility were proud and honored to serve there. It was the premier assignment for United States Army medical personnel.

There are "bad apples" to be found in even the most honorable institutions. The prestigious icon that Walter

Reed represented was not exempt from employing a few people who felt they were not getting their fair share of life's goodies. There are greedy people in all walks of life, and there are sticky fingers in every field of endeavor. Employees have been stealing from their employers since mankind first created the business of business. From paperclips and pens to pension funds, there are always those who feel they are entitled to more. And they try to take it.

Because most work environments do not offer the kind of unique opportunity that Walter Reed's nuclear medicine department offered, it was unusual for an employee to attempt to steal radioactive material from an employer. But anything can be stolen. If it can be sold, it is all profit. The entrepreneurial spirit is alive and well everywhere, and innovation and the willingness to take a risk can be remarkable when there is money to be made. Who would want to steal something that was potentially so dangerous? Why would anybody want to take something that had to be encased in lead to keep it from harming anyone and everyone who came in contact with it? Was there anyone who would want to buy a lethal blob of chemicals in a heavy lead container?

When a technology or a piece of equipment becomes obsolete and is replaced with something new, the old version is discarded. Those in charge move on to value and focus on how to use, operate, and protect the latest innovation, the newest technology. The old equipment is ignored and forgotten. It is no longer of significance, and no one seriously bothers to monitor what happens to it. It slips off the radar screen. This was how the Americium isotope, which had been vital to the operation of the once-lauded but now-outdated thyroid scanning machine of the 1970s, became unimportant. The nuclear medicine department at Walter Reed moved on to a new technology.

The old and unwanted machine and its radioactive isotope became superfluous. Someone had to dispose of what was no longer needed. If the person tasked with getting rid of the medical detritus decided to make his own what had been abandoned, who would know? The Americium isotope would vanish, and its disappearance would never be remarkable.

In the 1970s hardly anyone was thinking about "dirty bombs." The United States was still fighting the Cold War. The Russians were the bad guys who threatened the American way of life. The Soviet arch enemies had their own sophisticated nuclear weapons. The nuclear attacks that were most feared were those which would arrive on the warheads of ICBMs that raced through the skies to destroy American cities.

One myth, which circulated in the waning days of the Cold War and after the Soviet Union had fallen, was that Russian sleeper agents in the United States were armed with "suitcase nukes." Could a nuclear weapon be safely contained in something the size of a suitcase? Was this a realistic threat? The Russians were the nuclear threat. No one was worrying about radioactive isotopes, which had been discarded from a hospital's nuclear medicine department. No one imagined that this could be any kind of potential threat to the United States homeland.

Muslim terrorists were attacking and killing Israelis, but all of that was happening on the other side of the world. Middle Eastern countries were engaged in that fight, and the atrocities were between the Palestinians and the Jews. Even the Black September terrorists, which appeared on our television screens during the 1972 Olympic Games, had targeted, kidnapped, and murdered only Israeli athletes. No other nations were obviously at risk from these masked evildoers. Only Israel was threatened by Islamic terror. Had anyone even heard the word jihadist ... yet?

Decades later, terrorists from the nations whose citizens worship Allah would mobilize to kill us and take down our country's tallest buildings. But that would happen years down the road—in a different century and in a different millennium.

These future troublemakers first appeared in the American public's consciousness because of their manipulation of oil prices. We did not yet know that some of them would plan to kill us. Saudi Arabian princes and Iranian mullahs were initially a threat because they made us pay more money for barrels of oil and gallons of gasoline at the pump.

The OPEC cartel caused irritatingly long lines at the corner gas station. Middle Eastern countries, with their grossly misogynistic religion that required women to hide their faces and cover their bodies with sacks, were after our money. The United States was addicted to cheap oil, and these people were taking advantage of an opportunity. We did not fear them as a threat to our lives. They were a threat to our pocketbooks.

These countries would grow rich from our dependence on the oil they had to sell. Our view of Muslims in the Middle East would evolve over time from the image of camel-riding nomads in white robes and unusual head gear who lived in oil-rich desert kingdoms. During the intervening years, it began to dawn on us and gradually creep into the everyday reality of our lives that militant and murderous radical Muslims wanted to kill us and destroy our entire way of life.

In the 1960s and 1970s, planes were hijacked from Miami to Cuba by mentally ill individuals with axes to grind or by political fanatics. Passengers were terribly inconvenienced, but no one died in these bizarre events. We scarcely noticed when groups with different agendas began to hijack airplanes around the world. It was all so long ago and far away.

Then the Shah of Iran fell from power, and that country was taken over by theocratic fanatics wearing funny hats. The "Ayatollahs Assaholas" took our State Department personnel hostage for a year, and the fight with this Muslim country momentarily became distinctly personal. Jimmy Carter could not bring the hostages home. But as soon as the Americans, who had been held in Iran for more than a year, were once again on United States' soil, our country turned its back on the freakish fools in Iran and got on with our prosperity. Ronald Reagan was President, and we were bringing down Communism. We had bested our long-time nemesis, the Union of Soviet Socialist Republics, the Evil Empire. We were winning the all-important and all-engrossing Cold War.

Reagan recognized the threat from Islamic terror and bombed Libya for harboring the terrorists who had downed Pan Am Flight #103. In spite of the fact that our ally France would not allow us to fly through their air space to conduct these air raids against Muammar Gaddafi, we retaliated in force to punish the Islamic barbarians who had killed our children.

For almost eight years, Iraq and Iran were engaged in a brutal, back-and-forth war of attrition. There were unsubstantiated reports that Iran put its pre-teen boys into the fight at the forefront of the battle lines as "cannon fodder." What kind of brutal regime would do something like that?

It was on the news every day and every night, but we had stopped listening as it droned on day after day, year after year. This was a sectarian battle between two Muslim countries, between two different Muslim sects who held different beliefs. How could we be expected to understand a tortuous and on-going conflict between the Sunni and the Shia? This battle had been going on for hundreds of years. It was none of our business. This was not our fight. Who was paying attention to future threats and future wars? Who had ever heard of the Emirate of Kuwait?

All the signs were there that the Middle East would be the site of the next killing fields, and attacks from the savages of Islamic Jihad had already begun. In 1983, Muslim terrorists exploded a truck bomb at the entrance to the United States Marine barracks in Beirut, Lebanon. Two hundred forty-one American soldiers were murdered that day. Iran's Shiite henchmen Hezbollah had struck. The gauntlet was down, even though the United States might not have recognized it then for what it was. The age-old conflict between Western civilization and sharia warriors had been joined again with new ferocity. The attacks from Muslim terrorists who wanted to kill Americans were already underway. The slaughter had begun.

When he decided to steal the Americium isotope, which no one seemed to care about any more, the thief had no idea what he was going to do with it. Corporal George Faidley was a low-paid, low-ranking member of the U.S. Army Medical Corps. George was trained as a medic, but the Vietnam War was over before he could be sent overseas. In the post-Vietnam world at Walter Reed, there were more than a few medics who were no longer needed on the battlefield. After the war ended, there were too many military personnel available to do fewer and fewer jobs.

George became a kind of "gofer" and was called on to do those things that nobody else wanted to do. He ran errands for the administrative workers. He transported containers of supplies where they were needed. He changed light bulbs and carried paperwork from one department to another. He took out the trash when that was what had to be done. He did a little bit of everything. He was the almost faceless, almost nameless person in the organization that everybody asked to do things. Nobody really knew George.

George Faidley's superior, a civilian administrator in the Department of Nuclear Medicine, had delegated to George the responsibility of disposing of the obsolete Americium isotope. George was given specific instructions about how he was to get rid of the mysterious substance that was protected in its lead container. George figured the thing must be valuable if it was encased in lead. Everyone handled it with care and treated it with respect. New technology had made it obsolete. He decided nobody would miss it if it disappeared.

George would add this prize to the stockpile of other potentially valuable junk he had collected from the nuclear medicine department and from other places around the hospital. He was a thief and a pack rat. He went undiscovered because he stole only those things which nobody wanted any more. He mostly "recovered" items from wastebaskets and trash bags. He checked the dumpsters and the hazardous materials disposal bins on a regular basis.

It was easy to figure out how to circumvent the instructions he had been given for disposing of the radioactive material.

He found a container that was similar in size and shape to the lead receptacle which held the isotope. He filled his substitute container with objects that weighed approximately what the isotope weighed. He turned in the substitute container for recycling, disposal, or whatever they did with those things. No one even asked him to sign his name when he delivered the bogus container to be discarded. And of course, no one opened the container to see what, if anything, was inside it. Nobody was crazy enough to open the lead container that was full of danger. Those in charge knew better than to mess with radioactivity.

George took the stolen lead-encased Americium isotope to his garage and added this newest acquisition to his other "treasures." Although he had pawned a few things and sold some things from this salvaged rubbish heap, most of what he had stolen was still secure in his hoard. George knew he had something of value in the lead canister. He was not exactly certain what that value would turn out to be, but he was careful to keep the container intact and understood the importance of the protection the lead casing provided. Imagining that one day he would be able to sell his radioactive booty for significant money, he was willing to wait and guard what was valuable in his garage until a day of suitable opportunity arrived. Years passed.

Corporal George Faidley continued his career in the Army until he was let go from the military. He was immediately hired back as a civilian employee. George was angry with the government for taking away his military status. He hadn't actually lost his job because he'd been rehired as a civilian in the same position. But he didn't feel his civilian employment had the prestige of the medical corps rank he had enjoyed as a member of the military. He liked saluting and wearing a uniform. Those things had been taken away from him, and for what possible reason? He didn't understand it. If he still had the same job and the Army was willing to rehire him to do that same exact work, why had they deprived him of his military status? It didn't make sense, and it made George furious.

George kept working at Walter Reed because he needed employment, and he especially enjoyed the opportunities for petty larceny his job made possible. George continued his secondary occupation as a junkman. By the time he retired, his garage was overflowing with all kinds of "stuff" of dubious value. Almost everything in his cache was from the hospital. It was surplus or refuse, all of which was supposed to have been discarded.

George had learned to use a computer during his years at Walter Reed. He'd eventually purchased his own computer and became addicted to the internet. George discovered which of his "treasures" had value and which didn't. He found he could sell some of the things he had in his garage on eBay. George retired the year before Walter Reed moved to the campus of Bethesda Naval Medical Center. Life had become too confusing for George with all the changes, renaming, downsizing, and merging in the military. It was time to quit.

After his retirement, George spent a lot of time surfing the internet and inevitably discovered the dark web. It was only a matter of time until he found someone who wanted to purchase his prized radioactive leftovers, the Americium isotope he had liberated from the nuclear medicine department in the 1970s. He'd known it would be worth something someday. Finally, he was going to become rich in his retirement years. He had several buyers competing for his isotope. All he had to do now was wait for them to outbid each other.

Chapter 32

Looking for a Big Profit

George Faidley enjoyed organizing and reorganiz-ing his collections — looking at it, thinking about it, and selling some of it from time to time. He appreciated his stuff so much, he knew he would never be able to retire from his obsession with garbage. George Faidley loved eBay, Craigslist, and the dark web.

He finally decided which of the several bidders for his radioactive isotope would be the lucky buyer. It would be a simple transfer, and George had agreed to a price and a time and place for the exchange. Hoping to significantly pad his retirement income with the proceeds from this sale, George was demanding cash for his lead container and its contents.

George had never married and didn't have many friends. He didn't know his neighbors. Because he lived alone and no one missed him, it was weeks before anyone found George's body. Those who happened to notice he wasn't home thought he had taken a vacation. One of his neighbors finally became aware of the smell. She didn't know George Faidley even though she'd lived next door to the man for more than a decade. On one of her nightly walks, the neighbor's dog expressed an intense interest in Faidley's garage. The neighbor was overwhelmed by the smell when she approached the door of the garage. At first she thought a stray raccoon or cat might have become trapped inside and died there.

The neighbor didn't have a phone number for George, and her attempts to rouse him by knocking on his front door resulted in no answer. The terrible odor coming from the garage finally prompted her to call the Prince George's County Sheriff's Office. She met the sheriff's deputies at Faidley's garage. She almost fainted when the police raised the garage door, and the full force of the smell of death hit her in the face. The garage was so full of stuff, no one could immediately find what had died inside. But no one could doubt that something or somebody was dead in there. The neighbor almost fainted again when she saw all the dried, dark blood around the body. Once law enforcement officers saw a body, the neighbor and her dog were told to leave the scene.

Sheriff's deputies found the long-deceased George Faidley with his throat cut from ear to ear. He was lying on top of a dozen cases of Sulfa Silvadene. George had liberated the burn medicine when it had been thrown in the dumpster. Dozens and dozens of jars of the expensive medicinal ointment were now quite a few years past their use-by date. It was a mystery, even to George, why he had hung on to these cases of an expired cream no one would ever be able to use. The truth was that the large cartons pushed together made a kind of bed, a place for George to take a nap inside his garage when he wanted to catch some z's while going through his junk collection. The bed made of boxes had turned out to be his final napping place.

Investigators from the sheriff's office were puzzled and fascinated by the collection of things in George's garage. There were boxes of old office supplies, packages of unopened bandages, rusty surgical instruments, plastic containers of every shape and description, several sets of used melamine dinner plates and cups, two generators of questionable age and working condition, a mail cart, stacks and stacks of used file folders, and thousands of other things that might or might not have been useful to somebody once upon a time. There was a crate full of thousands of rusted paperclips.

The criminalists processed the crime scene as they would any other crime scene. These professionals had thought they'd investigated everything, but they had never seen anything quite like George Faidley's stash.

Prince George's County law enforcement were never able to solve George's murder. They could not come up with a motive or any explanation for the terrible way he had died. No suspect was ever found. George had no enemies, and George had no friends. His death was as strange as his life had been. The sheriff's office had nothing. Without much regret, this exceptionally odd murder was soon classified as an inactive case.

George had no will and no heirs. His estate consisted of the few pieces of furniture and the household goods he had in his rented house plus the contents of his garage. The crime scene investigators wondered amongst themselves if the TV show *Hoarders* would have any interest in George Faidley's abandoned stockpile. They thought it might have made a curious and entertaining show.

Somebody had helped themselves to George's Americium in its lead container. Law enforcement had no idea there had ever been a container holding a radioactive substance in George's garage, so no one ever looked for or ever found who had stolen this dangerous and valuable radioactive isotope. Who would ever have imagined that George was in possession of such an exotic and exceptional item? Nobody thought to look for what they didn't know was missing.

The radioactive Americium isotope was on its way to a mosque in Camden, New Jersey. The radical imam in that impoverished city had been asked to provide temporary storage for something that he was told would be important in a history-making strike against the infidels inside the United States. Although he had not been told the details of the attack, the imam expected it had something to do with the Democrat's nominating convention in Philadelphia that would be held during the summer in Philadelphia. The Camden mosque was one of the poorer places of Muslim worship in New Jersey, and it could not support itself on the money it raised from its congregation's donations. This mosque depended on Islamic organizations which raised funds nationwide, from the groups that supported the activities of global jihad.

The request that his mosque help with an important operation came with the offer of a significant financial bonus.

This money was a huge plus for the imam. He would never refuse to play a role in the struggle for Allah, even if he had not been offered compensation, but the additional money would be a tremendous help with the imam's always-strapped budget. Now the imam could put a new roof on his main building and have an additional electrical panel installed. The electrician had told him the mosque needed more electric power.

The imam welcomed the man who brought the isotope to the mosque. The cleric listened carefully to the instructions not to touch or damage the lead receptacle which held the radioactive material. The imam was told he would be safe from any radioactive emissions as long as he didn't tamper with the container. The Imam promised he would guard the treasured vessel with his life and would not breathe a word of its presence to anyone. He was told that his stewardship of the valued substance was a vital step in a critical campaign for Allah.

Several weeks later, two men arrived to pick up the lead container. They handled it with great care when they loaded it into their van. The imam had been wondering exactly what would be done with the mysterious and frightening thing he'd been harboring. He knew some basic facts about radioactivity. He knew about the fallout from nuclear weapons and accidents at nuclear power plants. Most people have heard about Hiroshima and Chernobyl.

The imam could not help but worry if his own mosque and community would be at risk if a nuclear event occurred in Philadelphia. Philly was just across the Delaware River from Camden, New Jersey. Would the prevailing winds carry the nuclear poison to Camden? The imam was ready at any moment to die for Allah, but he wondered if Allah expected even the youngest children who attended services at the mosque to die slow and painful deaths from radiation sickness. Did he need to prepare his congregation for sacrifice and death? His sermons often addressed the subject of giving everything, including one's life, for Allah. The imam wondered if he should ramp up his rhetoric and speak more directly and more specifically to get his people ready to die.

Chapter 33

Looking For Supplies

Since his retirement, Dean Abadi had devoted himself full-time to preparing for his *coup de grâce*, his ultimate tribute to Allah. Dean had anticipated the difficulties he would have in obtaining enough of just the right nuclear materials. He knew it would not be easy to find the technicians who possessed the necessary expertise required for such a sophisticated operation. He had been working on acquiring the materials and the people for more than two years. Terrorist organizations had financial resources, so cost was no object. Charities that fronted as humanitarian organizations had been raising money for terrorist causes for generations. Bringing his materials and people into the United States was going to be the challenging part of the undertaking.

Dean knew it was almost impossible to obtain useful radioactive material from sources inside the U.S. These substances were rare, and they were highly regulated, inventoried, and controlled. Every ounce had to be accounted for and disposed of properly. There were many rules and regulations. He might get lucky. Occasionally, something slipped through the system, but it usually wasn't worth the trouble. When he discovered the availability of the Americium isotope over the internet, Dean could scarcely believe his good fortune. He'd thought he would have to go to a third world or second world country to buy his nuclear materials. Even abroad, it was not easy to find someone who had it and was willing to sell it. As one might expect, the price was always exorbitant.

Because of the difficulties of obtaining radioactive materials, Dean determined it would be easier and safer to procure the rest of the ingredients he needed for his weapons from outside the United States. The former Soviet Union presented many opportunities for acquiring contraband of all kinds. After the failed communist empire disintegrated into a collection of independent states, weapons large and small, night-vision gear, radioactive waste, and countless other black market items were available for a price.

Lots of things were lost and stolen in the transition from a totalitarian state with a command economy to mafia capitalism. Nuclear materials were one of the things that had disappeared. For the right amount of money, almost anything could be made to miraculously reappear.

Dean had studied various kinds of radioactive isotopes and decided that cesium-137 would fulfilled the requirements necessary for one of his devices. Dean wanted an isotope that would disburse widely but not in high concentrations. He wanted to delay as much as possible the timeline for anyone becoming ill from breathing the radioactive particles in the air. Delay was critical because Dean's plan had two phases. He did not want the consequences of the first phase to be discovered until the second phase had become operational.

Cesium-137 seemed to have the attributes which made it an excellent candidate for use in Dean's special "balloon lifting" machines. No one had ever tried to disburse cesium-137 in the way that Dean Abadi envisioned doing. Because his invention was so innovative and experimental, there was a high degree of uncertainty about the way the machines would work. Would the air machines Dean had developed for spreading the isotope in the Quicken Loans Arena be effective and fulfill their promise? There was also uncertainty about how the isotope itself would behave.

Dean's technical experts had developed a method of cutting the cesium-137 with very finely ground silica. The substance, which would be blown into the air along with the balloons, would be invisible to the human eye. The concept was that the cesium-137 mixed with superfine silica would be spread throughout the Arena. The amount each person inhaled would be relatively small. It would not become obvious for several days that something terrible had happened.

Cesium-137 is soluble in water. When the isotope was breathed in by the people at the Quicken Loans Arena and once the fine particles of the lethal cesium-137 and silica mixture entered their lungs, it would be quickly absorbed by the body's soft tissues and other fluids in the body. Once exposed to water, a water-soluble compound called caesium hydroxide would be produced. This deadly poison would begin its journey through the bodies of thousands of unsus-pecting convention-goers.

Cesium-137 is difficult to handle. The man-made isotope is formed as one of the products resulting from the nuclear fission of uranium-235 and other fissionable isotopes in nuclear reactors and the making of nuclear weapons. Because of its high water solubility, extreme care must be taken when handling the isotope. Extraordinary protective measures are required when working with cesium-137. Dean trusted that his three technical experts were skilled in handling the dangerous substance and that they would observe the most stringent safety precautions.

Dean knew he had to bring his technicians and the Cesium-137 into the United States from abroad as surreptitiously as possible. He could not take the chance that one of the jihadists would have their papers challenged at an airport or a border crossing. They would all be traveling with and working on Dean's project using false passports and false identities. The plan for their transportation and the transportation of their radioactive materials via the tanker in the Pacific Ocean was conceived as having a high probability for success and would insure secrecy.

The short-term and long-term consequences of their plan, if it became operational and succeeded as they hoped it would, could not possibly be known before the fact by anyone except for a chosen few. Security was paramount and the young jihadists understood how important it was. There would be no trace, official or otherwise, that these people or these materials had ever entered the United States.

Dean's bomb technicians were not the typical jihadists who wanted to blow themselves up with suicide vests. There would be none of that purposeful self-sacrifice in this operation. These were serious scientists who hoped to change the world through the application of their special high-level skills. These deadly weapons had the potential to destroy the technicians who were constructing them. The strategy was to set up the attacks in such a way that the bomb makers would be able to escape without being harmed by their own handiwork.

They all planned to be far away from Cleveland and Philadelphia when the time came for their plans to reach fruition. After they had done their work for Dean, they wanted assurances that their true identities would not be compromised. They wanted to be able to return to their former lives and vanish back into the anonymity from which they had come.

Once the three had arrived safely in the United States, they would work in complete isolation. The empty storage shed on the grounds of the mosque was the ideal location for their workshop. The three technical experts would live at the mosque where everything they needed would be provided for them. They would eat, sleep, and pray with the imam at the mosque.

The two young men and one woman were highly-skilled explosives experts. Equally important was their training in the handling of radioactive materials, and they were committed to building flawless weapons. Dean was pleased that his plans and their implementation were proceeding on schedule. There were, as is always the case when plans confront the real world, some loose ends that had to be addressed.

Dean and the imam had thought about it for a long time before they'd made the decision to eliminate Aziz. Because

Aziz had been asking so many questions about the body found on the beach near Depoe Bay, they knew from their sources that he was under suspicion from law enforcement. Aziz had been a sleeper agent in place for many years, but things had changed. He was no longer trusted. He would not be able to handle the more sophisticated operations planned for the future. His superiors worried that he would talk if he was arrested. He was no longer up to the task and was a liability. He had to be eliminated.

Dean worried that Aziz's death would increase scrutiny of Aziz's life and particularly his activities in recent weeks and months. That was the chance they had to take. Aziz had always been a small fish. The typhoon had drowned Allah's martyr who had been supposed to set off his bombs and vest at the Seattle Space Needle. The freak storm had intervened, and the failure of the mission had not been Aziz's fault.

Aziz's mistake had been in asking too many questions after the fact. He had made a nuisance of himself trying to find out about the body and had drawn the attention of law enforcement by being too inquisitive. If he'd just stayed quiet and acted like he didn't know anything, he might have retained his usefulness. For some reason, he'd also become a suspect in a home invasion on the property next to the cove. No one could understand why he might have done a stupid thing like that. These blunders were all unacceptable, and Aziz had been permanently retired.

Dean felt certain they'd taken care of all the details involving their transfer of nuclear materials from the rafts to the Gator and then to the van. It had gone smoothly without anybody noticing or raising an alarm. The man who had shot Aziz with the silenced handgun was an excellent assassin and knew how to clean up after himself. Dean was sure nothing had been left behind in either Aziz's apartment or in the rental car. Dean could now focus on the future and the operation ahead.

His bomb makers were professionals, and they were working day and night to prepare the devious devices they would transport across the country to their ultimate targets. Dean had given a great deal of thought to the logistics of assembling and transporting the unique and innovative weapons. He wanted to opt for the safest and most efficient way to transport them.

He decided it would be better to assemble his inventions in Portland where the technicians had the luxury of time and friendly surroundings. It would be smarter to drive the already assembled weapons across country rather than try to assemble the bombs closer to their targets. Given what and where the targets were, Dean knew there would be security of every size and shape surrounding them. He decided it was smarter to have everything ready to detonate and bring the finished explosive devices to the targets.

Chapter 34

Looking For Cover

Assembling the deadly devices inside a workshop on the grounds of the mosque provided an almost perfect set up. The jihadists would not attract attention from neighbors. There would be no public record that anyone had put down a security deposit or used a credit card which would have been required to rent an apartment or a hotel room. ID was required to have gas, electricity, and water turned on. Because they were living at the mosque, all of the technicians' daily needs were provided for. The anonymity of Dean's people was guaranteed. As far as the world outside the mosque was concerned, Dean's team did not exist. They were invisible workers toiling for Allah.

Once the assembly of the complex and deadly weapons was completed, they would need to be transported to their destination. Dean purchased a motorhome to deliver his technicians and their prized cargo across the country to the targets. The motorhome was a way to keep the technicians in close contact with their work product and allow them to travel undetected almost all the way across the United States. They would never have to stay at a motel, use a credit card for any reason, or in fact be seen in public during the entire journey of thousands of miles. There would be no public transportation involved, and there would be no rental cars which required paperwork and a driver's license. Dean wanted to keep the operation completely off the grid. Having his technicians and their weapons together inside the motorhome and out of public view was the ideal way to accomplish this. Dean's operatives would never be seen, and their precious explosives would never be out of their control.

Dean had tried to think of everything. The motorhome would be stocked for the cross-country trip with the food his jihadists preferred. There would be no need for any of them to ever step outside the motorhome for meals or for any reason at all. While they traveled across the country, Dean did not want his people to be viewed by ubiquitous video surveillance cameras or to leave an electronic or paper footprint. These young warriors for sharia had arrived in the United States as ghosts, and they would remain ghosts for as long as possible.

A driver, known to Dean and to the imam and who was loyal to the cause, had been hired to drive the motorhome, to purchase gas, to buy take-out meals, and do whatever else was required during the trip east. He would pay cash for everything. Only the driver would ever leave the motorhome. Only the driver would ever be seen by the public, by the surveillance cameras, and in fact by anybody during the journey of several days. At the end of it all, that driver would disappear, never to be seen again. He would not be able to tell the story of his history-making drive across the United States.

There had been much discussion regarding the logistics of the operation and whether the motorhome should be parked in Cleveland or in Philadelphia. It was decided that the motorhome would go directly to the Philadelphia area and remain hidden there inside a warehouse in Camden, New Jersey. The technicians and their driver would live in the motorhome while it was parked inside the warehouse. There was a mosque next door to the warehouse. The jihadists would be able to pray and eat their meals at the mosque. The local imam was being paid to provide these accommodations. He was also eager to please and happy to contribute to the important work they were doing. He was at their service.

The motorhome would be unloaded at the warehouse, and preparations for the Philadelphia operation would be finalized first. The technicians would be certain everything for the success of their plan was in place before they left the City of Brotherly Love.

Once everything was ready for the Philadelphia convention, the materials necessary for the Cleveland operation would be transferred to a van. Loaded with the devices for the Cleveland attack, the van would deliver the three technicians and their cargo to the garage of a mosque near the Quicken Loans Arena. The van would remain out of sight in the mosque's garage while the technicians made their final preparations for the Cleveland operation. The three jihadists would live at the nearby mosque while they set the scene for death at "The Q." Every step had been carefully orchestrated, but even when a flawless scheme went operational, it occasionally ran into the unexpected. The random circumstances of reality sometimes interfered with the most perfect plan.

When all was ready and in place at the Quicken Loans Arena, one technician would stay behind in Cleveland to insure that everything went smoothly. Two technicians would return to Philadelphia to finalize the details for the Wells Fargo location. The Philadelphia attack would be larger and more dramatic than the one in Cleveland. The operation in Philadelphia was more complex. A number of things had to happen in the correct sequence for there to be success in Philadelphia. Philadelphia was a bigger city and closer to New York and Washington, D.C. The consequences of that operation would be catastrophic. They might even be cataclysmic.

Dean's contemplations and fantasies about what much of the USA would be like after his destruction was successful reminded him of a short story he had read when he was in school. *"By The Waters Of Babylon,"* written by Stephen Vincent Benét, had made an impression on Dean when he had read it as a high school sophomore. The story had stayed with him all of his life. He had never dreamed that he might be the instrument which would make this fictional tale into a reality of sorts.

Benét wrote his narrative in 1937 after the destruction of Guernica during the Spanish Civil War. This post-apocalyptic work of fiction was written years before the first nuclear weapon was ever created. Benét died in 1943. He would never have known the reality of what radioactivity could destroy and what it left behind. Benét's story was prophetic in a way he could never have imagined. Dean intended to bring an infidel civilization to its knees. He would make Stephen Vincent Benét's story of a modern-day City of Ruin into a breaking news account for the twenty-first century media.

Dean did not intend to be anywhere near Cleveland or Philadelphia for either political convention. He would be in Portland, watching the fallout from his brilliance on the news. His personal satisfaction would come from the successful execution of the intricate plans which had been a long time in the making. Dean had no need to become famous or for anybody to know what he had done. Just the opposite, he wanted to remain completely anonymous and continue living his life as he always had. No one would ever suspect that this mild-mannered, American-born, retired physicist and engineer had ever done anything remotely destructive or even exciting. A few people would know, but they would either be dead or were so committed to Allah that they would never breathe a word of who had been the mastermind behind the greatest terror attack on American soil. Imams didn't tell their secrets. The technicians who knew anything about Dean would, in one way or another, all be gone.

Why had Dean turned to jihad? Born in the United States, he had been given the best of everything his country could offer him. He had been a good student and popular in school. He had many friends. He'd had girlfriends in high school and in college. He'd made a bad choice when he married the sorority princess, but lots of people make bad choices in the marriage department. He'd had a successful, even a brilliant, career as a construction engineer. He'd never had children, but he'd never believed that was an empty spot in his life.

His parents had been non-practicing Muslims, and maybe he harbored some resentment that they had denied him his true heritage. Bethany Presbyterian Church was a long way from the world of Islam, but the religious teachings of his Sunday School had not been particularly onerous or demanding. Why Dean had turned away from the country of his birth was a mystery even to Dean. Islam and eventually militant Islam had offered him something which nothing else in his life had ever offered him. It was when he had embraced jihad that he felt as if he finally belonged someplace.

Chapter 35

Looking for Mold

etective Nathanial Broderick was desperate to check the mosques in Portland to see if any radioactive materials had ever been inside. After much consternation, he thought he had figured out a way to get access. It wasn't going to be easy, and technically, his authority for entering these places of worship would be questionable at best. He was so determined to find something, he was willing to take the considerable risks his plan involved.

Broderick would be setting up the operation on his own—without any official support. He would be flying under the radar screen of the FBI and all federal organizations. He would not have authorization from anybody to do what he was going to do. The only person with whom he was going to conspire was a friend who was a private investigator in the Salem, Oregon area. Broderick was going rogue. He had asked his PI friend to help him with his scheme.

Broderick had access to the technology that was routinely brought in to test a crime scene for possible radioactive contamination. This piece of digital equipment was a little bit larger than a cell phone. It could recognize and register tiny amounts of radioactivity. It would be useless in a dentist's office. Law enforcement's modern-day version of the Geiger counter was designed specifically to detect radiation in places where absolutely none is expected to be. Broderick had never been to a crime scene where the dosimeter had registered any radioactivity until it had been used to test the air in the car where Aziz had been murdered. After the positive reading in the rental car, Broderick had insisted that Aziz's apartment in Depoe Bay be checked. The dosimeter had yielded a positive reading when it was tested in the apartment. Radiation had also been found in Abigail Linder's cove.

In urban areas for the past several decades, whenever someone wants to construct a new building, they've been required to get a building permit. Every political jurisdiction in the country has different rules regarding these permits — the building codes that must be followed, the inspections that are required, the paperwork that has to be filed, and the countless other bureaucratic hoops through which a builder has to jump. The more recent the construction, the more extensive the process and the paperwork involved. Once a building has been permitted, inspected, and completed, if something is changed or added later to that building, new permissions are required. Sometimes old buildings are "grandfathered" for certain reasons to allow them to avoid costly code upgrades. Sometimes, changes and additions to existing structures are done illegally, without the necessary permits. It's a hurly-burly mishmash of rules and regulations, exemptions, variances, payoffs, grandfathers, and confusion.

Nathanial Broderick went to the city of Portland's Bureau of Development Services. This is the city office that officially issues Portland's building permits and keeps tabs on construction code regulations and site development activities. Broderick was hoping to find the plot plans and floor plans of several mosques he had identified as possible locations for radioactivity testing. But he had to obscure the fact that he was after these plans.

Broderick had researched the profiles of all the mosques in the Portland area. There were three he thought might be possible candidates for harboring illusive jihadists. The detective wanted to see the plans and building permits for these three religious complexes. The campus of a mosque usually consisted of more than a single building. There could be multiple structures on the site which might include a central building for worship services, housing for various clerics, garages and workshops, and sometimes even a school with everything that accompanies an educational facility.

Broderick knew he could not ask the city's Bureau of Development Services for floor plans, site plans, and other information for just a handful of mosques. That would be too obvious. The word would no doubt be reported back to somebody that he was targeting Muslims. Of course, that is exactly what he was doing, and for good reason. To try to hide which properties he was interested in, Broderick decided he would group his requests by neighborhood. He asked for the paperwork of several buildings and complexes within each of the areas surrounding the mosques that he had suspicions about. This required additional work and time. But asking for more paperwork than he really wanted would give some cover to his inquiries. He spent two days pouring over blueprints, drawings, plot plans, and reams of building specifications. He made sketches and took notes until he felt he had a grasp of the layouts of the properties and buildings that interested him.

The ploy that Broderick and his private investigator friend hoped to use to gain access to the mosques was going to be a phony "toxic mold inspection." Everyone has heard of toxic mold, and no one wants to have it on their premises. Just the mention of toxic mold got everyone's attention. Sometimes it has no discernable odor, and it can kill. It can live inside walls. One might never know it was there until someone became sick. Toxic mold is a real and dangerous threat in some places. But it was not a threat, as far as anyone knew, in the buildings Broderick's PI intended to "inspect." Broderick and his PI intended to take advantage of the fear of toxic mold to gain access to buildings that otherwise they would never have a chance of entering.

Broderick's PI would take charge of organizing the faux toxic mold inspections. Broderick would not participate. The mold inspection team would have to dress the part in hazmat suits, have the right equipment, and arrive in official-looking vehicles. They would have to appear to be legitimate in their search for toxic mold. Broderick worked with his PI to come up with a plausible story that would convince the imams at the mosques that their buildings needed to be checked for the dangerous substance. Once inside the right building, all Broderick needed was a positive reading of radioactivity. He would have found his source and his guilty mosque.

Letters with official city of Portland letterheads were sent to the mosques stating that the kind of drywall that was used in building the mosque had been shown to be susceptible to mold in other areas of Portland and in other cities nationwide. Broderick had the exact specifications of the drywall used in the building of each mosque. He had copied this information from the paperwork which had been submitted with the building permits for the mosques. The letter sent to each mosque would sound authentic, detailed, and official.

The letter would reassure those who received it that because of new technology for identifying toxic mold, the inspection could be accomplished by spending just a few minutes in each building. The inspections would be done free of charge and at the occupants' convenience. If mold was discovered, each specific area where it was found would be identified and mapped for extraction. The drywall company, each mosque was told, would be required to remove the moldy drywall and replace it with new, healthy drywall. It would be a painless procedure for the buildings' owners.

After the inspection, the inhabitants could rest assured their buildings were safe for habitation. The problem was, the phony letter explained, the moldy drywall had shown up in the Northwest and Southeast regions of the United States. These geographic areas had high yearly rainfall averages and therefore also had high levels of humidity. Blah. Blah. Blah. And so on and so forth. A phone number was given to call to set up the appointment.

The mold inspection scam was going to cost money. There were people to hire. There were protective suits, equipment, and a van to rent, and there were other props the "inspection team" would have to have to be convincing. Over the years, Nathanial Broderick had sent a great deal of business to his

PI friend. The PI owed Broderick, and Broderick had never been able to take any money for sending business to the PI. Covering the costs involved in mobilizing the phony mold inspection team would be a way for the PI to repay Broderick. The entire scheme would be done gratis. Broderick's friend had even hired a man for the inspection team who used to work for the EPA and had done real mold inspections before he'd retired. The guy knew the lingo and the equipment. He knew exactly what needed to be said and done so that the team would appear to be legitimately looking for toxic mold.

Of course, no toxic mold would be found. One of the PI's men would be on site with the rest of the hired technicians. This particular employee would be carrying the dosimeter, the device which was intended to detect radioactivity, not mold. Broderick worried that the deception would be exposed. He desperately hoped the team of pretend inspectors would find the mosque where the radioactivity was or had been. This was his last chance.

It took more than a week for the inspection letters to be delivered and for somebody at the mosques to respond. One mosque did not respond, and a phone call was placed to follow up on the letter. Finally, appointments were scheduled, and the inspection team was ready to make its visits. The ruse seemed to be convincing. The imams and other officials at the mosques appeared to believe that toxic mold might be a real threat to their places of worship.

The inspection at the first mosque was unremarkable. The clerics gave the team free access to all the buildings on the campus. They seemed to be skittish about allowing the strangers into their living quarters, but it worked out in the end. No mold was found, of course. More importantly, no radioactivity was detected.

The second mosque was a larger facility, and the imam there was not as agreeable to the demands of the inspection team. The imam wanted to restrict the access of the inspectors. He told them there were a couple of outbuildings on the grounds that were off-limits. This presented a problem which required some negotiations and did not reach a satisfactory resolution. The inspectors did not want to accept these restrictions and insisted they had to check all buildings. It was a standoff as the two sides tried to come to an agreement. The imam was adamant about the inspection team not going into one of the out buildings. Finally, the inspection team agreed not to go into that one particular building.

However, the imam's refusal to allow inspection in one of the outbuildings was a huge red flag for the people on the team. They insisted on closer scrutiny of the areas where they were allowed to go. They insisted that if mold was found in any of the other buildings on the campus, they would have to inspect the building that was off limits.

When the team reached the parking garage of this second mosque, the radiation detection device went crazy. The garage where the mosque kept its vehicles was definitely ground zero. The team paid special attention to all the other structures on the campus and got radioactivity readings of varying strengths in several of them. The pretend inspectors made a note of the exact location of the building that the imam would not allow them to enter. They told the imam that no mold had been found in any of his buildings. Because no mold had been found elsewhere, the inspectors told the imam they would not insist on entering the forbidden building. The mosque received its bogus clean bill of health.

When the news was reported back to Broderick, he was jubilant that he had found his culprits. He continued to be angry and worried about what these people intended to do with their radioactive material. But Broderick felt vindicated. His hunch had been spot on, and the time, trouble, and expense of the pretend mold inspections ruse had paid off. He was not exactly sure how he could legitimately proceed from this point, but he had his mosque and his guilty imam. Broderick was sure Aziz's murderer and his associates were, or at least had been, living somewhere on the grounds of this one particular mosque.

Because the imam had been so adamant about denying the mold inspectors access to the off-limits outbuilding, Broderick was certain the radioactive substances these jihadists had smuggled into the United States through the cove near Depot Bay were in that building on the campus of the mosque. Broderick's next steps would have to be carefully staged. His brilliant discovery of the location of the mystery travelers and their dangerous cargo had been accomplished without any official authorization. Only by revealing that he had been engaging in illegal activities, could Broderick let the FBI know what he knew. It would be tricky.

The team had to keep one more appointment at the third mosque, even though they had already found what they were looking for. They did not want to arouse suspicion, so they kept the appointment they had scheduled. The inspection team visited the third mosque. No mold was found, and no radioactivity was found. The toxic mold inspection team was disbanded. Mission accomplished. The PI's operatives, who had taken on the role of mold inspectors for a few days, changed their costumes and their hats and moved on to pretend to be something else.

Chapter 36

Looking for Evidence

Nathanial Broderick put the full-court press on his fellow law enforcement colleagues. He had decided to try to enlist the FBI and other federal agencies into the investigation of the Portland mosque. He could not tell them how he knew there was radioactivity inside the mosque because he had obtained that information without a warrant and under questionable circumstances. He found himself in a difficult situation because he was a detective with the Oregon State Police, but he had no official connection to Multnomah County where Portland was located. The city of Portland's police department was another branch of law enforcement, separate from the sheriff's office officials who had jurisdiction in Multnomah County. Law enforcement organizations everywhere are territorial. Sometimes the locals cooperate with the state police and the feds. Other times they dig in their heels, and sometimes they are even obstructive. It was complicated.

The FBI had taken jurisdiction over Aziz's murder case because of the radioactivity detected at the murder scene and in Aziz's apartment. The tough sell for Broderick was to link the murder of Aziz to the mosque where radioactivity had been found. Law enforcement was encouraged, at least in theory, to co-operate, but jurisdictional issues always created difficulties. This case was no exception.

Broderick told the FBI and others he had received a "tip" from an informant that there was something radioactive in a certain mosque. The FBI, of course, wanted to talk to the informant themselves. This was a problem for Broderick because in fact there was no informant. Broderick was frustrated that he couldn't convince the FBI to go into the mosque. Because of the current environment of extreme political correctness and because federal officials were generally so protective of any and all Muslims, it would be almost impossible, even if they wanted to, for the FBI to get a search warrant to allow them to enter a mosque to investigate.

Even if every FBI agent in Oregon were convinced there was something radioactive inside that mosque, it would be difficult to get a warrant. Broderick was going to have to find another way to get the information he needed. He was going to have to find another way to convince the FBI there was something dangerous in that mosque.

Broderick realized he might already be going down a slippery slope. By planning, authorizing, and participating in the phony toxic mold inspection scheme, he had already technically broken the law he had sworn to uphold. He had not trespassed personally on any of one of the three mosque properties. But that point would become moot if the scam were ever uncovered and became a court case. His name would be front and center in a lawsuit for an illegal search. He would lose his job.

Now he was focused on a way to get into the building the imam had declared off limits to the mold inspection team. Broderick felt certain that whatever he was looking for would be in that building. He felt such an urgency to proceed, to do something that would move his investigation forward, that he was shocked at his lack of fear about breaking the law again. He was determined to get into that forbidden building and obsessed with his desire to find out what was inside. It no longer seemed to him like he would be taking that much of a risk. It had become something he absolutely had to do. Nathanial Broderick wondered if he had already slipped across the line from being an enforcer of the law to being a vigilante. At this point, did it even matter to him that he had crossed that line?

He decided to call Abigail. He understood events more clearly when he talked them over with her. She was a smart woman and had an excellent analytical mind. She had imagination and could think outside the box. She liked having a problem to solve, and he always came away from a visit to her house with a new perspective or a new insight. And then there was the excellent Anne Marie who seemed to honestly enjoy cooking for him. He hoped he was not becoming a pest, but both Abigail and Anne Marie always welcomed him as if they were genuinely delighted to see him. Abigail enjoyed being involved in a real mystery, and Anne Marie loved to have her cooking receive the compliments it deserved. There were quite a few reasons to visit the cottage outside Depoe Bay.

Broderick called Abigail and told her he had news and wanted to bring her up to speed on the case. She had been a victim of a home invasion incident when Aziz had picked the locks and searched her house. She had discovered the dead body and the backpack bomb on her beach. She had discovered the remnants of the rubber raft in her cove. She had seen Aziz searching the cove a few days later, and she was the one who had called attention to the fact that the sand and dirt in the cove had been torn up by an ATV.

Broderick didn't feel he had to justify his visits to the writer's house, but in case anybody wondered why he kept going back to talk to her, he had lots of reasons why he might want to check back with Abigail Linder. She was the one who had brought Aziz to his attention, and she was an integral part of the case.

Broderick was anxious to meet with Abigail, but their lunch had to be postponed twice. It was delayed once because Abigail had the flu. Then there was a fierce January storm. Broderick was so eager to talk to her that he would have driven out in the storm in spite of the high winds and the freezing rain and snow. The coast road was closed and said to be impassable. Broderick thought he could make it through with his four-wheel drive. He didn't quite have the nerve to breach the roadblocks in order to enjoy spiced cider and the most heavenly chocolate chip cookies in the world. His sense of urgency never left him, but he decided to do the reasonable thing and wait out the storm.

Chapter 37

Looking for Lunch

I was delighted to hear from Nathanial that there was news about the case. He wanted to bring me up to date on the latest. He sounded excited. We set a date for lunch, and then I came down with the flu. It was one of those illnesses that sneaks up on you. One day you just feel more tired than usual, and the next day you feel a little better. The following day you ache all over, but it isn't quite bad enough to keep you in bed or from going out in the car. Then one morning you realize you don't think you have the energy to get up. You tell yourself you will be fine if you just have a few more hours of sleep. Finally, I gave in and admitted that it was going to be a bad case of the flu. I had chills and fever and a horrible cough. I didn't feel like eating anything and only wanted to sleep.

Anne Marie was worried about me, especially when I lost my appetite. She knew for sure at that point that I was seriously ill. She wanted to take me to the doctor or have the doctor come to the house. I realized I didn't even have a doctor in Oregon, but Anne Marie had a doctor and thought she could convince him to make a house call. I didn't think there was a doctor left in the world who still made house calls. I put Anne Marie off and insisted that I was fine and getting better. However, one morning when I woke up, I suspected that the flu had turned into pneumonia. I was getting worse.

Anne Marie's doctor came to the cottage and listened to my chest. Sure enough, I had pneumonia and needed serious antibiotics. Anne Marie got the medications from the drug store, and she even came in on Saturday and Sunday to check on me. She was worried because I was all by myself. When you feel as bad as I felt, you just want to be left alone. I appreciated her coming by the house, and I knew her concern was real. I don't think of myself as old, but when one is in one's seventies, pneumonia is not something with which to trifle.

The giant Augmentin capsules did their thing, and I began to improve. Anne Marie convinced me to drink countless cups of green tea with honey. When I was feeling a little bit better, she made my favorite chicken noodle soup with her homemade noodles. She walked and fed Gaela. I could barely make it to the bathroom or let Gaela in and out of the back door. Putting Gaela's food into a bowl was beyond my skill set for several days, and neither Gaela nor I would have made it through without the amazing Anne Marie.

When I was finally well enough, Nathanial and I made another appointment to meet over lunch at my cottage. Then a horrendous January storm hit the Oregon coast, and we had to delay our meeting again. The roads flooded and were completely impassible. My dirt road driveway was a sea of mud. We'd been warned in advance, so Anne Marie had brought in plenty of groceries ahead of the storm. She made extra soup and put it in my freezer. She left my favorite meals in the refrigerator. She was worried that I would starve or have a relapse of my illness. She was leaving nothing to chance.

I had pretty much recovered from the pneumonia and was taking it easy. From the shelter of my house, I watched the ferocious wind as it churned the ocean swells into spouts of white and gray. It was like watching a battle between the wind and the water, and I fell asleep at night wondering which would win.

Being housebound by the weather reminded me of the first storm I had experienced shortly after my arrival in Depoe Bay the previous fall. So much had happened since then. I knew the rhythms of living on the Oregon coast now. I had a mystery to occupy my curiosity. I had a wonderful housekeeper and cook, and I had a new friend in Detective Nathanial Broderick.

I turned on my gas fireplace. I read, and Gaela and I watched TV from the warmth and comfort of the couch. Many people lost power, and I was once again thankful I had made the decision to install a generator. I slept a lot and ate the meals Anne Marie had made and left for me. I was fully recovered from my bout with pneumonia when Nathanial finally came to the house for lunch.

Anne Marie made her famous tomato basil soup. The previous summer, she had canned tomatoes from her garden. Anne Marie and my gardener had conspired to bring some of my basil plants indoors, and she was keeping these wonderful herbs alive in pots in the kitchen. So, even in the dead of winter, she had fresh basil to cut in strips to flavor and garnish the soup. The soup was so sweet made with the homegrown tomatoes, I had to ask if she'd added any sugar. She said she didn't need to add sugar, that her tomatoes were the sweetest. The steak sandwiches with sautéed onions and horseradish mayonnaise were something new, and Anne Marie had made two sandwiches for Detective Broderick. She had buttered and grilled the rolls in the skillet, and the steak was perfectly cooked between rare and medium rare. Yum!

I told her she didn't need to make me any dinner as I was completely stuffed after the delicious lunch. She smiled and said there was leftover steak, au gratin potatoes, and Brussels sprouts for dinner. She'd made cherry pie for Nathanial's dessert. I could have had some pie, too, if I'd been able to move from my chair where I was immobilized by a food coma. I wondered if Nathanial was ever going to get around to talking about the case. I told him he'd better get to it if he expected me to stay awake to listen to him. The man could really eat!

He told me everything. He told me about his private investigator friend in Salem and the pretend mold inspection team. I'm not a lawyer so I didn't know how badly he might have broken the law. I told him I appreciated his ingenuity in getting access to the mosques. I was shocked to learn that the hypersensitive Geiger counter thing, the dosimeter, had given a positive reading in one of the mosques.

When I heard about the dosimeter readings, I assumed that federal agents had immediately swooped down on the mosque and arrested a whole passel of conspirators. Case closed. But Broderick set me straight about how things worked with this politically correct and Muslim-centered Department of Justice. I was furious that he could not go in and get the bad guys. This was something which was radioactive! It was dangerous. This was serious business. Why didn't somebody do something?

Nathanial told me he needed to get into the building the imam had declared off-limits during the mold inspection ruse. He said with the current attorney general setting guidelines for the FBI, he would never be able to get a warrant to search that building, no matter what kind of evidence he presented. Muslims and their mosques were off-limits for investigations. Period!

I told him it was time for somebody to call the fire department. The gas fireplace was blazing beside us. He glanced at the fireplace and gave me a puzzled look. I explained. "Somebody is going to have to get into that off-limits building and see what's in there. There doesn't have to be a real fire. It will be a false alarm. But somebody needs to call the fire department and report a fire at the mosque. When firefighters respond, you ride along with them. Of course, when you arrive, there won't be a real fire there. But you will have to insist that an inspection team go into every building on the grounds. No exceptions."

I continued with my stream-of-consciousness idea. "The fire marshal has the responsibility to refuse to take 'no' for an answer. He should insist on going into every building, including the suspicious shed that the imam insists is off limits. Be sure you or somebody takes the Geiger counter dosimeter thing along. When you get to the suspicious building, the shed, you will discover inside whatever there is to discover. Everyone will forget that the fire was a false alarm. There will be so much hoopla about the nefarious activity that is going on in that outbuilding, no one will have time or energy to focus on why there was a false alarm in the first place. Bingo! You have found your smoking gun and you have caught the imam with his pants down. Can they cut my head off for saying that?"

"You would have made an excellent criminal, Abigail. It scares me sometimes that you might go over to the dark side. Law enforcement would be forever chasing their tails, trying to catch you."

I laughed and accepted the compliment. At least I think it was a compliment. "No worries there, Nathanial. I am the most law-and-order person of any law-and-order person you will ever meet. One of the reasons I began to write my thrillers was to point out the weaknesses in our systems and to make people more aware of what they had to look out for. Sometimes what is quite obvious to one person is invisible to another. It takes all eyes open and watching constantly to keep us safe these days."

"If you are so law and order, does that mean you are going to turn me in for my fraudulent toxic mold inspections? I deserve to be turned in for that, you know." He was laughing, but I could tell it had bothered him a great deal to have to circumvent the law in order to find out what he needed to know. He had seen no other way than to do what he had done.

Chapter 38

Looking for the Smoking Gun

fter the mold inspection team had come to the mosque and tried to gain access to the building where the "dirty bombs" were being constructed, the imam was worried that someone from the health department would come back and try to have another look at that shed. He didn't think the mold inspection people would get a search warrant because he didn't think they would go to the trouble to get into the one building to which they'd been denied access. They'd seemed to be satisfied when they left that they had accomplished what they'd come to the mosque to do. They had not found any mold, and without inspecting all of the outbuildings, they had given the mosque a clean bill of health.

When the imam told Dean Abadi about the mold inspection, he asked if the Imam had checked with the Multnomah County Health Department about the authenticity of the letter the mosque had received and the legitimacy of the inspection team that was sent. The imam told Dean the letter had been written on an official letterhead, and there had been a phone number in the letter for him to call to set up an appointment for the inspection. He had not called the Multnomah County Health Department's general number to see if they had really sent the letter. The imam was not as suspicious as Dean was.

Dean and the imam discussed the situation and decided they did not want to draw additional attention to the mosque by calling county or city officials after the fact. The inspection was over, and no mold had been found. The inspection team had stayed away from the forbidden building and had accepted that they would not be able to check it out for mold. The imam felt the incident was finished. Dean was not so sure. Dean was by nature less trusting .

They decided their work had reached a point where it could be safely moved to Dean's garage. Because of the mold inspection, both Dean and the imam agreed that everything needed to be transferred away from the grounds of the mosque. The three young engineers who had arrived by sea would live with Dean and continue their work at his house. Dean used his van to transport the technicians and the devices they were working on. Dean felt more secure having the work going on where he was in complete control. He could watch every move the team made, and no one could gain access to his garage without his permission. There would be no mold inspections on his property — by the county or by anybody else.

The young people were not as happy to be staying with Dean as they had been living at the mosque. They liked to pray five times a day, and living at the mosque had made that quite convenient. The Imam had a cook who came in three days a week to cook for him. She also cooked for the three jihadists and made the young people's favorites. The three technicians had liked living at the mosque with the imam.

Life at Dean's was more Americanized, and the young people were not Americans. Dean made an effort to accommodate his guests. He hired the cook from the mosque to come to his house to fix their meals. The three jihadists had settled into a routine at the mosque and had been comfortable with that arrangement. But they accepted the fact that they had to move their operations to Dean's house for security reasons.

Neither Dean nor the imam believed there was any reason to think they were under suspicion. There was no way their activities could have been compromised. They had been extremely careful with every detail of their plans and with the execution of those plans. They thought they had operated flawlessly and had successfully covered their tracks. There was no way anybody could possibly know what had been going on at the mosque. Dean's house was completely off the radar screen, or so Dean believed.

A few days after the bomb-making operation had been moved to Dean's garage, the fire department arrived at the gates of the mosque. Someone had called in an alarm reporting a fire. Several fire trucks showed up at the entrance to the mosque to fight the fire. Ambulances and EMTs would assist by taking care of anyone who had been injured. The imam told the firemen that there was no fire. He did not want anybody from the fire department on the grounds of the mosque.

The imam protested vehemently when the fire marshal

told him they were going to enter the grounds of the mosque, and they were going to do a thorough inspection of all the buildings. There would be no exceptions. Every building, no matter how small or how dilapidated, would be inspected for possible fire. The delegation from the fire marshal's office directed teams of firefighters to begin the inspections.

The imam thought the false alarm and its report of a non-existent fire was dubious. He thought sending the fire marshal to investigate every building on the grounds of the mosque was at least a case of overkill. The outbuilding where the young engineers had been working had been off-limits to the mold inspection team. Now the fire department was insisting they had to inspect everything.

All of this made the imam quite anxious. He was afraid their plans had been found out. Maybe Dean was right to be paranoid about the mold inspections. The imam was relieved that they had already moved the operation to Dean's house. Thank goodness their work was no longer going on at the mosque. There was nothing for the fire department or anybody else to find. The whole thing with the fire alarm smelled to high heaven, but the imam still did not think there was any way his mosque could have come under suspicion.

The fire marshal's inspection seemed to be taking a long time, and the imam was impatient and annoyed with the whole thing. There was nothing to see at the mosque, but the fire department insisted on looking for it. One of the men from the fire department carried with him the extra sensitive radiation dosimeter. He accompanied the fire marshal's team and recorded extremely high levels of radioactivity in the suspect outbuilding. This was the shed the imam had not allowed the mold inspectors to enter. Something radioactive had been inside that building. But whatever had once been inside the outbuilding was no longer there.

All that was left in the shed was a high reading on the dosimeter. The evidence Broderick had so badly hoped to find had disappeared, and it was another dead end for his investigation. He was discouraged that all of his attempts to nail the source of the radioactivity had come to nothing. It seemed as if there was no place for his case to go.

The imam at the mosque was now quite angry. He was suspicious about who had called in the false alarm which brought the fire trucks and the fire marshal. The imam had not wanted to cooperate with the fire investigation. He now insisted that all first responders leave the mosque property as quickly as possible. He let the fire marshal know he thought the fire alarm had been intentionally called in to harass the mosque, to make trouble for an Islamic place of worship. He implied the mosque was ready to file a federal lawsuit for unlawful search and seizure and for discrimination against the Muslim community.

The imam was acutely aware that local law enforcement had its eyes on Muslims and their institutions. Wherever Muslims were under extra scrutiny, the imam was going to do everything he could to try to put a stop to it. The charade of pretending the mosque was not on law enforcement's radar screen was at an end. The local authorities were no longer trying to hide that they were looking at his mosque. The imam knew that he was protected at the federal level because of current policies. If the imam was going to get the locals to butt out, he was going to have to take his case to the feds.

After the false alarm fire, Dean was furious. He knew the mold inspection and the fire alarm were indications his mosque was being watched. But he could not figure out what anyone had done to reveal themselves. He thought back over all of his own actions and everything that had happened with his young scientists. He could only figure that something about Aziz's murder had put the authorities on to the Portland mosque. Maybe he should have paid more attention to the imam's opinions about Aziz?

Dean and the imam had argued about how to get rid of Aziz. They both felt he was a liability and agreed he had completely outlived his usefulness as a soldier serving the cause of Allah. The imam was in favor of leaving Aziz to his own devices in Depoe Bay, to allow him to live out his life there. It would not hurt anyone for Aziz to believe he was still of value to the cause of jihad even though he would never again be called on to assist in a mission. The imam did not think it would be dangerous to leave Aziz alone, a sleeper agent fast asleep, never to be awakened again.

Dean Abadi had not agreed with the imam. Dean wanted Aziz eliminated. Dean wanted him dead. Dean knew that Aziz was already being watched and that Aziz could be arrested and forced to talk. Dean was not willing to take the chance that Aziz was a weak link who might ruin everything they had worked so hard to accomplish. The imam had not wanted to send one of the engineers back to Depoe Bay to make contact with Aziz. Once the three had been collected from the cove along the Pacific coast and transported to Portland, they were safe. The imam did not want one of them to go back out into the public—especially to take a ride on a bus to meet with Aziz. Dean and the imam had argued about this, and Dean had prevailed.

Dean argued that Aziz's death could not occur in Depoe Bay. It had to look like a big city mugging gone wrong. It had to happen in Portland. which was the closest city with the appropriate criminal element on which the murder could be blamed. Everyone knew Aziz did not own a car. The only way Aziz could drive to Portland would be to rent a car. He had to believe he was on a mission in the service of Allah. Aziz had to believe he was doing all of this for jihad. Dean and the imam had come up with a plan to induce Aziz to drive to Portland where he could be murdered in an urban area and in a public place.

The technician who killed Aziz was an expert assassin. He had been trained to do many things. He did not want to expose himself by riding on a public bus to a small town in Oregon to meet with a has-been jihadist who'd been in place as a sleeper agent since before 9/11. But the jihadist followed the orders he was given. He was a good sharia warrior.

Even the method of Aziz's death had been a point of contention between Dean and the imam. The assassin was highly skilled in the use of the long knife, and that was the weapon he preferred to use to kill. But slicing someone's throat from ear to ear was not the "American" way to kill. Americans kill each other with guns. The parking garage murder scenario called for the use of a handgun. The assassin had been trained in the use of firearms, but he was not as comfortable with a handgun as he was with a knife or even an AK-47. He finally agreed to use the hand gun on Aziz in the parking garage, and he used a silencer. He fired two shots into Aziz's head and left no fingerprints. It was a professional hit.

The assassin had no idea he had left traces of radioactivity behind. It was the trail of radioactivity that linked Aziz's murder to his apartment over the t-shirt shop, to the Pacific Coast cove in Depoe Bay, and to jihad. The murder was not an urban mugging or "burglary gone wrong." It was the radioactivity that had been found in the rental car that ultimately led investigators to a Portland mosque.

Chapter 39

Looking for a Jihadist

*After the fiasco at the mosque, Detective Broder-*ick was completely demoralized. He knew something radioactive had been there, but he had no idea where that something was now. In spite of detecting radioactivity at the scene of the false fire alarm, the authorities finally shut down the investigation for lack of evidence. They had no useful leads. Broderick was surprised there was so little interest in finding the source of the radioactivity.

The detective suspected pressure from the feds might have led to the investigation being quashed. An implication that anything or anyone Islamic might be involved in suspicious activity was discouraged. Investigations into anything Islamic usually did not get off the ground and were frequently ordered to be shut down. Broderick was given other cases to pursue. He was told to suspend all investigations having to do with the radioactivity case.

Spring came to Depoe Bay, and Nathanial Broderick was disappointed that he didn't have any reason to visit Abigail Linder and her housekeeper Anne Marie. He occasionally called to give her the update that there was no news. She always invited him for lunch, but since he had nothing to offer in the way of new information and had nothing to discuss with her, he didn't feel he deserved a lunch.

Broderick knew something was going on. He knew something was going to happen. He felt it in his gut. But he had no clue what it was that was going to happen—or where or when whatever it was would happen. Radioactivity was a new element in the terrorism landscape. It was what law enforcement feared most. What good thing could possibly result from a shipment of radioactive material being stored at a mosque?

One day, Broderick was having a slow day and decided to take another look at the file on the Aziz investigation. It had now been designated as an inactive case. It could not be downgraded yet to a cold case, but no one was still working on any aspect of the investigation that had to do with radioactivity. Broderick read through every page in the file and was almost at the end when he saw a piece of paper he hadn't seen before. He had read through these same papers so many times in the past, he felt he knew every detail of the case by heart.

Today there was a folded piece of paper in the file that he didn't recognize. There wasn't any date on the paper, but Broderick was sure it was something new. He did not know how it had made its way into the file. He wondered if he had missed it in the past. But here it was, and it was important.

Months earlier, Nathanial Broderick had requested that the FBI find out who in the Portland area had purchased, in the year prior to the arrival of the rafts in the cove, a very specific model of the John Deere Gator. He didn't think there would be many people on the list. His intention had been to cross reference the list of people who had purchased a Gator with membership lists from Portland's mosques.

Because law enforcement at the federal level of government had pretty much put a stop to any investigations into anything having to do with Islam, there were not going to be any membership lists from any mosques available to anybody. Before the fake mold inspection had identified the mosque where the radioactive material had been, Broderick had little hope of linking the purchase of a Gator with a particular mosque, let alone to a member of that mosque. This line of inquiry had become another dead end.

Nathanial Broderick had forgotten about his request for the list of Portland area residents who had purchased specific Gators. He'd made the request about the Gators before the mold inspections and before the fire alarm at the mosque. Because of those two events, Broderick did not have to search the membership lists of multiple mosques in Portland. Now he only had to focus on one mosque, the mosque where the radioactivity had been found. He was betting that whoever had purchased the Gator belonged to that radioactive mosque. He was certain whoever owned that Gator had driven the people and the cargo from their arrival in the cove, through the woods, and to the main road outside Depoe Bay.

There were fifteen people on the list of those who had purchased the specific model of the Gator that Broderick was investigating. Three names stood out as sounding somewhat "Middle Eastern" to Broderick. Having a Middle Eastern sounding name did not mean one was a terrorist or that one was a Muslim. But it gave Broderick a small ray of hope and perhaps a small lead in his inactive case. He hoped he had a way to get started again with the investigation.

Broderick ran background checks and internet searches on the three names he thought might be members of the suspect mosque. He found that one of the Gators had been purchased by a man who owned a vineyard in the Willamette Valley. The man had a Greek name and attended a Greek Orthodox Church. Another one of the Gators had been purchased by a man who owned a dairy farm outside of Portland. That man was a Ukrainian immigrant and did not appear to have any religious affiliation. He might be a possibility.

The third Gator purchase was made by a man named Dean Abadi. He had lived in Cleveland, Ohio and Chicago, Illinois, before he'd moved to Portland many years earlier. Among other affiliations with several civic organizations, Abadi was listed as having belonged for many years to Bethany Presbyterian Church in a suburb of Cleveland. The retired physicist and electrical engineer did not have any known church affiliation in Portland—at least that Broderick was able to find. None of the three likely candidates appeared to be a Muslim. None would be attending services at a mosque. This seemed to be yet another dead end in a sea of dead ends.

Detective Broderick wondered what Abigail would say. He decided she would tell him that perhaps the man who purchased the Gator did not have a Middle Eastern sounding name. Or, maybe he had converted to Islam from whatever religion he had previously practiced. She probably would suggest that he find out where each one lived and watch their houses to see where they went and what they did with their time.

One technique that law enforcement uses to determine if anything untoward is going on in a particular household is to check utility bills. If the energy bills at a certain address increase suddenly and dramatically, there is a good chance that someone has begun cooking methamphetamines in that house. Although Broderick was not looking for a meth operation, he was looking for someone whose lifestyle had changed and whose energy and water consumption profile had suddenly increased.

The operation involving the radioactivity had moved away from the campus of the mosque. Where had it moved? Had the person who had purchased the Gator taken the people and their work, whatever it was, into his own home? It was certainly worth a look.

Broderick was interested in a time frame that covered the period when he suspected the terrorist operation had moved out of the mosque. The vineyard owner's and the dairy farmer's electricity, gas, and water bills varied as one might expect them to with the fluctuating seasonal demands of planting and harvesting. But Dean Abadi's utility usage had spiked after the phony mold inspection and before the false fire alarm—at just the right time for Broderick to suspect that something drastic had changed in the Abadi household.

Broderick decided to start his surveillance with Abadi who lived in Portland. Dean Abadi was a retired construction engineer and lived alone—at least most of the time—in an expensive house in an upscale Portland neighborhood.

Chapter 40

Looking For a Candidate

Both political parties promised infighting and fireworks this year. There had been much more confusion than usual during the primary season for both Republicans and Democrats. There would continue to be controversy and even chaos at the conventions. At the Democrat convention, there would be stark disagreements about choosing a candidate. The candidate the Democrat machine was supporting might be a criminal who had openly stated that it was "her turn" to be the president.

Various factions of the Republican party would object to the candidate who had received the most votes in the primaries. He was not really a Republican, they claimed. He was a populist. Both political parties would argue over the issues. They always did. The American people seemed to be angry about the last eight years. No matter what their ideological beliefs were, they saw the economy in the dumps and the world set afire by terror attacks. Many said openly that they no longer recognized their own country.

The fundamental transformation that had promised "hope and change" had been a disaster. The Republicans were going to nominate a billionaire businessman and reality TV star who had never before held political office and might be certifiably nuts. The Democrats were going to nominate a political retread with terrible judgment who was a serial liar and who had barely escaped going to prison by handing out who knows what payoffs and manipulations. What was the country coming to? The world had gone insane. Politics in the USA was not far behind.

The conventional wisdom about the Democrats was that the socialist congressman from a small New England state had thrown a monkey wrench into the plans of the presumptive Democrat nominee. No one had ever expected that anybody would give "the anointed one" a run for her money. But the old white man, the socialist, had done just that.

The current vice president had been discouraged from running because he could never have withstood the scrutiny of a primary contest, and he was too old. He seemed to be a good guy who was fairly well-liked, but he was not that smart. He had several huge plagiarism scandals in his background from law school and from previous presidential runs.

The thorn in the side of the Democrat Party's coronation ceremony had come in the form of that socialist congressman from New England. He currently called himself a democratic socialist, but that was just to allow him to get into the Democrat primaries. He had messed with the sitting president's grand design.

The president's chief of staff had secretly alerted the FBI about a scandal involving the presumptive Democrat nominee's email server. The original plan had been for the "party favorite" to be indicted just before the Democrats held their nominating convention. The current president would swoop in and put in his own vice president, the man who could not survive the scrutiny of a primary contest. If the president's own vice president won the election, it guaranteed that the sitting president would have a third term. The president's legacy would be perfectly preserved. Democrats would be in the White House again, and the sitting president's leadership of the Democrat party would not be challenged by any other antagonistic faction within the Democrat Party.

The continued presence of the socialist challenger in the Democrat Party and his huge success as the people's choice had thrown off the party faithful's plans. How could the existing president insert his vice president as the nominee, if there was this other extremely popular nominee waiting in the wings? The Democrat interloper had won several state primaries. He was clearly popular with the people. The millions who supported the socialist congressman would be enraged if the nomination was given to someone who had not competed in the primary process. The indictment of the "entitled" candidate that the people seemed to be rejecting would now have to be called off. It would be an interesting political year. It would be a mess.

Dean had been a responsible citizen in his former life. As a Presbyterian and a man who had identified with the country of his birth, he had registered to vote. He had voted in almost all important elections. Since his conversion to radical Islam, he viewed American institutions through quite a different prism. His plans to attack the political process of the United States had been formulating in his mind for several years, but the icing on the cake came this election cycle when the two major political parties chose their Presidential candidates.

Although it would not be official until the conventions in Cleveland and Philadelphia, both of the "presumptive nominees" were people Dean thought were beneath contempt. He loathed and despised both of them. He believed the woman was a criminal and the man was a maniac. These choices confirmed for Dean that the United States was indeed in decline and deserved to be brought down.

Dean remembered the Democrat's designated candidate from previous escapades and wondered how such a toxic human being could ever be elected to anything. He especially remembered the terrible "health care plan" she had dreamed up in her younger days. She couldn't even get that hot mess passed through a Democrat congress. The urban myth was that she was smart, but her record of non-accomplishments and downright failures was stunning. She had even failed to pass the Washington D.C. bar exam back in the 1970s. She was a terrible candidate that nobody really liked.

Republicans were going to nominate a flamboyant and "very, very rich" (his words) candidate. He had managed to mobilize into a populist movement the anger many Americans felt about the state of their country and the state of the world. Dean could not comprehend why anyone would vote for the Republican candidate either. The businessman and flamboyant TV personality had never before held any public office. He was not a real Republican and had in fact belonged to the Democrat party or some other political party for most of his life.

Allbert could only imagine that his appeal was some kind of a reaction to the disasters of the current regime. People were disappointed by eight years of laziness and criticizing the United States. The choice … to gather around the arrogant woman who was the offering of the Democrats or to gather around the Republicans' unpredictable and seemingly unstable egomaniac … astounded Dean.

Dean had grown to despise the United States, its citizens, and its political leaders. He was now even more convinced that his plans would be a tribute to Allah. He believed that by ridding the world of these two terrible political choices, he would be doing the people of the United States, and especially the people of the world, a favor.

Dean would weep no tears for anyone who died in the attacks at either convention, but he was particularly pleased that both front-runners in this presidential election cycle would be destroyed. In his opinion, both nominees were repulsive candidates who were not liked by their own parties or by the people who were going to hold their noses and vote for them. Dean had come to despise Americans and the American political process.

Dean was now an enthusiastic believer in sharia law and had committed the rest of his life on earth to try to bring this Muslim system of beliefs to as many places around the world as he possibly could, including to the United States. He had totally lost any belief he might have had in the U.S. Constitution. He had converted, and he had become a believer in sharia law and in the rise of the caliphate.

Dean himself did not fully understand why he had found such comfort in Islam and why he had turned so harshly against the country in which he had been born and raised. Dean did not understand all the reasons why he had become such a virulent advocate for terror and was in fact planning the most horrendous attack in history on the American homeland. He did know that the prospect of the destruction he would bring thrilled him to his core.

Dean was not entirely sure the air-circulating machines he had designed and helped to build for use at the convention in Cleveland would work. These machines were something entirely new and not thoroughly tested. But he was almost certain the Philadelphia plan would work perfectly. All he had to do was get his machines, his weapons, and his people to their target locations. He was anxious to get the entire operation and the young people out of his house.

Never having had any children of his own, he was not used to having other people of any age living with him—let alone these youthful zealots. He was not a tolerant man. He had engaged the cook from the mosque to feed his house guests, but they were not happy when they'd had to leave the mosque. They understood why the move was necessary, but they were unusually religious and wanted to pray at the mosque several times every day. They prayed at Dean's home, but for these non-Americans and devout jihadists, it was not the same as praying at the mosque. Twice a day, Dean drove them to the mosque in the van. He considered this an imposition on his time and on his good will. More than an imposition, he considered the twice daily trips to the mosque a huge security risk.

Dean was an American, and his home was very American. The young people who were working in Dean's garage were not Americans. They were much more comfortable in the traditional Islamic surroundings of the mosque. Dean himself was anxious to move the three young technicians away from his home, into the motorhome, and on to the political conventions. He wanted them on their way as soon as he could get rid of them. He felt somewhat guilty about not wanting to have them around. He knew they were fanatics who were willing to give their all for Allah, but he honestly didn't like any one of the three. They were smart, but they were spoiled. Dean found them to be petulant and rigid. They annoyed him. He would be happy when he had his house back to himself. He wondered if maybe he was more of an American than he wanted to admit.

Dean did not want the bomb technicians on the road for too long, but he wanted them to arrive at their target locations in plenty of time to prepare for the attacks. Timing was critical, and it was tricky. The motorhome was ready. Living in close quarters in the motorhome with these temperamental geniuses would be a test of everybody's patience.

The cook was going to accompany the three, in addition to the driver. Dean felt it was ridiculous to send the cook along to cater to the three young people, but they insisted on it. Dean proposed that the cook make meals ahead to refrigerate and freeze. That plan would have required the meals to be carried in the motorhome, and the young people would have to thaw and heat the food in the microwave. This plan was turned down by the prima donnas who would not lift a finger to cook their own meals, even in a microwave.

Dean knew he was lucky to have these brilliant technicians working on his project, but he personally could not stand their entitled attitudes and their unwillingness to do anything to take care of themselves. Dean especially had not liked doing their laundry while they were staying at his house. He decided the motorhome was going to leave sooner rather than later.

The imam had originally intended to accompany the bomb makers to their target locations, but when the cook was added to the travel group, there would not be room for the imam. There were only four beds in the large motorhome, and the couch could be made into an additional place to sleep. The cook was going. The imam was not. There would not be anyone along on the trip to ride herd over the young people and make sure security and other protocols were followed. It was not ideal, but it was the way it had to be.

Dean had planned every detail of the operation. In theory, his plan was perfect. Many plans are perfect in theory. Dean was smart enough to know that, in the real world, problems might arise and plans might have to change. He was trying to adjust, but he was frustrated for many reasons. He would be glad when the bomb makers were on their way and out of his house. He'd had enough of babysitting for a while.

The motorhome could not be loaded at Dean's house. His garage was not tall enough to accommodate the motorhome which was the size of a Greyhound bus. Dean could not have a motorhome parked outside his house for several days, let alone have people coming and going while they packed it full of radioactive materials, explosives, and electronics.

The motorhome had to be parked and loaded at the mosque. The parking garage attached to the mosque was the only practical location. The bomb components would be transferred back to the mosque from Dean's home via the van. It was not ideal to move these fragile and volatile experimental machines too many times. But the reality was that when the preparations were completed, adjustments had to be made for security reasons. The three young technicians moved their things back to the mosque for the final stages of loading the motorhome. They were happier there. Dean was happier, too.

At last, the motorhome was ready to go. The components for the devices and the bombs were safely stored and securely cushioned in the baggage compartment underneath. When one is dealing with radioactivity, extra precautions must be taken. Safety measures are paramount. Fortunately, as difficult as his technicians had been, they were quite cognizant of the care that had to be taken with their radioactive materials.

The cook had insisted that an extra refrigerator be installed in the motorhome. The converted bus would not be stopping to shop at grocery stores during the trip across the country. The extra refrigerator was small, but it was awkward to try to find a spot for it inside the motorhome. It took up a lot of the living space, but it was necessary to keep the cook happy. The cook had to be kept happy to keep the young jihadists happy. Things were getting complicated.

Security procedures required that the three young people and the cook never leave the confines of the motorhome. Their foreign appearances and heavily accented English might draw attention if they were to appear or speak in public. Only the driver who had been born in the USA and who spoke perfect American English would be allowed to step outside the motorhome during the journey. He would pay cash for everything he bought along the way. There would be absolutely no paper trail.

The driver would be exclusively in charge of filling the vehicle with gas. All the motorhome's systems had been checked and rechecked, and there should not be any mechanical problems or breakdowns. The driver had experience with motorhomes and knew all about hooking one up to services along the route. He was well aware of the various maintenance duties that had to be attended to during the trip. Hopefully, there would not be any emergencies.

Dean Abadi had invested a great deal of himself in this project. He had planned it for so long, and he had such high hopes for what the results could be. It was a relief when the motorhome finally pulled away from the mosque. The bombs and their unique delivery devices, which he had worked so hard to build, were at last on their way to the targets. Dean was alone again in his home. He cleaned up his garage and decided he would get rid of the Gator and the van. He did not intend to use either one again. They were just taking up space. He would sell the Gator and the van and buy a BMW.

Chapter 41

Looking for a Gator

Detective Broderick and the private investigator who owed him some favors were going to cover the surveillance of Dean Abadi's house. No one in law enforcement except Broderick felt Abadi was a priority, so no other resources were going to be allocated to the stakeout. Abadi may or may not own the Gator that had been driven through the woods at Depoe Bay. That Gator might be owned by the Ukrainian dairy farmer, by the Greek owner of the vineyard, or by someone else entirely. Broderick could not cover the house twenty-four hours a day, seven days a week. He was concerned that they would miss something critical with their spotty surveillance program.

Broderick was pleasantly surprised when he had a hit on the first day he spent watching Abadi's house. When he observed a dark green van back out of the man's garage early in the morning, he made a decision to follow the van and abandon his watch on the house. The van drove several miles across town where it pulled onto the grounds of the radioactive mosque and into its parking garage. The mosque was the same one where the toxic mold team had registered radioactivity and the same mosque where the suspect outbuilding had subsequently sent the dosimeter into paroxysms. Bingo!

Broderick was now absolutely certain he had his man in Abadi. In spite of the fact that he had supposedly been a Presbyterian earlier in his life, Abadi had just now driven his van to the suspect mosque. Here was the connection Broderick had been hoping to find. The detective waited in his rental car outside on the street for more than an hour until the van exited the grounds of the mosque. Broderick followed when the van returned to Abadi's home. The detective was confident he was watching the right house. He was now certain that Dean Abadi was the Muslim who owned the Gator that he'd been searching for.

The van made a second trip to the mosque later that day. Twice a day on subsequent days, the dark green van left Abadi's garage and drove to the mosque. After an hour or more, the van returned to Abadi's house. Broderick assumed Abadi was a religious man to want to drive twice a day to a mosque to pray or attend religious services.

Broderick needed to get inside Dean Abadi's garage. He wanted to see if the Gator was stored there, and he wanted to see what else was going on inside the garage. But he would have to be careful. Another phony health department raid was not going to cut it with a private citizen's home. Broderick wanted to go in while the van was at the mosque, but he didn't know if there were any people still at the house. He decided it would be safer to approach the garage at night when most people are sleeping.

The next day, however, Abadi's van did not leave the garage. Broderick thought it was odd that all of a sudden, the pattern of Abadi's behavior had changed. Something was up, and Broderick was beside himself because he did not know what it was. Maybe Abadi was sick? When three days went by without the van making a trip to the mosque, Broderick decided he needed to transfer the focus of his observations elsewhere.

There was not any good place to watch the mosque unless one was on the grounds. Broderick couldn't do that and had to observe from the public street, but he couldn't see much of anything from where he had to park. He decided the best thing to do was to make a list of all the vehicles that drove onto and left the grounds of the mosque. He wrote down detailed descriptions of each vehicle that entered and left. He wrote down the license plate numbers. He snapped a photo of each vehicle when he could. It was tedious work, and it probably would not yield any useful information.

Most of the vehicles that entered the mosque's grounds eventually came back out. Broderick made a note of the ones which did not come out after a few hours. These might be worth looking into. The second day while he was watching the mosque, he saw an enormous motorhome pull out of the main entrance. The motorhome was oversized. It was as big as a Greyhound Bus and was the largest motorhome allowed to drive on a public highway.

Where had that enormous thing come from? It must have been in the garage next to the mosque. It could have been there for days or weeks. Would anyone risk transporting something radioactive in a motorhome? Broderick did not know if the appearance of the motorhome had anything to do with the arrival of the people and their radioactive materials that had passed through Abigail Linder's cove in Depoe Bay. He wrote down the Oregon license plate number and a detailed description of the motorhome. He would check out its ownership. It might be worth following the motorhome to see where it was headed. On the other hand, the vehicle might have nothing at all to do with the radioactivity. It might just be that the motorhome was owned by a visiting sheik who liked to travel and had several wives.

After two more days of observing the mosque, Broderick decided he was not going to learn anything more of importance there. He made plans to go back to Dean Abadi's house and break into his garage. Broderick was not sure what he would find, but he would take along his Geiger counter dosimeter, the ultra-sensitive radioactivity detector. He wanted to know if the Gator he was looking for was stored in Abadi's garage. He also wanted to know if radioactive materials had ever been there.

Broderick again attempted to get some back-up manpower to help him with his plans, but he knew his superiors were tired of hearing his theories about the Gator and Dean Abadi. Broderick had become a one-man band in his quest for the illusive radioactive elements. Broderick knew that nobody in law enforcement would support his plan to break into someone's garage without a warrant. That part of his operation would have to be kept off the books. He decided he would not have anybody stand guard while he broke into Abadi's garage. What he planned to do was risky, maybe too risky, but Broderick sensed he was on to something important. He could not let it go.

The next night, Broderick waited until after dark to make his move. There was a person door on the side of Abadi's garage. It was locked with several padlocks which surprised Broderick. What could be in the garage that was so valuable? What would require this degree of security in the lock department? To gain entry, he used his lock picks with great care. He did not want to alert Abadi that there had been a break-in. Broderick had to spend some time picking the various locks, but finally he was inside.

It was a three-car garage. The long-sought-after Gator was parked in one space. The dark green panel van was parked in another. Broderick's radioactivity dosimeter was registering off the charts. He ran it over the Gator and the van. He ran it over the empty space in the garage. The radioactive materials Broderick had been searching for had definitely been here. There was no question about it. But where had they gone? Where were they now? That was the question. He now knew where the materials had been, but it seemed he was always at least one step behind. He was always finding where what he was looking for had been, but he was never in time to actually put his hands on it.

Broderick knew he had been in the garage too long. Picking all the locks had required extra time. And he had thoroughly searched the garage in hopes of finding a clue about where the radioactive materials had been taken. Broderick didn't want Abadi to know that anyone had been inside his garage. The detective would be sure he left everything just as he'd found it. This included the locks which he intended to put back exactly the way they had been. Broderick was working on putting the locks back in place when he heard someone approach the side of the garage. As he finished with the last lock, he realized somebody was just around the corner of the building.

The detective didn't have time to hide. He only had time to run. He took off into the trees behind the garage but did not make his escape in time. He heard the gunshot at almost the same moment he felt the pain in his thigh. Then he heard another gunshot and felt the pain in his side. He heard a few more shots fired. By then he was safely in the woods where he thought no more bullets could find him.

Broderick had been injured in the line of duty before, so he knew these gunshot wounds were serious. He had to make it to his car, and he absolutely could not be caught by either Abadi or by the police. He couldn't let anybody know he had been inside Abadi's garage. Detective Broderick's actions constituted breaking and entering and trespassing. What he had done was against the law. There had been no warrant, and Broderick knew he would be in serious trouble if he were caught by law enforcement. If Abadi caught him, he knew he would probably end up dead.

At last Broderick had the evidence he needed to get a search warrant for Abadi's garage and home. But it didn't look like he was going to have the chance to get that warrant now. Broderick knew he was in trouble. He knew he had to focus on conserving his energy, saving himself, and getting to a safe place. He moved through the woods as quickly as he could. He was carrying the Geiger counter dosimeter. He absolutely could not drop it. It was the one thing he could not leave behind.

Broderick was bleeding profusely. He thought he was making his way in the direction of his car, but he was dazed. He couldn't remember exactly where he had parked. Could he make it there before he collapsed? He was growing weak from loss of blood, and his mind was fuzzy about where he had left his car. He became increasingly disoriented. He needed to stop and apply pressure to his wounds, but he couldn't take the time. If Abadi decided to call the police, it might be only minutes before they arrived. But if Abadi had something to hide, and Broderick knew that he did, maybe he wouldn't call the police.

Broderick was still cogent enough to realize he had to continue to focus on survival. He knew he had to immediately get as far away as possible from Abadi's property. He stumbled and recovered. He stumbled and recovered again. He didn't hear any sirens, and that gave him hope. Maybe no police were coming. Maybe he would make it. He made a few false starts out of the woods as he struggled to head in the right direction. He didn't think Abadi had followed him. Maybe Abadi had just wanted to scare away an intruder.

Broderick finally found his rented sedan parked on a side street. He fumbled in his pocket for the remote key opener. He fell inside the car and collapsed across both front seats. Eventually he roused himself enough to be able to assess his injuries. He realized he was badly hurt. He would have to get professional medical attention, but first he needed to apply pressure to the wounds to try to stop the bleeding. He tied his belt around his thigh, and that seemed to slow the flow of blood from the leg wound.

He had also been hit in the torso, and it was the wound in his side that concerned him the most. He took off his shirt and found where the bullet had entered. He'd been lucky. It was a through and through, just like the wound in his thigh. There would not be any bullets to dig out of his body. But he knew he had left behind a great deal of blood. He took his shirt and pressed it against his side, packing it hard into the wound as tightly as he could. No vital organs appeared to be hit, but he was still losing blood. There was a first aid kit in the console of the car, but what good would a few Band-Aids and a couple of aspirin do to help his current situation? He grabbed his jacket from the back seat and secured it as tightly as he could around his body and the shirt he had packed into his side to staunch the blood.

More than anything, he wanted to lie down. He struggled to remain conscious but thought he had slowed his blood loss. After a few minutes, he imagined he was feeling less light-headed. He was desperate to tend to his wounds. He needed to get out of the neighborhood and get help. But all he could seem to think about was finding a place to lie down. Where in the world would that be?

As he concentrated on trying to drive, Nathanial Broderick went over and over in his mind attempting to remember exactly how he had left the locks on the person door at Abadi's garage. Had he finished putting back the last lock? Had he left any of his lock picks behind? Had he left any trace that he'd been inside the garage? How far away from the garage door had he been when he was shot? Had he left a trail of blood from the garage? In the woods?

Nathanial Broderick had been staying at a motel in Portland while he was doing his surveillance of Abadi's house and the mosque. The motel was several miles from where Broderick had parked his car for the nighttime break-in. He thought there was about a 50/50 chance he could make it back to his motel. He did not want to go back to a place where he had checked in under his real name, but at this point he didn't have a choice. He drove just under the speed limit, trying hard to keep himself from slipping into unconsciousness. He did not need to be stopped for speeding right now, and he did not need to pass out behind the wheel and cause an accident.

Broderick parked his rented sedan outside the door of his room at the back of the motel. The driver's seat of the car was now completely soaked with blood. Because he kept such odd hours doing his surveillance work, he'd requested a room at the rear of the motel. He'd wanted a room at the back because he had hoped his late-night comings and goings would not be noticed or bother anybody. He was now even more thankful he had made that request. He struggled to find his room key. It had fallen out of the pocket of the jacket he'd tied around his body. Broderick finally found the key on the floor of the sedan behind the driver's seat.

He let himself into his room and fell onto the bed. He felt as if his life were slipping away from him. He didn't think he could stay conscious and knew he needed to get help before he passed out. Doctors had to report gunshot wounds to the authorities. Broderick knew he couldn't answer any questions about his gunshot wounds so he knew he couldn't call a doctor for help. But he was desperate for some medical care.

Years earlier, Broderick had been in the military. He'd kept up with a couple of his buddies. He thought he might be able to call on one of them who had been a medic and had served with him in Iraq. The man had gone back to school on the GI bill after he'd finished his tours in the military, and now he was a CPA in Portland. Broderick didn't know if his friend would be willing to help him out. He hadn't talked to Arnold Moore in at least a year. They'd lost touch, but Broderick felt as if making a call to Moore was his only chance to have treatment from somebody who knew even a little bit about what they were doing.

Broderick called the phone number he had for his friend and got an answering machine. He left a message and asked Moore to call him back on his cell phone as soon as possible. He told his friend he was in bad trouble and needed help.

The detective fell asleep on the bed in the motel room. Broderick was awakened with a start when his cell phone rang an hour later. It was Arnold Moore calling him back. Nathanial told him he had been shot and couldn't go to a hospital.

"I thought you were the police, Broderick. What do you mean you can't go to the hospital? Have you gone rogue?" Arnold Moore couldn't understand why his formerly straight-arrow buddy wasn't able to go to a doctor or to an emergency room for medical treatment.

"I'll explain it all when I see you, but I need help right now. I am fading fast, and you are my only chance." Broderick told Moore he had been shot in the leg and in the side and gave him a cursory description about how serious the gunshot wounds were. He gave his friend directions to the motel. He told him to bring bandages and antibiotics.

"You know I haven't worked as a medic in years. I'm a CPA now, and it's been almost a decade since I treated a gunshot wound. I wouldn't want me working on me if I were you."

Broderick convinced his friend that he was his only hope for survival. He fell asleep again while he waited for Arnold Moore to arrive at the motel. He'd left the door of the room unlocked. Moore stopped at a pharmacy to get supplies on his way to the motel. When he arrived, he cleaned and dressed Broderick's wounds. He stitched up Broderick's leg but felt the wound in his side should not be closed yet. He did all he could to keep everything as sterile as possible to minimize potential infection. He told Broderick that infection was the main danger he was facing. He didn't think Broderick would die without a blood transfusion, but he wished he could hook up an IV for his former Army pal.

"I'm not going to ask you what happened, and you are not going to tell me. If I were working right now as an

EMT, I would be required to report to the authorities that I have treated a gunshot wound. Since I am now a CPA, I am going to skirt the law and fail to report this to anybody. I've done all I can do for you, though. I can't take a chance that I might be arrested. I have a wife and two small children, and I can't afford to risk losing my livelihood. I was happy to do this for you, but this is it. I don't know what else to tell you. You need somebody to help you change the dressings on your wounds. The wounds will need to be watched carefully. Dehydration and infection are real and serious possibilities. You need professional attention. This is nothing to fool around with, Broderick. You need to get somebody you trust to take you home with them and take care of you. You need somebody to make sure you are drinking plenty of fluids. You need somebody to feed you. What you really need is to be in a hospital. You're already stiffening up, and by tomorrow morning you will be too stiff to walk around by yourself. You will need help going to the bathroom. You need to be sleeping and resting on sheets that are changed every day, if not more often. I have brought you all the antibiotics I could find around my house. I don't have any painkillers I can give you, and I can't prescribe anything for you. Only a doctor can do that. I wish I could do more, but I can't take the chance."

Broderick was enormously grateful that his friend had been willing to do all he had done. He realized he'd imposed on the man in a way he should not have and would not have if he'd had any other choice. Nathanial Broderick was so tired. He just wanted to sleep and sleep. He had to get more help, and he didn't know where that help would come from. He knew he could not call on any of his law enforcement colleagues or anybody associated with his work.

Nathanial was desperate to get out of Portland. He wanted to go home to his apartment in Depoe Bay, but he knew that was a bad idea. He would have to walk up two flights of stairs to get to his condo. It had a great view of the water, but he would not be able to negotiate any steps at all in his current condition.

He decided to call Abigail Linder and ask for her help. She had a hard time getting around, but she was not hung up on convention. She might be willing to help him. At least she and her housekeeper would be able to feed him. He hated to impose on Abigail's good will, but he was out of options. He wanted to be away from Portland in the worst way. He made the call and told Abigail everything that had happened.

Abigail did not let him down. "I am coming to get you right now. You can stay at my house, and Anne Marie and I can clean and dress your wounds, keep you hydrated, and feed you. Give me the address of your motel, and I will program it into my GPS. Pack up everything you'll need for the next few weeks. Make sure your motel room is paid up for the next month. Call the desk and tell them you will be out of town for several weeks but want to keep your room. Tell them you are leaving your car parked in the parking lot while you are traveling overseas for business. That should satisfy them. They won't care if you leave your car parked there as long as you've paid ahead for your room. You want anyone who might be watching you to think you are still doing surveillance in Portland.

Abigail continued to give directions. "When I get there, I'll put a blanket over the blood in the driver's seat of your car. If anyone looks in the window, they won't be scared out of their mind at the sight of all the blood that you're telling me is there. I should be at the motel in a little more than two hours. Leave the door to your room unlocked. I am starting for Portland now." Abigail wasn't one to waste words or time.

Broderick had tried to be careful not to get blood on the bedclothes in his motel room. He'd put down towels which were now soaked with blood. There was blood on the bedspread, and he struggled to the bathroom to try to rinse it out. There was also a lot of blood on one of the sheets, so he bundled that up with the towels to take them away from the motel with him. He threw his clothes into a duffle bag, unlocked his room door, and went back to sleep. When he woke up again, Abigail Linder was standing over his bed with her cane in her hand.

Chapter 42

Looking For Healing

"**C**an you walk to my car? It's parked right next to yours." I slung the strap of Broderick's duffle bag over my shoulder. We leaned on each other as we limped out the door into the motel parking lot. Less than fifteen hours had passed since Broderick had been shot, and it was thankfully dark again as we struggled to reach my car. Broderick carried the bundle of the bloody sheet and towels. He left the wet bedspread on the bed to dry. He was terribly stiff, just as his CPA medic had predicted he would be. Every step he took was excruciatingly painful. I helped him into the passenger seat of my SUV. It was not an easy feat. I tossed my cane into the second seat with Broderick's duffle bag and the bloody linens.

Broderick gave me the key to his rental car which was parked next to my Suburban. I could see the driver's seat was soaked with blood. Once daylight arrived, anyone who looked in the window of the car would see the enormous amount of blood on the driver's seat. I'd brought some old blankets with me, and I spread the bedding over the driver's seat of the rental car to hide the blood. It was shocking to see how much blood Nathanial had lost.

I was relieved he had parked at the rear of the motel. If I hadn't covered up the blood, someone walking by the car would have had no trouble seeing the blood-soaked seat. It was alarming. It looked like someone had been murdered in the car. If anyone saw it, they would call 911 or at least notify the motel's management. Broderick was lucky that no one had yet sounded the alarm about the blood in his rental car. I wondered if Nathanial needed a blood transfusion.

I hoisted myself into the driver's seat of my SUV, and we were on our way back home to the cottage in Depoe Bay. Gaela sniffed Nathanial briefly when he got into the passenger seat. Then she settled down into my lap where she always rides when I drive my car. I was terribly worried about Nathanial. He was as pale as a ghost and looked like he was close to death. I hoped and prayed he looked worse than he really was. Broderick lowered the back of the passenger seat all the way and fell asleep as soon as he allowed himself to relax.

I had brought a small cooler which held water and Gatorade. Whenever he woke up from his restless sleep, I insisted that he drink as much as he could. It felt like the two-hour journey took two days. By now Nathanial was in considerable pain, and he didn't have any pain killers except for Advil. He knew he shouldn't take too many of these. But he was desperate and kept popping them with his sips of water. We eventually had to stop so Nathanial could pee. It wasn't easy getting him out of my vehicle and then back into it. We both knew it was imperative that he drink plenty of water so he didn't get dehydrated. But stopping alongside the road was dangerous for many reasons.

We finally made it to my cottage. I felt as if I'd been driving forever. I had called Anne Marie and asked her to meet us at the house even though it was a long time past midnight. Broderick was now so stiff he was almost unable to move. It took both Anne Marie and me working hard to get Nathanial out of the SUV and into the house. Anne Marie had made up a cot in the living room, and Nathanial collapsed on the clean bed in gratitude. I wondered where in the world she'd found a cot on such short notice. The woman never ceased to amaze me. It was past time to change the dressings on the detective's wounds, but he begged off until morning. Anne Marie had warmed up some chicken noodle soup for him, and she insisted that he eat all of it. She also had brownies, and he ate three of those.

Anne Marie had set up a TV tray next to the cot. The TV tray served as a bedside table, and Anne Marie put a small bucket of ice, a plastic cup, and several bottles of water on it so the patient could take a drink whenever he was thirsty. We helped him to the bathroom. He would have to get there by himself if he woke up again before morning. I left my cane by his bed. I had a spare someplace. Being cared for by two old women who had no idea what they were doing wasn't an ideal solution for Broderick, but it was better than going into shock or dying from an infection, alone in a motel room.

By morning, Nathanial had developed a fever. We realized we should have changed his dressings the night before. We should not have allowed him to talk us out of it. Neither Anne Marie nor I was trained in any area of medical care, but we did our best to clean and put new bandages on Nathanial's wounds. He started taking the antibiotics his friend Arnold Moore had left with him. He said he realized that he should have started taking those the night before. Anne Marie and I were so worried about Nathanial, but we knew we couldn't call in anyone who would report a gunshot wound to the police. We also knew we could not allow this young man to die of an infection.

Anne Marie kept Nathanial well-fed, and the two of us changed his bandages twice a day. His fever seemed to be responding to the antibiotics, but in a couple of days, Nathanial had used up all of the medication Arnold Moore had given him. He was also about to finish the supplies of antibiotics that Anne Marie and I had been able to find in our homes. He needed to have another prescription if he was going to continue to fight the infection and have any hope of recovering.

The morning Nathanial was going to run out of antibiotics, Anne Marie came to the house with an older man. She introduced him to Nathanial and to me as Dr. Hubert Miller. Nathanial's eyes registered surprise and alarm that Anne Marie would bring a physician to see him. She knew what the stakes were.

Miller shook hands with Nathanial and said, "I am a retired neurosurgeon, and I don't want to know how you acquired the wounds in your leg and your side. I just want to look at them, debride them if necessary, and prescribe some antibiotics for you. If you have fallen and these injuries are the result of a farm or construction accident, that is none of my business. My business is to heal, not to report injuries to the authorities. If anybody wants to take my medical license away from me, that's fine. I stopped renewing it six years ago and have no intentions of ever needing a license to practice medicine again. Just so we understand each other."

I had been very upset about Nathanial's wounds and the lack of any professional consultation for him. I knew only one internist in Depoe Bay, but Anne Marie, bless her heart, had come through by bringing Dr. Miller to the house. I was overjoyed to have a real surgeon, even a retired neurosurgeon, look at Nathanial's leg and side. The leg wound was easy to see, and it appeared to be healing nicely. The wound in his side, which was just under Nathanial's right arm, was more difficult to evaluate. This wound was hot to the touch and could be the cause of Nathanial's ongoing low-grade fever.

Dr. Miller did a thorough examination of the wound under Nathanial's arm and found a small abscess. He incised and drained the infection and cleaned it up. The procedure was painful for Nathanial, and he did his best not to pass out or scream. Dr. Miller told Nathanial he was going to write a prescription for antibiotics. He was emphatic that Broderick had to continue to take the antibiotics for at least fourteen more days.

The doctor apologized because he could not prescribe any pain pills. That required a narcotics ID number, and Dr. Miller no longer had one of those. He still had his prescription pad, so he was able to write a prescription for the antibiotics, but pharmacies were much more particular about who prescribed narcotics. Dr. Miller knew his old prescription pads would not pass scrutiny for pain killers.

Nathanial was in a lot less pain after the retired surgeon had drained the abscess under his arm. Without the pain, he was able to sleep all night. Anne Marie filled the new prescription for the antibiotics, and Broderick's elevated temperature subsided within a few days. Dr. Miller had complimented Anne Marie and me on how clean we had kept Nathanial's wounds and what a nice job we had done with the bandages. Anne Marie had sent Dr. Miller home with a box of homemade chocolate fudge cupcakes with almond buttercream frosting. Anne Marie always knew exactly the right thing to do.

Nathanial had called in to work and taken two weeks of vacation the morning after he'd been shot. He couldn't tell his superiors why he was asking for time off, and he couldn't tell them why he wasn't coming back to work any time soon. He was anxious to continue the investigation but realized his immediate responsibility was to get well, to save himself.

After two weeks under the excellent care of Anne Marie and me, our patient asked for his phone. This was a good sign. It meant he was feeling better. He wanted to check his emails. He looked in his duffle bag, and the phone wasn't there. Anne Marie had washed all of the bloody clothing he had been wearing when he'd been shot. She'd also washed the bloody towels and the sheet from the motel. Most of the blood had come out of his shirt and pants, but his jacket would never be the same again. The phone had not been in the jacket.

Broderick had used his phone when he was at the motel, but he hadn't seen it since. He wondered if he had left it in his room. He said he thought he remembered putting it in his jacket pocket before we left. I remembered that we'd struggled to get him into my SUV. The phone could have fallen out of his pocket during any stage of that ragged journey.

Anne Marie searched my vehicle, and sure enough, the phone was on the floor underneath the passenger seat. It must have fallen out of Broderick's jacket sometime during the trip from Portland. Of course, the battery was dead. Anne Marie drove to the mall to buy a charging cord for the phone since neither my phone charger nor hers would work with Nathanial's phone. Finally, Broderick was able to check his emails. Most of them were of no interest to him, but one was marked urgent and was from someone at the OSP.

The email was about the motorhome Broderick had seen driving out of the grounds of the mosque when he was doing his surveillance in Portland. He had forgotten all about the motorhome after he was shot. The license plate had turned out to be stolen, which was not a surprise to Broderick. The important information in the email was that a motorhome, exactly matching the description he had written down, had been purchased the year before by an LLC that could not be traced to Dean Abadi. The size and description of the motorhome were the same as the one Broderick had suspected might have belonged to Abadi, the motorhome he'd seen exiting the grounds of the mosque. When the motor home had been sighted, the colors and exterior paint design were identical to those on that motorhome. This was a smoking gun Broderick had been hoping to find. He hope this would finally get the attention of his superiors and the FBI. He already knew Abadi was his man. All he had to do now was find the motorhome. He felt a tremendous urgency to get on with it.

Nathanial wanted to get dressed and go immediately to his office to plead his case with his boss. However, just the little bit of exertion required for him to check his emails had exhausted him. He was not able to dress himself, let alone go into his office. He argued with me about this. He stressed how important it was that he get this information to somebody. He finally wore himself out presenting his case to me and fell asleep.

I was worried that he would work himself into a frenzy over the need to communicate the important information to his boss. I was worried that Nathanial would have a relapse. There seemed to be little I could do to help him with the case. But I was a writer, so I started writing an email on

Nathanial's phone addressed to his boss. I hit the high points about the ownership of the motorhome and the radioactivity and decided I would let Nathanial fill in the details and finish composing the email. At least I'd given him a place to start.

I knew I was clever with words, and I'd been able to communicate information to Nathanial's superiors without giving away how Nathanial had made his discoveries. I focused on Nathanial's surveillance outside the mosque property when he had seen the huge motorhome leave. I didn't tell any untruths, but I did word the email carefully. Nathanial's supervisor did believe him that radioactivity had been found on the mosque's grounds. Because the motorhome had been sitting in the parking garage at this same mosque, I thought the connection would get his boss's attention.

In the email to Broderick's boss, I drew Abadi into the case as an important player by making a big thing out of the fact that Abadi had been the person who had purchased the Gator which had been driven through the woods in Depoe Bay. The information that Abadi had purchased a Gator came from the FBI. Of course, I could not mention the fact that Nathanial had found that Gator in Abadi's garage. My email suggested that the authorities needed to get a search warrant and look for the Gator in the garage. Because we knew Abadi had bought the Gator, I was able to suggest with some certainty that it might still be at his house. Somebody in law enforcement just had to find the Gator before Abadi sold it or moved it. Also in my email, I pointed out that Dean Abadi had probably purchased the huge motorhome that had been observed leaving the mosque.

Nathanial was out of sorts when he woke up again. He had to admit to himself that he was in no condition to go into work. He read the email I had composed and grudgingly admitted that it was exactly what needed to be said to motivate the people in his office to get back on the case. He agreed it might help to mobilize a search of Abadi's house and garage. The email might also prod law enforcement to begin looking for the motorhome. Nathanial was certain that the motorhome had something to do with the radioactivity. He was frantic about finding it.

I pulled out all the stops to try to make Nathanial settle down because I was concerned about his health. I promised him I would do everything I could to see that the case went forward. The truth was, I didn't think I could do much at all for him on that score. I urged Nathanial to complete the email I'd started and send it as soon as possible. I tried to get him to focus, and he finally decided to work on the email which he sent off to his boss's phone later that evening. Nathanial seemed to relax a little bit once he had told his boss about Abadi's Gator and about the motorhome.

Nathanial's first excuse for not going into work had been that he was taking some vacation days. Everyone in his office had been urging him to do this, so they were happy when he'd decided to take time off. After he had used up his vacation, he called in and said he had the flu. He would be out for another week or ten days.

He could never let anybody in his office know he was recovering from two serious gunshot wounds. No one could ever know about those. The case against Abadi might collapse if anyone found out that Nathanial had been inside Abadi's garage to obtain evidence. Because Broderick had broken into Abadi's garage without a warrant, Abadi could get off—if his case ever went to court. There had been no other way, but Broderick's discoveries were "fruit of the poisoned tree"— to use the phraseology of defense attorneys everywhere.

Nathanial had to be completely well and able to hide his injuries when he went back to work. Nobody else was going to carry the ball for him on this case. It was up to him.

Chapter 43

Looking For Death

*Because of the tight timeline between the sched-*uling of the Republican and Democrat conventions, the jihadists had little time to travel from one location to the other. They needed to have everything ready in Philadelphia before they headed to Cleveland. There would not be much time after the end of the convention in Cleveland to get back to Philadelphia and put things in place there. The team was currently working in Camden, New Jersey, and everything would be ready for the attack on the DNC convention at the Wells Fargo Center before they left for Ohio.

The plan for the job in Cleveland had been years in the making. On the final day of the Republican convention, in addition to all of the other hoopla, there would be the usual extravaganza of balloons. Dean Abadi and his technical team had devised the air-blowing machines which would recycle the balloons that fell from the ceiling and landed on the floor of the Quicken Loans Arena. Dean's invention would blow the balloons back up into the air. The design of the device was based on the adaptation of an ordinary leaf blower and included a modified air compressor and a small battery-powered generator. Dean had used his engineering expertise to make the prototype for the invention. The machines were rectangular, had a low profile, and were about the size of an ordinary air purifier. Each was designed to be inconspicuous.

A white box truck that had the bright purple and gold logo of the *Let Us Entertain You* party company painted on its side would be used to transport the "air machines" to the Quicken Loans Arena. *LUEY*, the company which was now owned by Dean Abadi, had been hired to help produce the grand finale at the Republican National Convention. *Let Us Entertain You* and all of its trucks and personnel had been carefully screened and vetted. *LUEY* employees had been issued special security badges which allowed them unfettered access to set up for convention events.

The company's party vehicles could come and go as they wished, and they could park anywhere that was convenient. *Let Us Entertain You* trucks had been entering and leaving "The Q" for days before the convention began. Security was unbelievably tight at the Republican National Convention, but *Let Us Entertain You* was already inside the security perimeter. The fox was in the hen house.

Forty of the small air-circulating machines had been built and would be brought to the Quicken Loans Arena on the morning of the convention's final day. The machines would be distributed around the perimeter of the convention center and bolted temporarily to the floor in out-of-the-way places behind and underneath support structures and convention seating. They would scarcely be noticed.

It was always a letdown when the balloons that had dropped from the ceiling sat on the floor until people kicked them out of the way. Delegates stepped on them or picked them up and popped them. Some of the fallen balloons just sat there until they died a natural death from loss of helium. They were in the way all over the floor, and their drama was so short-lived as to be almost a waste. *Let Us Entertain You* would wow the Republicans with their invention which would blow the grounded balloons back up into the air when they landed on the floor.

The air would continue to blow and boost the balloons up into the air for unending excitement. Celebrating with great hilarity, everyone would be oohing and aahing over the fact that the balloons were no longer just sitting there dead on the ground. Convention participants would marvel at how the balloons were being kept aloft as the magic machines blew them off the floor and up into the air over and over again.

What only Abadi's people knew was that each of the new contraptions, which blew air up and around the convention hall and rebooted the balloons, would be spreading death in the form of cesium-137 throughout the arena. The air that recirculated around and around the thousands of people who were gathered for the finale of the convention was radioactive. Convention goers could not see the superfine mix of silica and cesium-137 that was filling the arena and filling their lungs. Everyone who drew a breath inside the Republican Convention would be contaminated with the radioactive isotope. It was a low-tech version of a dirty bomb. There would be no explosions. There would be no immediate realization that anything was wrong. It was a silent and secret delivery system for the lethal poison.

The curious air blowers would slowly and insidiously circulate the balloons and the radioactive air around and around the arena full of people. Cesium-137 chloride is soluble in water. If Dean had wanted to achieve an event that affected its victims rapidly, he would have added the cesium isotope to the water supply at "The Q." He wanted just the opposite. He wanted an event that would affect its victims as slowly as possible. The best case for Dean's purposes would be that none of the thousands who were being contaminated would become ill with radiation poisoning until they returned home from the convention. The delay would make tracking down the source of their strange illnesses much more difficult.

The early stages of radiation sickness present with symptoms that could be indicative of any number of illnesses. Loss of appetite and fatigue might just be the result of exhaustion from having attended a grueling political convention, the consequence of having endured a long plane flight or a long drive, or a reaction to the oppressive summer heat. Nausea, vomiting, and diarrhea could be signs of a twenty-four-hour virus or the flu. Fever usually indicates that one has an infection of some kind. The symptoms are so non-specific, they could be caused by anything. It is not until someone who has been exposed begins to suffer seizures or lapses into a coma that a serious illness is even considered. It is a long leap from the appearance of any of its almost ordinary symptoms to the definitive diagnosis of radiation sickness.

The three-person team from Portland would be the ones who brought the devices into "The Q" and installed them in the convention hall. The technicians would set things up so that all of the balloon recycling devices would be electronically activated as soon as the red, white, and blue orbs began to fall from the ceiling. When the last balloon recycling machine was bolted into place in the Quicken Loans Arena, two of the jihadists returned to Philadelphia to put the finishing touches on the surprise they were preparing for the Democrats. There was work to do in Philadelphia.

One of the technicians remained behind in Cleveland to troubleshoot anything that might unexpectedly go wrong. But he would not be anywhere near the Quicken Loans Arena when the balloons began to blow around in the deadly air. By the time the balloons came down, he would be at the Cleveland bus station waiting to ride the bus to Columbus. He would observe the activation of the air-circulating machines through an app on his cell phone.

If something went wrong and he couldn't fix it through his phone, he had a team in place at "The Q" to fix it. He could walk them through almost any scenario, but he was confident that the subtle weapons he and his fellow jihadists had put in place would function perfectly. There would be no need for troubleshooting and no need to fix anything. He would board the bus to Columbus as the Republicans were caught up in the amazing balloon extravaganza.

According to the plan, no one would realize anything untoward had happened on the closing night of the Republican National Convention. The hope was that many hours would pass before they began to feel the effects of radiation poisoning. Some might not begin to feel ill until days later. Everyone would have gone home, back to the safety of their houses in Des Moines and Tucson and Greenwich. Hopefully, no one would put together the pattern of isolated illnesses until the Democrat convention in Philadelphia was well underway. That was how it was supposed to happen. It had taken health professionals weeks to track down the source of the Philadelphia Legionnaire's Disease catastrophe in 1976.

The Democrats had scheduled their Philadelphia spectacular directly on the heels of the Republican event in Cleveland. The Republicans' convention occurred first so their site could not be blown up. That would obviously put everyone on alert. Death to the Republicans would be slow, insidious, and done in such a way that no one would figure it out until it was too late to stop the catastrophic attack in Philadelphia from going forward. In the end, they all would die.

In Philadelphia, the two jihadists who returned from Cleveland would put the finishing touches on the weapon they were building—innocuous pieces of air conditioning equipment that would become a dirty bomb. In Philly, the plan was for the air conditioning system at the Wells Fargo Center to fail on the next to the last day of the convention. This breakdown had been orchestrated so that when the AC failed, it could not be repaired in time. An entire temporary air conditioning system would have to be brought in.

Only Emergency Cooling and Heating, the company which was secretly owned by Imam Muhammad Muhammad, would be able to provide the units which were large enough to cool the convention center for the final day and night of the Democrat National Convention. ECH's temporary equipment would have to function successfully for an entire day as a real and viable cooling system. It would operate normally to cool the convention hall until the DNC convention drew to its four-day close.

The timetable was set so that on the last night, when the most important politicos in the party took the stage to speak, the temporary cooling system's units would blow up.

Towards the end of the evening, the explosive devices planted inside the replacement cooling units would be activated. The timing mechanism guaranteed that the dirty bombs would detonate just as the Democrats were ending their final evening of celebration, when the maximum number of participants was present at the Wells Fargo Center. The bombs which had been hidden in the temporary air-cooling units would explode.

These explosions would be gigantic and devastating bombs full of another radioactive isotope. This time the isotope would be the Americium which had spent one of its former lives in a thyroid scanning machine at the old Walter Reed Army Medical Center in Washington, D.C. The entire temporary cooling system that contained the Americium would be blown to kingdom come along with all of the delegates, dignitaries, and politicians at the convention. There would be nothing subtle or mysterious about this detonation or the fact that it would contaminate everything in its radius with deadly radioactivity. Philadelphia would be nuclear ground zero, contaminated for decades, even centuries.

The whole world would know that a nuclear weapon, a crude one to be sure, had been detonated in the United States. It was an act of war. The war had begun many years before, but the United States had been late to realize it was under attack. The war was an unconventional one, and the U.S. had not figured out that the battlefield was now in their own backyard, not just in obscure places half-way around the globe.

Homeland Security had wanted to keep this from happening, but they had to be right every time. Terrorists only had to be right once. This summer, the messengers of terror would be right twice. The leadership of both political parties would be destroyed. It would not just be the two people at the top of both tickets. Congressmen, congresswomen, senators, governors, and all the people down the line who'd attended their political conventions as delegates would be killed. Both parties would be decimated. There would be no one left to fight back against the onslaught of sharia law and the worship of Islam in the United States. It was the day of reckoning. "Kill them wherever you find them" was the scripture of the day.

The current administration in power had done everything it could do to block investigations of Muslims. The desire to pretend that terrorism had nothing to do with a religion had contributed directly to the success of the lone wolf attacks that occurred in the United States. No one would be allowed to investigate the mosque which had been complicit in the planning of this apocalyptic act of vengeance. Current government policies had paved the way and made Dean Abadi's personal jihad a piece of cake, easy as pie.

Chapter 45

Looking for Help

Nathanial could not keep himself from calling his boss the day after he'd sent the email. His boss was polite on the phone and acknowledged that Broderick had made a breakthrough. He asked how Broderick was doing. His boss obviously did not feel the same sense of urgency about the motorhome that Nathanial was feeling. No one at the OSP had yet done anything to move the investigation forward. It was all Nathanial could do not to scream at his boss. New cases had come to the desks of law enforcement, and the Gator tracks on the beach at Depoe Bay were old news.

Nathanial finally could not restrain himself any longer, and he went in to work. It was a mistake, but he felt he had no choice. I drove Nathanial to his office to meet with his boss. The detective was going to try to convince him to begin an official search for the motorhome and to seriously

investigate Dean Abadi and his property. Nathanial Broderick argued his case in person and finally got his boss to agree
to put out an APB for the motorhome. It was something, but
the motorhome could be anywhere by now. It had left the
grounds of the mosque more than three weeks earlier.

When Nathanial returned to the car, he looked like death
warmed over. He collapsed into the passenger seat of my
Suburban. I'd brought a thermos of green tea with honey,
and I also had two bottles of cold water ready for him. He
grabbed a bottle of water and drank the entire thing. Then
he opened the thermos and started on the tea. He was worn
out from his interaction with the people at work and was
obviously not ready to be back on the job.

"All right, Abigail, you don't have to say it. I'm in terrible
shape and in no condition to try to go back to work for a
while. You were right. I admit it."

"What did your boss have to say to you? I'll bet he didn't
tell you that your 'vacation' had done you a world of good."

"He told me I looked like shit, and what the hell was I
doing back at work? He told me that, in my battle with the
flu, the flu had won. He said not to come back into the office
for at least ten days. I don't want to talk about it anymore."

"Did he say he would put out the APB on the motorhome
and get a search warrant for Abadi's home?" When Nathanial didn't answer me, I looked over at him and wasn't at all
surprised to see he was sound asleep.

We reached my cottage just as Anne Marie was getting
ready to leave. Nathanial had not fully recovered his usual
vigorous appetite. Anne Marie had made a special dinner for
us which combined several of his favorites. When we opened
the door, the aroma of roast leg of lamb filled the air. Anne
Marie had made the roast with her famous garlic, black

pepper, Kosher salt, and brown sugar rub. She had made delicious gravy from the pan drippings. The leg of lamb was resting on the top of the stove, and roasted potatoes were in the oven. There were peas in the microwave. It would be a wonderful meal.

My mouth was watering, and I hoped the food would be appetizing enough to tempt Nathanial. I didn't want to eat by myself, but he wasn't looking too good after his trip to the office. He'd always been such a good eater, and it made Anne Marie and me sad to see him "off his feed." Anne Marie had turned herself inside out preparing things she knew he loved. Some days he ate with almost his usual gusto. Other days, he picked at his food. He was not himself. He had sustained life-threatening gunshot wounds and had fought back from a dangerous infection.

I was still worried about him and wondered to what extent his lack of appetite was due to depression. It would not be any wonder if he were depressed. His whole life was centered around his work, and now he couldn't do his job. I didn't know how to help him. Anne Marie had certainly done her part by making the wonderful food she hoped would nourish Nathanial's body and soul. I didn't have such a straightforward way to help this young man we had both come to care about. I wished I had some kind of a magic potion that would heal all of his wounds—physical and psychological.

Chapter 45

Looking for a Motorhome

In the end, the route the motorhome had taken from Oregon to the East Coast was not of importance. By the time the APB on the motorhome was put out by the authorities, the motorhome was parked out of sight in the warehouse in Camden, New Jersey. The cook had already flown back to Oregon. After returning the two technicians to Camden in the van, the driver put a different stolen license plate on the motorhome and drove a circuitous route through North Carolina, Tennessee, and Texas. He would leave the motorhome in Texas with the conversion company that was going to sell it on behalf of Dean Abadi's LLC.

At the end of the convention in Cleveland, the deadly air pumps would have served their purpose. A special clean-up crew was hired to remove them. The forty devices would be unbolted from the floor of the Q, collected, and loaded into a *Let Us Entertain You* box truck. The truck would be returned to the company's headquarters. The clean-up crew would be contaminated when they touched the pumps and carried them to the truck.

Someday, somebody might put the pieces of the puzzle together and figure out how the radioactive-laden air had been blown throughout the convention center. By the time that happened, the collection of small air-blowing pumps, which had kept the balloons dancing in the air, would have disappeared forever. How the deadly radioactivity had been spread so successfully inside "The Q" might always remain a mystery. It didn't matter to Dean as long as the infidels were dead.

The technician who had stayed behind in Cleveland to troubleshoot would arrive by bus in Columbus, Ohio and take a taxi to the Columbus airport. From the Columbus airport, he would board a non-stop flight to Los Angeles, and from L.A., he would travel on to Indonesia to resume his position as a science teacher at a madrasa in Medan on the island of Sumatra. His colleagues would ask him how he had enjoyed his sabbatical in Amsterdam. A look at one of his passports would show that he had just spent eight months in the Netherlands.

By the time the dirty bomb actually exploded, the engineers would be long gone from Philadelphia and the Wells Fargo Center. The day before the close of the Democrat National Convention, one of the technicians would fly out of Philadelphia International Airport nonstop to London. He would spend two days at a hotel in that city and then fly back to his home in Saudi Arabia. He had several passports. There would never be any way to trace his real journey or figure out that he had spent time in the United States.

The morning of the last day of the convention in Philadelphia, the female engineer would take a bus to Port Authority in New York City. There she would board another bus and proceed to the JFK Airport. She would switch passports and identities, alter her appearance with a quick change in the ladies' restroom, and fly to Paris. From there she would take the fast train to Brussels where she would don her hijab again and disappear back into the Muslim community of Molenbeek. Life would go on as it had before the three had boarded a tanker out of Jakarta many months earlier—before they had conspired to change the world forever.

Dean Abadi would be watching television far away from Ohio and Pennsylvania when he hoped to see the results of his plan come to fruition. No one would ever know that he had been the mastermind behind the brilliant plan of what would amount to the deployment of nuclear weapons inside the United States. Who would ever suspect a man who had been a Presbyterian for most of his life?

Chapter 46

Looking for Ghosts

inally, Nathanial Broderick's health was restored, and he was ready to return to work. He had moved from the cot in my living room back to his own condo. He was trying to have a normal life and had returned to his job searching for terrorists and radioactive materials. He was discouraged that there had not been a sighting of the suspicious motorhome anywhere in the USA. Could something that gigantic completely disappear into thin air? Nathanial guessed it had probably been repainted and no longer resembled the motorhome he had seen leave the mosque in Portland. He was certain it had carried the radioactive material someplace, someplace still unknown to him.

All of his efforts to get a search warrant for Dean Abadi's house had been turned down by DHS. They said search warrants for Muslims had to pass a different and more stringent test. Mosques and homes of known Muslims had been placed off limits for any searches by local law enforcement. They were essentially untouchable. Broderick was told he did not have probable cause to get a warrant for Abadi's house. Only the feds were able to give permission to search the homes of Muslims and their mosques. The feds now were entirely hands off when it came to investigating anyone with an association to Islam.

Meanwhile, Dean Abadi had decided he no longer had any use for the Gator, the van, or the motorhome. He advertised the Gator on eBay. The Gator was almost new, and a survivalist from rural Idaho bought it. The man paid cash and brought a flatbed to transport the Gator back to his remote cabin in the wilds. In three days, the Gator had a new Idaho registration and a new license plate. It disappeared into the woods for the next two decades. Dean donated the van to the Salvation Army in Sacramento, California, radiation included, and took a tax deduction.

Dean had owned the motorhome for less than a year. He was resigned to the fact that he would take a financial beating when he sold it. He didn't care about that. The Texas company which had originally done the conversion of the basic bus body into a luxury motorhome contacted him to tell him they had a buyer who was anxious to purchase his motorhome. The potential buyer didn't want to wait for a custom designed motorhome to be completed, and they were crazy about Dean's. Dean agreed to the sale price, and the motorhome's exterior was repainted to suit the tastes of the new owner. The motorhome received a good cleaning and never returned to Oregon. It found a happy home, radioactive cargo hold and all, in a gated community in Palm Beach, Florida.

The true ownership of Emergency Cooling and Heating, the company that furnished the temporary air conditioners to the Wells Fargo Center during the DNC convention, was hidden by many layers of holding companies and obfuscation. It would take considerable unraveling to find the imam's name anywhere even remotely connected with the ownership of Emergency Cooling and Heating. Imam Muhammad Muhammad had arranged to sell Emergency Cooling and Heating, which had its offices in Cherry Hill, New Jersey, through the maze of legal machinations he had used to purchase the company the previous year. Money had already changed hands, and sale papers had already been signed. The sale was scheduled to become final on the first of August.

Dean Abadi loved the name of the party company he had bought in Cleveland. He almost decided to keep *Let Us Entertain You* as an investment, but sanity prevailed. He made the decision to sell it. *LUEY* had a great reputation, and he had no trouble unloading the company for a good price. Dean already had his money. That sale would become final, and the new owners would officially take possession on the first of August. No one would ever be able to find the name Dean Abadi or the name of the imam, Muhammad Muhammad, anywhere in the complex and copious paperwork which accompanied the purchase or the sale of either of these businesses.

Dean Abadi was a ghost as far as any kinds of nefarious activities were concerned. He remained a retired construction engineer who lived a quiet life in Portland, Oregon. He attended his mosque regularly. He was an excellent example of a "good Muslim," a peace-loving member of the peace-loving religion that was Islam. Dean Abadi would continue to live his quiet life until he got another bright idea about how to serve Allah with another act of mass murder. He was a true sharia warrior.

Chapter 47

Looking for an Ending

I *wrote the final words at the end of the last chapter* of my suspense thriller. I was pleased with the book and satisfied with the way I had ended it. I'd struggled with the conclusion of the action but felt I had finally got it right. I closed my laptop. I knew I would be back the next day for revisions and many rounds of editing. It had been months since I had finished a novel. It was always a good feeling, and I liked my latest effort. It had an unusual ending. I don't like confusing endings that try to fool the reader, but in this case I'd decided on something less conventional than the usual wrap up at the end of the book. I wonder if I ought to send it to a new publisher under a new pen name.

I had missed writing. I'm a writer, and writers have to write. My imagination is just too vivid and active for me not to make up stories in my mind. I definitely did not want to go back to the publicity tours and book signings or any of those aspects of being a writer. But there are plenty of novelists who refuse to reveal themselves to the public. Publishers don't like those writers because publicity is good for sales. I didn't need the money so I didn't care if my books sold millions of copies or not. More writers seemed to be getting into self-publishing these days. Maybe I would look into that again.

Nathanial Broderick came by regularly to say hello. Anne Marie, Nathanial, and I had become good friends. Nathanial was coming for a crab and lobster dinner tonight, and he was bringing the seafood. To accompany the crustaceans, Anne Marie had made a large bowl of her special potato salad with vermouth, basil, red wine vinegar, and sweet gherkins. She had also left a platter of mozzarella and tomato salad in the refrigerator. There was a mustardy remoulade dipping sauce and cut up lemon wedges for the cold Dungeness crabmeat. Melted butter was waiting on the stove. It just needed to be reheated for the lobster. There was French bread warming in the oven. I love lobster and crabmeat. Nathanial was delighted to be bringing the cooked shellfish. He'd invited Anne Marie to join us for dinner, and once again she told him she didn't like seafood.

Nathanial also brought a bottle of white wine to go with the dinner he was offering as a gesture of thanks to me. He said he would never be able to repay us for saving his life and taking care of him after he had been shot. I didn't want any thanks or repayment. I just wanted to talk and eat. I enjoy Nathanial's company. I wish he would get a girlfriend but was flattered that he wanted to spend time with me.

Anne Marie had set up a table on the porch for the seafood feast. There was a cool breeze coming from the ocean. The sun was setting over the Pacific, and it was a perfect summer evening. We ate every bite of the crab and lobster that Nathanial brought. Anne Marie had left a cherry cobbler in the oven. Nathanial insisted on cleaning up, and he put the dishes in the dishwasher. We settled into a comfortable discussion of Broderick's last case. It had been so terribly frustrating and had gone wrong at almost every turn. He asked me what I thought he should do with the case going forward. He wondered if he should try to go forward with it at all.

I shared with Broderick that I'd been writing a novel about the case. I had written my story as a fictional account, but I'd stayed close to the real facts of his real-life case. I told Nathanial that I'd gone ahead and finished the story with an ending drawn strictly from my writer's imagination. In the absence of any more information about how the real case might be resolved, I'd decided to finish the book based on my own fictional ideas.

"I don't presume to know how this case ends in real life, of course, so I made up an ending. That's all it is, a made-up ending. A lot of the story will sound familiar to you, and I have borrowed heavily from the things you've told me. I haven't put any facts in there that aren't known to the public. I made up what happened to the nuclear material after you lost track of it. I made up what happened to the motorhome and to the jihadists who arrived by raft in the cove. I made up a lot about Dean Abadi and tried to figure out why he did what he did. I made up the reason for bringing the radio-active stuff into the country. I changed every name. You are welcome to read what I have written, but you have to remember ... it's fiction. That's the bottom line."

We inevitably got into a political discussion as we wondered what in the world the current U.S. government was doing by blocking almost all investigations into terrorism and Muslims. We looked out over the Oregon coast. I had lived in Depoe Bay for less than a year, but it absolutely felt like home to me. I'd come to this place to escape my East Coast life and to become a recluse, an eccentric hermit who saw no one and never went out. I had to concede that I was not as anti-social as I had thought or hoped I might be. I wasn't going to be able to give up writing, and I wasn't going to be able to give up talking to people. I love people. And I absolutely cannot help myself when it comes to a mystery.

I was looking forward to the fall. There were too many tourists in Depoe Bay in the summer. It was close to the end of July, and the vacationers could not be gone too soon for me. Schools started in the middle of August these days, so family vacations would be ending in a few weeks. I was looking forward to the cooler weather, the rain, and the wild winter storms. I looked forward to not waiting for a seat at my favorite restaurants.

I love the Oregon coast, and I love my life here. I feel as if I've made a great decision to settle in my cottage by the sea with my dog and best pal Gaela. What life could be better than mine? I have a housekeeper who is a treasure, and I have a friend in the Oregon State Police. Nathanial gave me a kiss on the cheek and said goodbye. He had cleaned up the kitchen. We will have lunch next week.

I let Gaela out for a last run in the backyard. When I was ready for bed, I decided to turn on the TV and try to catch the late local news. I don't like politics or politicians. I accept them as necessary evils that come along with democracy which hands down beats all other forms of government in the world. I especially did not like politics this year. I've avoided turning on my television set because I could not abide political ads or the political nominating conventions which had been taking place in the Eastern Time Zone. I was hoping those loathsome events were finally finished. Had the last night of the Democrat Convention been the night before, or was tonight the last night? One could only hope that it was all over. The cable news blah, blah, blah gives me a headache.

Maybe it was safe to turn on my TV set again? Maybe it was safe to watch the news again? It wouldn't be safe to watch the news again until after November, and maybe it would never really be safe to watch the news again … ever. The results of both of the conventions had been known for months. What was left to decide? What was left to do? All the self-congratulatory hoopla and verbal baloney that circulated at these things, apparently an expression of some kind of fun for both parties, was ludicrous—in my opinion. I lifted Gaela up onto the bed and found the remote control for the TV. I turned it on.

Acknowledgments

Heartfelt thanks to my readers and editors. I couldn't have done this without you. Thank you to Jamie at Open Heart Designs who does everything to turn my manuscript into a book. Thank you to my photographer Andrea Burns who always makes me look good. Thank you to all the friends and fans who have encouraged me to continue writing.

About the Author

CAROLINA DANFORD WRIGHT *is a grandmother. She uses a blue and white cane. She has lived in many places and traveled far and wide. Carolina has had several fulfilling careers and began writing mysteries when she was seventy. She believes that behavior has consequences and that it is critical to fight for truth and justice. The women of the Granny Avengers series echo Carolina's crusade to help right the wrongs of the world.*

MORE FROM
LLOURETTIA GATES BOOKS

HENRIETTA ALTEN WEST
THE REUNION CHRONICLES MYSTERIES

1. *I Have a Photograph*
2. *Preserve Your Memories*
3. *When Times Get Rough*
4. *A Fortress Steep & Mighty*
5. *The Wells of Silence*
6. *Going Home*
7. *I've Got some Real Estate*

MARGARET TURNER TAYLOR
www.margaretttaylorwrites.com

BOOKS FOR ADULTS

Traveling Through the Valley of the Shadow of Death

I Will Fear No Evil

THE QUEST FOR FREEDOM SERIES

1. *Russian Fingers*
2. *Do You Know Who I Am?*
3. *No More Secrets*

BOOKS FOR YOUNG PEOPLE

Secret in the Sand

Baseball Diamonds

Train Traffic

The Quilt Code

The Eyes of My Mind

*Available in print and ebook
online everywhere books are sold.*